Life Sentences

Life Sentences

Short Stories

Edited By

Anthony B. Pinn
and
Gregory M. T. Colleton

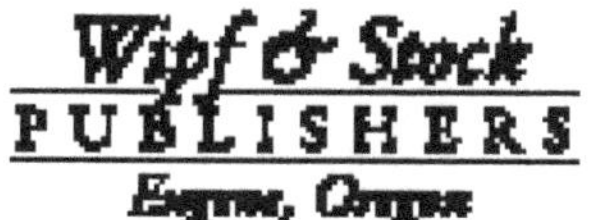

LIFE SENTENCES
Short Stories

ISBN 13: 978-1-4982-4995-9

Contents

List of Contributors / vii
Introduction / xi

The Preparation

"Casper's Ghost" by David A. Nelson / 3
"Sonny's Slips" by C. Kelly Robinson / 12
"Có Mang" by Corina Marie Ahn Knoll / 22
"Friends of Distinction" by Ian Edelman / 38
"Faithful Afflictions" by Anthony B. Pinn / 45

The Journey

"Indira Shaves Her Legs" by Faynessa Armand / 61
"The Inner Harbor" by Stanley N. Bernard / 66
"Circus" by Matt Rhodes / 77
"The Darkness Away" by Michael Gavin / 84
"Old Friends and New Lovers" by Annette B. Almazan / 99
"Lost Your Way to Heaven" by Edwardo Jackson / 106

The Crossroad

"S" by E. A. Bagby / 123
"The Storm that Loved a Bike" by Diane Glancy / 129
"Dead Canadian Girlfriend" by Philip Stone / 138
"Reds" by Gregory Pace / 150
"Jack and Jill" by Gregory M. T. Colleton / 162

Contributors

Annette B. Almazan received her JD degree from the University of California at Los Angeles in May, 2002, and her BA in English (Honors) and Philosophy from Georgetown University in May, 1997. She is currently an Assistant District Attorney at the Queens County District Attorney's Office (NY) and was previously a Clinical Fellow with the D.C. Street Law Project at Georgetown University Law Center. Prior to becoming an attorney, she was a high school teacher at Yerba Buena High School in San Jose, CA, as part of Teach for America.

Faynessa Armand is a native of Los Angeles, and a writer since the age of six (She and her sister wrote Flintstones scripts and plays for the garage). A practicing teacher, she has published many short stories (*Belletrist Review*, *Berkeley Fiction Review*, *A Place to Enter*, *Flying Horse*, *Santa Barbara Review*, *A Community of Voices*). She won the fiction award at the Santa Barbara's Writers Conference in 1996 and continues work on stories and novel ideas.

E.A. Bagby, a native of New Mexico, lives in Chicago, where she divides her time between writing, acting, and music. She is a founding member of Sansculottes Theater Company, with whom she has cowritten several shows. In 2006, Sansculottes and Chicago's Storefront Theater produced her musical *Practical Anatomy*, and Chicago ScriptWorks staged a reading of her screenplay *Bellham*. Bagby's writing has also appeared in *Conversely*, *Dramatics*, *The Tap*, and *The Writing Group Book*. Press 53 will publish her novella *Lost Children* in September 2007.

Stanley N. Bernard is Director of the PARK Project, an innovative project helping children with emotional and behavioral health challenges in Bridgeport, CT, funded by the Substance Abuse and Mental Health Services Administration (SAMHSA). Bernard holds a Masters Degree in Public Health from Yale University and is currently a doctoral candidate and Kellogg Fellow at Columbia University. Bernard is a published poet, husband and father of four.

Gregory M. T. Colleton is a screenwriter, actor and director. Born in Evanston, Ill., Colleton attended Macalester College and later joined the Teach for America program where he taught composition, history and violin to middle school kids while spreading the gospel of Michael Jordan. He resides in Los Angeles, but dreams of living back near the Windy City.

Ian Edelman was born and raised in New York City. He credits getting De La Soul's "3 Feet High & Rising" for his Bar Mitzvah and skateboarding in crack era NYC as the two biggest creative influences in his life. Ian now lives in Los Angeles with his fiancée and their dog Lola.

Michael Gavin lives with his wife and daughter in Catonsville, Maryland. His poetry and fiction have appeared in literary journals throughout the country. The short story that appears in this anthology is a chapter from his first novel manuscript, *Westbend.* When he is not working as an associate professor of English at Prince George's Community College, he yearns for the Cubs to win the World Series.

Diane Glancy published three books in 2005. *In-Between Places*, University of Arizona Press; *Rooms New and Collected Poems*, Salt Publishers; and *The Dance Partner*, Michigan State University Press. In 2007, Arizona published a new collection of poems, *Asylum in the Grasslands.* Glancy is a professor at Macalester College where she teaches Native American Literature and Creative Writing. She currently is on a four-year sabbatical/early retirement program. She will hold the Richard Thomas chair at Kenyon College in the spring of 2008 and 2009.

Edwardo Jackson is a graduate of Morehouse College and has an MBA from the University of Phoenix. The winner of the 1993 NAACP ACTSO Silver Medal in Playwriting, he is an author, screenwriter, and actor, as well as a President of the entertainment promotional company JCM Entertainment, LLC and co-founder of JCM Books. His works include *Ever After* (2001), *Neva Hafta* (2002), *I Do?* (JCM Books, 2006), as well as the stories "And Then She Cried," featured in the anthology *Proverbs for the People* (Kensington, 2003), "Broken Rules" in the anthology *Intimacy* (Penguin Plume, 2004), and "Postcards from Hell" in the *Truth Be Told* anthology (Montage, February 2006). Originally from Seattle, WA, Jackson resides in Southern California.

Corina Marie Ahn Knoll was born somewhere in Korea but grew up in Iowa, a state known for its plentiful corn and bacon. She attended one of the Midwest's finest liberal arts colleges (Macalester College) where she learned the intricacies of communication and sociology. Now residing in Los Angeles, Corina edits for a magazine and spends her free time playing soccer and watching the Food Network. She is extremely skilled at filling out Mad Libs and using her jazz hands.

David A. Nelson was born smack dab in the middle of Brooklyn during the "Summer of Love" (and a slew of inner city race riots). When he was ten years old he found a Super 8 camera in his father's closet and has been writing and making films ever since. Admitted into the Dramatic Writing and Film Production Dept of NYU on a scholarship, he came up through the ranks of Spike Lee's 40 Acres and a Mule working as an assistant editor on films such "School Daze," as well as music videos and commercials. He has been a sought after music video director for more than 10 years, working with artists including Outkast, De La Soul, R. Kelly, Jermaine Dupri, 2-Pac Shakur and George Clinton. He recently made his feature directorial debut with the sports-fantasy sequel "Like Mike 2" for 20th Century Fox. Nelson also made his documentary directing debut with the award winning short, "Positively Naked," which premiered on HBO/Cinemax in 2006. He lives in Los Angeles with his wife and fiery red-headed daughter.

Gregory Pace began writing fiction at an early age. Born and raised in New York, he later lived in Atlanta, GA, where he attended college. After beginning graduate work in film and television, his hunger for all things creative took him to Los Angeles, where he currently works as a screenwriter.

Anthony B. Pinn is the Agnes Cullen Arnold Professor of Humanities and Professor of Religious Studies at Rice University. He is the author/editor of seventeen books, including *African American Humanist Principles: Living and Thinking Like the Children of Nimrod* (2004) and *Terror and Triumph: The Nature of Black Religion* (2003).

Matt Rhodes was born in Iowa and raised in Ohio. A financial analyst, poet and occasional journalist, his work has appeared in various local magazines and web sites and most recently *The Sporting News*. He is a graduate of Northwestern University and is working toward an MBA at the University of California, Berkeley. He lives in San Francisco.

C. Kelly Robinson is a graduate of Howard University and Washington University in St. Louis. He is the author of five published novels, including *Between Brothers* and *No More Mr. Nice Guy* (Villard/Strivers Row) as well as *The Perfect Blend* and *The Strong, Silent Type* (Penguin/NAL). Robinson is a 2001 recipient of the Individual Award for Achievement, a recognition from the National Council on Communicative Disorders. He lives with his family outside Dayton, Ohio where he is working on a new novel and several nonfiction projects.

Philip Stone is a graduate of the University of Illinois in Urbana, where he majored in rhetoric, and studied film. His spare time is spent playing drums with the nationally touring rock duo, *Sanawon*, co-hosting and editing Donkeypunchradio.com, and moving luggage at a downtown hotel where they don't tip as well as they should. He lives in Chicago with his wife, his computer, and his drumsticks.

Introduction

In retrospect, the idea for this book began almost 10 years ago, at Macalester College in St. Paul, Minnesota, when a graduating senior came to his professor for advice about his future. The young man had a variety of options: go to graduate school, enlist in a teaching program or return home and join his cousin's garage band. At 21 years old, the garage band seemed to be calling his name, but it wasn't the only voice he heard. "Why can't the decision be clearer," he asked with some frustration. "No, you've got it all wrong," said the professor from behind his desk, "this is the fun part. This is what it's all about." The professor shifted in his chair and smiled, as if he had waited years to be on this side of the conversation. "If you already knew which door to enter, then you'd just walk in, no questions asked. But you have options. You're like a hotel and there are doors all around you. The question isn't simply which door do you choose, but rather what happens when the door that you do choose isn't what you expected."

Now here we are editing a book together. It might appear an odd grouping. We are at different stages of our lives, involved in disparate professional realities, and living in and dealing with radically different cities. But what we continue to share is a belief that life isn't easy. Relentlessly life confronts us with difficult choices and options. Seemingly, no matter how well we plan, or how considered we thought we were in our choices, there's no finality, enduring clarity or lasting stability. Life just continues to come at us and outside influences carry "big guns."

It's bigger than just us. Economic collapse, social upheaval, environmental destruction, the joy of friendship, the pleasure of community, social justice, personal angst—it's all bound together. And while this bleak reality often feels cold, it gives a shade of meaning to what seems a world out of control. As a result, a pressing question became obvious: Why?

In response, a turn to one of the sacred books of the Bible seems only natural, or at least not unreasonable, all things considered. The "Preacher" in the Book of Ecclesiastes, that biblical book sandwiched between the wisdom of the Proverbs and the untamed sexuality of The Song of Solomon, gives a spin on this question: everything happens within its time. Life is thick, and messy, full of pleasant adventures and painful encounters:

> To every thing there is a season, and a time to every purpose under the heaven: A time to be born, and a time to die; a time to plant, and a time to pluck up that which is planted; a time to kill, and a time to heal; a time to break down, and a time to build up; a time to weep, and a time to laugh; a time to mourn, and a time to dance; a time to cast away stones, and a time to gather stones together; a time to embrace, and a time to refrain from embracing; a time to get, and a time to lose; a time to keep, and a time to cast away; a time to rend, and a time to sew; a time to keep silence, and a time to speak; a time to love, and a time to hate; a time of war, and a time of peace. (Ecclesiastes 3:1–8)

This pretty much captures it. Our existence is just that complicated, beyond simple rationalizations and grand schemes that explain away our discomfort. It involves change that must be handled—as best as one can, as bizarre as our efforts may appear.

In theory, this is what most of us do with at least a little grace and maintaining something that resembles dignity. But, when the truth is told, handling change isn't as easy as it sounds. There are no perfect answers, and the concerns are rarely that dramatic. But, they do exist. And as a result, more often than not, our lives become an individual journey, a quest really, for the best kind of response—to make the most appropriate choices from all possible options.

We found this oddly intriguing, and decided to invite others to think about this dilemma and the Preacher's response in Ecclesiastes, not for overtly religious or spiritual reasons, but simply because of its more earthy and mundane appeal—its take on why life happens the way it does and our decisions in its aftermath.

In these short stories by established authors and those not so established, an exploration of life as change takes place. These writers come from a variety of backgrounds, perspectives and differing levels of familiarity with the short story genre, but what ties them together is a willingness to creatively explore the raw and more uncomfortable dimensions of life—big events and small happenings, all bound up by a recognition of the inevitability and (dis)comfort of change. Each has a story to tell, a creative and imaginative angle on life as it happens somewhere, to someone. This is an experiment, a recognition of and confrontation with the depth of culture and culture's life maps—the ways in which the joys and troubles of life are given meaning. It involves an attempt to address these large (and small) challenges and dynamics of life without the jargon of the professional philosopher or theologian, but rather through the more "earthy" language of popular culture—the short story. In short, we are creating life sentences.

Some of the stories are dark, others much more hopeful. But for those who will read through these stories looking for the thread, the common theme, it's simple: life is change—sometimes pleasant and sometimes painful—changes of heart and mind. The stories are arranged in light of the undertone of movement, of an approach toward and arrangement of time and space, echoed through the Preacher's words. While not thematically rigid, the placement of the stories speaks to postures toward life and relationships consistent with the Preacher's orientation: Preparation. It also speaks to the rhythm of life suggested by the Preacher, a rhythm that resembles playful intentionality: Journey. Finally, the third section of the book suggests the dilemma, the contractions and paradoxes often entailed by life: Crossroads. Of course, there are other ways these stores can be arranged, and we imagine readers will make their own thematic and conceptual connections to and between the stories told in this volume. And that is as it should be.

In the following pages, writers share their vision of this unpredictable process. This, we believe, is the beginning of something important, a discovery of why, an excursion with courageous and talented souls, and their extraordinary fables. The beginning of something you now hold in your hands. Read it and reflect on it, in light of your own stories of life and the wisdom of the ancient preacher: "To everything there is a season."

So it begins; but not without a word of thanks to friends and family that encouraged us along the way. We also thank the contributors whose good humor and patience over the course of a good number of years is appreciated. We would also like to thank Stephen Finley, Margarita Simon, and Derek Hicks, PhD students at Rice University, for editorial assistance. Finally, the editors would like to thank Wipf & Stock Publishers for supporting this project, believing in it, and bringing it to an audience beyond a captive group of people who owe us money.

Breathe deeply . . .

Anthony B. Pinn and Gregory M. T. Colleton
2007

The Preparation

Casper's Ghost

By
David A. Nelson

"FIGHT!"

The word rang out like a shot from a starter pistol and sent a swarm of kids racing across the schoolyard. Not away from the storm's center but rushing headlong into it. Granted, this was before the days when children running across a schoolyard meant that some ostracized outsider got his hands on his Daddy's nine millimeter and decided to live out his ultimate video game revenge fantasy. It was a scrap, a scuffle, a challenge of physics, where two objects couldn't occupy the same space at the same time and one of those objects had to get it's ass whooped. Don't get me wrong, these battles weren't trivial, or benign in any way. Everything was at stake. Reputations were lost, bones broken, shirts and egos torn apart and discarded. These were power plays that could determine the tone for the rest of the school year, maybe even for the rest of our lives.

I walked up to the edge of the circle. I knew who I'd find in the middle, I just hoped I was wrong. Some members of the congregation were already chanting, "a fight, a fight, a nigger and a white, if the nigger wins then we'll all jump in." And then the response, the same song with the alternate ending; "if the whitey wins we'll all jump in!" It was clear that it was a race fight, black versus white. It made it easier on the crowd to pick their favorite. Like always chose like. Racial tensions were high in the fifth grade. I could hear the obligatory prologue to the fight shouted by the two opponents in the center of the circle. "I'ma hit you so hard I'ma kill you're whole family!" and the less poetic, "yeah, I'm going to kick your ass first!" I stood up on my toes and saw the two combatants, Casper Carter and 'The Fonz.' The two most feared students in all of P.S. 98. This was no pre-show attraction, no under card, this was the heavyweight title bout for sure.

This was Midwood, Brooklyn back in the 1970s. Public School was not that different from jail. Schoolyard/prison yard—we were all doing our time. The lunchroom was where it was most obvious. United we stood, but divided we ate, separated into groups by race, religion and the kids from the science club. If you were smart you stuck to your own. Back then all the black kids had afros and dressed like Sly and the Family Stone even though they were in the fifth grade. They were bused in from God knows where and would shake you down in the hallway for money or candy or they'd just go, "let me hold your pen for a minute?" and that meant you weren't ever getting it back.

ᔓ ᔓ ᔓ

I had my run-ins. Once during a free period in the middle of the day, amidst the cacophony of screaming kids running at top speed in every direction across the concrete schoolyard, I ran to catch a pink Spalding in a game of "off the wall" and accidentally caused a four-kid pile up. It was me and three inseparable mini-Super Fly's tumbling in a blur of burgundy bell-bottoms and floral print shirts. Suddenly, I was surrounded. There were three Afros bobbing back and forth spitting racial epithets and blame for the collision; "what the fuck?" "Why don't you watch where you goin', Honkey!" and "you dead, white boy!"

Since all eyes where on us and I was the guy who just scuffed their white patent leather shoes, not to mention their egos, there was no walking away. Next came a brief flurry of faux karate kicks and jabs. To picture it now, it seems like some hack idea for a concept film, "a blaxploitation flick—only with little kids acting in all the parts . . ." Either way I was still getting beaten up by three four-foot pimps in a schoolyard and felt like I was in one of those dreams where you're wearing a lead jacket swimming through glycerin.

Thank God for Casper Carter. He came over to the scene of the scuffle and in his deep voice barely whispered, "quit it." The three hoods stopped their Jim Kelly acrobatics immediately and quickly strutted away. "You alright?" Casper asked. "Yeah." I replied, laboring to keep lower eyelids from releasing tears that I did not want to let flow. He raised his hand like an Indian Chief, I put mine out and he slapped me five and walked away. Right then and there everyone knew that the three little pimps wouldn't think about starting with me now. Casper squashed it, and Casper and I were cool.

For a long time Casper was known as the toughest kid in the school. After him was Makeeba Johnston, and that was because she was wild and most boys wouldn't hit her back. Casper was at least a foot taller than everyone else and he didn't have an Afro. He had a close shaved head with a collection of bumps and scars that let you know you had no idea of the meaning of the word "hard-knocks." He was known as Casper because that was his name and when he left the room he'd say, "I'm ghost."

ᔓᔕ ᔓᔕ ᔓᔕ

We went back too; I met Casper in the fourth grade when I hit a three-point jump shot in gym class that won a heated half-court four on four. Casper said the team was now "The Brooklyn Globetrotters *and the White Boy!*" with me being the said "white boy." After that we were friends. As much as we could be. He lived somewhere in Bed-Stuy and got bused in to school every day. He came to a few of my birthday parties at The Roller Palace and sometimes would come over after school. But there was always a distance. He felt out of place and defensive. One day my Grandma called from her apartment a few floors up to check in on me because she saw me come home with a bunch of kids from school. He asked why she called. "No reason," I said. He said, "she's nervous 'cause she saw a black kid in y'all's apartment." "That's not true," I told him, and wondered to myself if it might be. Things got worse when Alex Haley's "Roots" came on. I entered the auditorium for morning attendance and the tension was unmistakable. Casper was angry and ready for a fight. I went up to him to say, "what's up?" and he cut me off, "fuck you. Your great grandparents owned my great grandparents!" I explained to him that my great grandparents were from Russia where everyone hated them, "that's why they came here." I told him that my ancestors were slaves too and then we were cool again.

Casper would occasionally walk over to the table where I sat with a group of middle class white kids, momma's boys from Midwood cowering into their Wonderbread sandwiches lest they get eye contact with someone and get asked the Zen riddled question; "What'choo look'n at?" There was no way to respond without causing a ruckus and getting their night braces bent out of shape. To answer, "Nothing" was an insult and would result in a fight; to say "You" or anything else for that matter would be a challenge worthy of a fight to the death, or at least until some underpaid custodial worker got bored and broke it up. So most kids just stared down at their hot-lunches or Mom packed tuna sandwiches. The teachers thought we were a well-behaved group, little did they know they were not the authority we respected. It was the bullies from the outer neighborhoods. These were the neighborhoods where our parents, while driving through, would lock the doors and tell us how they remembered when they used to be exclusive for doctors and lawyers and the well to do.

Casper never bullied me and I think that's because he had respect for me, probably because of how I handled myself during the potato chip incident. He would come over to the White boy table and sometimes ask for some potato chips that my Mom packed in a ziplock bag for me. I'd give him a few. I guess in a way it was kind of payment for him squashing the beef between me and the three four foot pimps and any future bullies who thought about stepping to me. But I also knew that he didn't have money and didn't really see much of his own Mom, and just got whatever slop was on the menu for hot lunch that day. So I gave him some Ruffles and that was that. Some of the other kids from Casper's neighborhood would stop by our table once in a while and they would go through the other kids lunch bags and take pieces of their stuff, Milky Ways, Now & Laters, Sugar Daddy's, whatever they wanted.

I was left out of this pillaging, until one day one of the kids stood over me and said, "yo, give me some of your chips!" I tried to ignore him but he wouldn't let up. "You better hand over those chips, boy." I looked up slightly to catch sight of Casper and saw him pretending not to hear. I realized I was on my own. "Gimme some or I'ma take the whole bag, fool," he said. I turned around to face him. "What's your name?" I asked. "Fuck difference does it make what my name is? My name is the kid who ate your potato chips." A short kid from their group egged him on, "Kalil, take all his shit!" I spoke again looking him dead in the eye, "Kalil—listen to me, my mom works real hard to take care of her children. She comes home after work, cooks dinner, and cleans the dishes. She wakes up early in the morning to make sure we have breakfast, then she makes lunch and packs it for us to take to school. The last time I checked, she didn't adopt a little black boy with braids. So these aren't your potato chips. They're mine. My hard working Mom gave them to me and there's no way in hell I'm giving any of them to you." And I turned around and resumed eating my lunch. My heart was pounding out of my chest and I was expecting to get hit in the back at any second. But next thing I knew Casper and his whole crew were laughing hysterically at how I played Kalil. Kalil was embarrassed and just grabbed a chocolate bar out of Michael Zalinsky's hand and walked away; "Fuck all y'all bitches then!" was his salutation.

After my "Potato Chip Rebellion," a few things happened. No one messed with me in the lunchroom, Casper treated me with a new found respect, and all the Wonderbread boys expected me to come to their aid any time someone approached our table with candy bar extortion on their mind. I told them it wouldn't do anything, that they had to stick up for themselves or they'd always be picked on. They chose to give up their Almond Joys. Sometimes you feel like a punk, sometimes you don't.

A lot of drama took place in the lunchroom, fist fights, first kisses, bonds and betrayals. But none more incredible than when The Fonz got put back into the sixth grade and entered our lunchroom for the first time. The Fonz was from somewhere else, Albania or Lithuania or somewhere. He looked thirty compared to the other kids in school anxiously awaiting even a sign of puberty. When the bell rang, he literally had a three o'clock shadow. No one wanted to mess with him even though we knew it was kind of ridiculous to dress like The Fonz. A "Happy Days" lunch box was one thing, but actually coming to school in character seemed fanatic and only added to his reputation for being unhinged. Plus, he didn't say anything, not even "Aayy" or "Woa." I'm not even sure if he spoke English or if where he came from everyone dressed like The Fonz, but I wasn't about to ask him. We saw him walk in, wearing his customary costume, black leather jacket with the collar up, blue jeans cuffed at black motorcycle boots, bad attitude painted across his face. The Fonz looked angry and defensive, everyone would know he got put back a grade because he couldn't cut it where he was and he was ready to break the collarbone of anyone who had something to say about it.

The Fonz was looking for a place to take his seat, when from between two tables, chasing after one of his friends Casper came running out and accidentally smashed into The Fonz sending his food tray crashing to the floor. The lunchroom fell silent. I don't even think Casper knew who he bumped into until a thick Slavic accent broke the silence, "pick it up, you black bastard." Casper turned around in disbelief. Did he just hear what he thought he heard? "What?" he asked the leather clad antagonist. "You heard me. Pick it up. Or if you want me to kick your ass?" It wasn't really fear that flashed across Casper's eyes as much as unfamiliarity with the events that presented themselves. It was pretty well understood that you didn't mess with Casper Carter unless you were suicidal or just plain crazy. The thing was, no one knew if The Fonz was either or both. One thing was certain, there was not an ounce of fear on his face. Casper said, "I could clean it up with your fake ass leather jacket if you want." "Or I can clean it up with your fake ass jacket," The Fonz retorted, at a slight disadvantage due to the fact that he hardly spoke English. "I ain't even wear'n my jacket, fool! You should watch where you're going too!" Casper shouted. The Fonz said, "Fuck you—niggers." Yes he did. Children of foreigners always seem to learn the bare essentials needed to get by before truly mastering the language.

At this point for all intents and purposes Casper should have knocked The Fonz's front teeth out, but I knew that Vice Principal Darwick had already given him two warnings for fighting in school. One more meant permanent expulsion and relocation to a school in his own district. Our public school was a white-collar country club compared to the maximum-security schools in Bed-Stuy. I wished I could walk over and deliver a line as cool as he did for me, something that would dissipate the tension and have the fight avoided altogether, something like "Cool it" or "Sit on it Fonzie." But, I didn't command that kind of power in the lunchroom and The Fonz already used the N-word. There was no way to diffuse this bomb that was ignited the moment The Fonz entered the room. These two preteen titans would have to battle. But it wouldn't happen here. They both knew they were already in hot water and this would only make it boil. "After school—you're dead!" Casper fired. "You won't be alive either way also!" was The Fonz's reply.

ଓ ଓ ଓ

The rest of the school day went by in slow motion. Casper skipped class and rumors started to spread that he had already left school because he was scared to fight The Fonz. I didn't think it was true. But what if it was? He'd never be able to come back. The dethroned King never hangs around the palace. He'd have to go into exile, cast out somewhere into the bowels of Brooklyn. In between classes the hallways were buzzing, kids were choosing sides and placing bets, not for money or anything, they'd just twist pinky fingers and say; "I bet Carter gets his ass kicked!" or "He's chicken, he's not even going to show. I heard he already went home." There was a definite divide, the white kids wanted Fonzie, the black kids had Casper's back. Little skirmishes broke out throughout the day, mostly pushing fights and racial slurs, but no big brawls. It was a pressure cooker and it probably could have broken out into an all out race war if the right buttons were pushed and the third graders were armed.

My cafeteria table fell right in line with the masses, fantasizing out loud about how Casper would get his ass kicked and that his friends wouldn't bully them anymore. They imagined a life where they wouldn't have to give their lunch candy away to anyone. Arty Dekakis was rooting for The Fonz. "He's going to cream Casper, totally annihilate him," he said. "Idiot," I thought, he's just going to be giving his Bubble Yum to Fonzie next week if he wins. "Who do you want?" they eagerly asked me. "I don't care," I said. "Bullshit!" Richie Samuels accused. "Pick one," they demanded, "whose side are you on?" "Casper smashed into him in the lunchroom and didn't even say he was sorry! Plus, he always takes my chocolate," Zalinsky said, trying his best to push my swing vote toward the populace. I didn't answer. "You want Casper!" they charged. "So what?" I said, "I hope they don't fight, but if they do, I hope Casper wins, alright?" "That's cause you're a nigger lover," one of the Wonderbread Boys spit out. "Are you? Are you a nigger lover?" they all asked. I told them all to shut up. They confirmed that I was and they were downright mad at me for not giving them the answer they wanted to hear. "Casper's friends always come over here and take our stuff," they complained. "They're not his friends. And that's because you don't stick up for yourselves," I reminded them. "You're stupid if you like them! They hate us too, you know," they informed me. "I didn't see any of you help me when I got jumped during lunch last week," I accused them. They all walked away without saying a word. I knew then that we wouldn't be friends like we had been in the past. I wasn't that sad. I remember right then and there feeling like I just got older, like I changed. I used to care so much what they all thought of me. I always wanted to impress them, in sports, with my grades, everything. But it didn't really matter. We were different, and right then I realized I was glad to be.

I had a minute before my homeroom class and so I went into the boy's bathroom. When I entered I heard a slow rhythmic banging. It came from the last stall. I walked to a sink in front of the stall and started to wash my hands. The banging continued. Someone was punching the metal wall and I heard low moans between each hit. "Casper?" I asked. "Who's that?" he said and opened the stall. I asked him if he was all right. "I'm cool. Just getting ready," he said. He looked up at me, "so I guess you want me to lose too, huh?" I told him I didn't. "Not even cause I take your potato chips?" he asked. "I pack extra," I told him. I let him know that I thought that the other guy was a weirdo. I told him I call him "The Fonz" because of how he dresses. "He's big," he thought out loud. I didn't answer. "I could lose," he said. He let himself hear the words for a second and then with a sense of dread in his voice said, "I can't lose, you know?" "No. No way, you can't," I said, trying to instill confidence. "Do you have to fight?" I asked him. "Always," he answered. We were silent for a moment and then he took a deep breath and said, "wish me luck." "Good luck," I told him. "Luck ain't got shit to do with it, son—its skill. Skill and balls," he said with a half smile. I wished him luck again anyway. "I'm ghost," he said and left the bathroom.

ꕥ ꕥ ꕥ

It was three o'clock, school was out. I walked out thinking that maybe both parties forgot, or were just on to more important things or possibly were just willing to let it slide altogether. I almost let myself believe it when

I heard the word fired across the yard. "Fight!" I followed the bloodthirsty crowd to the gathering circle. The oddest part was that it always seemed like the crowd was angrier than the two boys who were about to fight.

They faced each other. "Ok, now I beat up the big bad black boy," The Fonz said. "Beat this! Fake ass, Fonzie!" Casper yelled and came out swinging. The Fonz was fast; he ducked Casper's swings and connected with a right hook to the side of Casper's head. This shocked Casper and maybe scared him a little, but his fear quickly turned to rage as he charged The Fonz again. They crashed like battering rams and locked together as each threw a flurry of punches. Some hits connected, others didn't. The crowd roared with vicarious pleasure. The two fighters separated for a second, and as they parted, The Fonz threw another punch that just caught Casper on his lip. It drew blood. It probably looked worse than it was, but blood ran down his mouth and dripped onto his already stained T-shirt. The crowd was now bloodthirsty; even some of the black kids were cheering for The Fonz. There's nothing like seeing old idols fall. Casper was a great street fighter, but it seemed like The Fonz was trained. He appeared to move much faster than you would expect for his sheer bulk. Casper threw hard punches, each one seemed capable of demolishing small buildings, but he couldn't connect. The Fonz threw him down hard to the concrete a couple of times.

Casper was getting roughed up pretty bad. This was the guy who spared me from getting my own ass whooped and there was nothing I could do to help him. I was no match for The Fonz. So, I did the only thing I could do and just yelled out my support, "c'mon Casper, kick his ass! Stop playing with him. It's your fight!" Some of the black kids looked over to me wondering why I was cheering for the opposing side. A few white kids seemed like they were ready to challenge me for being a traitor. But I didn't stop, I kept telling Casper to stop playing around and really fight him. Then Casper got up and grabbed The Fonz around the waste, charging him like a wild bull. The Fonz grabbed onto the back of Casper's pants and tried to perform some kind of wrestling throw. Casper broke free and informed everyone that The Fonz was indeed "gay" because he was now trying to undress him. "You want my big black dick, don't you?" Casper inquired as he grabbed his own crotch.

Then quick as lighting Casper threw two punches that both connected, catching The Fonz off guard and knocking him down to the ground. The Fonz seemed stunned by the strength of the punches. He got up and Casper connected again with another combination. It truly became Casper's fight. Once he actually got hit, The Fonz lost his confidence and his edge. Casper kicked The Fonz in the ass while he was down on the ground. Arty Dekakis let out a barely audible cheer.

When The Fonz got up, his mouth was bloody and he was barely holding back tears. Casper went over and pulled his fist back; The Fonz cowered from the impending punch. Casper didn't throw the punch, he just yelled, "who's the nigger now? Nigger!" The Fonz turned and pushed through the crowd running toward his home. Casper didn't say anything, he just put on his worn denim jacket, picked up his book bag and walked toward the school bus that would take him back to his neighborhood. He was bruised, but not broken. It was still his school.

When I returned the following week, I found out that Principal Buntner had learned of the brawl, and since the park was officially school property, he had Casper expelled. He would now attend school in his own neighborhood, a fate no one was sure he would survive. The Fonz got his first warning from the Principal and he started coming to school dressed like a normal kid, or at least like a normal kid from Albania or Lithuania or somewhere. I still ate at the Wonderbread boys' table, only we didn't talk as much anymore. I was just doing my time praying that I was destined for greater things, or at least something outside of Midwood. Casper never returned to our school, but one thing is for sure, he did leave a hero, undefeated and undisputed, at least in my mind. I don't know what ever became of Casper Carter, but I am often haunted by his ghost.

Sonny's Slips

By
C. Kelly Robinson

THE EVENING Misty swooped into my office lobby, I didn't even see her coming. I was at the receptionist desk reviewing the day's billings with Ms. Watson, when I felt a whoosh of cool air against my neck. I turned around and there she was.

Misty hadn't changed a lot since the funeral. Three weeks had passed since we'd put Sonny in the ground, and she was wearing the same black nylon sweat suit she'd sported at her brother's memorial. Her hair was different, of course; the girl revamped her hairdo weekly. Today she had a short natural, her tight, kinky curls tinged in burnt sienna.

Looking down into her eyes, I slid my hands into my pockets. My knees felt ready to buckle and I could feel Ms. Watson's hot stare singe my back. "Hi," I said, catching my breath, "back in town already?" At the funeral, she'd sworn she was moving to L.A. for good. Not that commitments carried much weight with Misty.

Reaching up to clench my shoulders, she planted a wet kiss onto my left cheek and stepped around me to trade glares with Ms. Watson, who stood over her whirring copy machine with arms crossed. "I know you not gonna sit there and not speak," Misty said, her luminous eyes shining with feigned innocence.

Ms. Watson, a forty year-old grandmother with the old soul of a "real" Grandma, cocked her head sideways and peered over the rims of her wire-rimmed glasses. "Baby, don't start none, won't be none. We all love you here, but now is not a good time . . ."

Slinking away from the desk, I let the girls get reacquainted and went to my office, ducking as I entered a space designed for a man of average height. I'd had a full day and would have been happy to leave the place in disarray for the night. Damned if some misguided desire to impress didn't take me over. Moving furiously through the windowless rectangle, I ran a dust rag over the TV and DVD Player in the far corner, straightened up the posters and plaques that had fallen from the walls, and collapsed into the seat of my grandfather's wide cherry wood desk.

I looked toward the floor and remembered one last thing, something I was afraid that Misty would notice. Sonny's poster. The one from '97, when he came in off the bench and helped Jordan lead the Bulls to the championship. It was a marvelous poster; a shot of my boy, my most famous client and a friend I'd loved like a little brother, standing before the world tall and proud. He looked like a champion unbowed by his life-long struggle with a knotted tongue. Like many kids from the streets of Brooklyn, Sonny fought the impact of an invisible father, a suffocating housing project, and a home ravaged by crack pipes and pimps. For him, life's demands hadn't stopped there. An extra weight had leapt from the shadows and wrapped about his shoulders, leaving him grasping for the simple words that came naturally for everyone else. As his speech therapist since his years starring with the Maryland Terrapins, I had tried to shepherd Sonny past the impediment of his stutter, help him cut through the thicket of sports agents who declared him damaged goods and the NBA coaches who questioned his intelligence. The Sonny in this poster, his shoulders high and his eyes ablaze, had won the battle. He had not won the war.

I held Sonny's poster in a tight-fisted grip, turning the crumpled mass over and over in my hands. The night of his death—an apparent suicide—I'd ripped it down in a fit of rage. Misty would notice its absence. My hands shaking, I yanked the bottom desk drawer out and felt near the back for my safety stash, a flask of sweet suds. I'd embraced the flask, for the first time in years, on the same night I ripped Sonny from my wall.

I downed two swigs and shoved the flask and the poster's remains deep into the drawer, just as Misty cracked my door open. As she approached, I jammed two sticks of Trident into my mouth. "I hope you made up with Ms. Watson," I said, my mouth smacking with the sloshing of the gum. "You should call before showing up here, Misty. Not that you're not welcome, but well . . . you know. Ms. Watson's protective of her turf." My office had been one of Misty's many places of employment. She'd assisted Ms. Watson for about three months, until we realized she thought nine to five meant ten–thirty to two.

She walked past my two low metal chairs and perched on the desk corner closest to me. "Ancient history, okay?" She was leaning over me and removing her sweat jacket, flooding me with the smell of her vanilla-scented perfume and her Strawberry Bubblicious-stained breath. "Sorry that ain't work out, I know you only hired me as a favor to Sonny." She paused and looked around at the posters on the wall, sweeping over James Earl Jones, Marilyn Monroe, and Bo Jackson. "Sonny always loved you for helping me. He loved you, period."

My chest muscles flexed and I couldn't meet her eyes. Next I knew she cupped my chin with a hand and forced my gaze to hers. At twenty–four, she was more than ten years younger than me, but damn if I didn't feel like the child when I was in her hands. Especially without Sonny around to keep me honest. "I know you loved him back, Lyle," she said. "You helped him stand on both feet, be the man he could be. You know that wasn't the Sonny we . . . lost. I want you to help me prove it."

Inhaling her scent, I felt my breath growing shallow. "Misty . . . what?"

"Look at these," she said, laying a stack of small square paper slips across my desk and shifting her bosom smack into my face. I looked past her and examined the slips as she kept talking. "Found them in Sonny's place last night. Went over to help Deidre clean up." Deidre was Sonny's widow. Deidre wasn't speaking to me, but I'd heard through the grapevine that she and Sonny's kids were moving out of his estate in Silver Spring, to stay with her parents. Sonny's main remaining asset had been heavy life insurance policies; he'd as good as thrown them away when he slipped the noose around his neck.

"Are these betting slips?" I held one up to the light and recognized the markings from slips my Pop collected at the horse track, years ago. It had started as a recreational hobby for Pop, but by the time he took me along he was risking my college fund on those unpredictable creatures. I never understood the pull it had on him, at least not until alcohol got me. That burning liquid was the deranged lover I'd spurned repeatedly, only to see it resurface with every crisis that crossed my path.

Misty interrupted my reverie. "Let me save you some time," she said, draping an arm around my shoulder, "see the stamp at the bottom of these receipts? Silver Fox Enterprises. That's Grady Worrill's place."

My eyes narrowed at the mention of Grady's name. I'd attended high school in Baltimore with his nephew Ike; the Worrill family had been notorious throughout Baltimore even then, twenty years ago. Grady, the patriarch, led a crew of siblings, nieces, and nephews in the family business. In addition to a car wash, massage parlor, and a pharmacy that dealt in stuff that came without prescriptions, they took bets on sporting events via the Silver Fox bar. Any loser with a few dollars was welcome to risk them.

Sonny's signature was scrawled on every damn receipt, and the results weren't pretty. Last year he'd lost twenty thousand by siding with

Purdue over Washington in the Rose Bowl; he'd also selected FSU over Oklahoma in the Orange. This year he'd been fool enough to take Ohio State over Michigan and Indiana over Maryland in basketball, dropping another seventy–five thousand in the process. Sonny wasn't stupid; he was sentimental, always believing in underdogs because he was one himself. He'd told me about the gambling once a few years earlier, but I'd thought he'd let it go. Between my counsel and the sharp pay cut he took when the Bulls waived him, he should have known better.

I ran a tape totaling the net losses on Sonny's slips while Misty sat perched on the desk, looking over my shoulder. Her warm breath made the hairs on my neck stand straight, but I kept hitting my adding machine's keys until the last slip was accounted for. "Three hundred twenty–one thousand dollars, seventeen cents. Jesus." I looked over my shoulder. "Did he have that kind of money?"

"There was some old bonuses, from his first couple years in the NBA, that Deidre got him to set aside in savings or stocks or somethin'." She sighed. "He *tried* not to touch it . . ."

"He'd been out of the NBA for two years, Misty," I said, frowning, "no way could his deal with NBC or his little gigs with the rappers cover this."

She grabbed my chin again, with a force as savage as it was desperate. "I know. If you were Grady and someone owed you that big, what would *you* do?"

Ms. Watson was clearing off her desk for the evening when Misty and I passed her, headed for the front door. She shot me a glare that pulled me to her side. I looked over my shoulder at Misty, who held the door open, before whispering, "what?"

"It won't look good, you leaving with her," she said loud enough for Misty and anyone in the hallway to hear. "You insist on winding up on your ass, huh Lyle? Them white boys ain't playing with you." She was referring to Alex and Bo, the two therapists with whom I'd shared office space for five years now. "They'll leave you stone cold, they see you go off the deep end. You got young kids, boy—"

"And a mother of my own," I said, teeth clenched. I patted Ms. Watson's hands and spun around, following Misty.

It was deceptively sunny outside, despite the temperature being in the low fifties. As I climbed into the driver's seat of Misty's Mercedes SUV, which she had parked on a crowded block of 13th Street, Ms. Watson's reference to my girls hit home. It was after six, and they were due out from soccer practice shortly.

I revved the SUV's engine and pulled into traffic. "Give me a minute," I said, grabbing my cell phone from my windbreaker. Reaching Ma, I explained I'd need her and Pop to get the girls and keep them another night. I got no complaints, just some rightfully concerned probing. Ma knew I was going through a rough patch, but she expected more advance notice than I could give right now. For six years, since Michele had decided I could raise our children better without her along for the ride, I had done pretty well, dodging the bottle and plugging forward. No doubt, though: my ex-wife's abandonment had taken me to the edge of the abyss, and losing Sonny had nudged one foot over the black hole.

"Thanks for driving," Misty sighed as I zoomed toward New Hampshire Avenue, "you sure you don't mind helping me out?"

I fought back a grim smile and patted her hand, which was alarmingly close to my lap. Was this about helping her or about helping me? "We all deserve to know what really happened, Misty. You don't owe me anything."

When she didn't respond, I looked over to see a tear rolling down her right cheek. Head down, she muttered, "I told him not to keep messing with Grady's business."

It was overcast by the time we arrived in Hyattsville. Misty led the way into the Silver Fox, a red brick, two-story storefront slumping with age. I hadn't been through the place since my college years, when I was a marginal Morehouse basketball star looking for summer thrills, but I knew enough to know I didn't want to walk in there looking like trouble. At the Fox, a six foot three, two hundred fifty-pound stranger was liable to get his head bashed in.

We opened a front door with smudged glass and stepped onto creaky wooden floorboards. Straight ahead was a sunken bar framed by loud red carpet and plaid wallpaper. The flashy colors, combined with the harsh white light bulbs overhead, made for a blinding effect.

Misty walked over to a man crouching behind the bar, his butt up in the air as he knelt down to lift a cardboard box packed with spirits. She leaned over the counter, her eyes dark and determined. "Grady in?"

Ike, Grady's nephew, turned and stood to face us. I recognized him instantly—the head shaved as bald as mine, the mouth full of flashing gold teeth, and the short, wiry frame of a flyweight boxer. He scowled like we had stole something and started to push his shirtsleeves up both arms. "I look like Grady to you? He ain't here, get the freak out."

"Ike, we just need a minute." I stayed at Misty's side, not wanting to take a menacing step toward a cat who'd packed heat since our days in junior high. My hands fluttering in the pockets of my slacks, I fought the urge to feel like a "little bitch," as the kids liked to say. No point in raising the temperature until I had more facts. Today was about Sonny, but I didn't want it to be my last day.

"I know you?" Ike arched his back and walked out from behind the bar. "You look familiar."

I went ahead and reminded him of our glory days. It took several examples to jar his memory, but he came around. "Lyle Wickham. You was da man back in the day. Dude, between the big gut, mangy beard, and chrome dome, I'd never have known ya."

"Ike, look," I said, "we're just trying to understand Sonny's debts to Grady. You know, whether there were any issues."

"Any issues?" Ike walked past us to a corner opposite the bar and grabbed a pool stick. "He was in hock to us, nah mean? Was Grady happy about that?" He pulled out a racking triangle and filled it with a rainbow of balls, before pausing to size both of us up. "Don't know about the trick here, Lyle, but you went to Mo'House. You're smart enough to figure that shit out."

From behind me, I heard Misty shift. Her voice was clear and crisp, her tone eerie in its calm. "What do y'all do to folk you ain't happy with?"

Leaning nonchalantly over the pool table, Ike flicked a cool glance at us as Misty and I edged toward the table. His gaze met mine again, a wary beam declaring *damn right, you best act like you know your place*. "What you want me to say, girl," he said, taking a shot and scattering the balls, "somethin' you can run and take to the po-lice?"

"I ain't here to cause you trouble, man," Misty said, her voice caught between a plea and a threat, "I just want my brother's rep fixed on the street. People sayin' he a punk, that he did himself—"

"Not my problem," Ike said, flicking a wrist dismissively. "Everyone should have the problems your boy had. What happened to him, happened 'cause he didn't handle his business."

As I stepped to the edge of the pool table and placed a firm hand in front of Misty, keeping her from getting past me, I felt my stomach lurch. The sickeningly sweet odor of the liquors surrounding Grady's bar and the emotional tension was about to do me in. I wanted nothing more than to shut these two up and down the open bottle of Scotch on Ike's counter.

I turned toward Misty. "This is pointless," I said, more for her protection than any other reason. "Ike and Grady may have had issues with Sonny, but they didn't—" I stopped when her face contorted suddenly and she gripped my arm, sinking her long nails into my forearm.

As I yelped in shock, Ike stepped back from the table, opposite us, and sucked his teeth, the gold flashing off the overhead lights. "It's none of your damn business what we did, okay? Grady always handles his business. Folk who place bets with him know they gotta pay up when everything's due or they gon' be sorry. Beyond that, I don't personally be getting my hands dirty." He paused for dramatic effect. "So I wouldn't know what went down with Sonny. I *do* know we'll never have another bad debt from that muthafucka."

"They killed him!" The SUV's insides shook with Misty's thunderous shriek as I pulled away from the curb. She grew quiet and for a few moments the only sound was the misting rain and the whirr and hum of her luxury car's engine. "They killed him," she said softly, and began to weep almost imperceptibly. Wrung out from emotion, I continued to slip through traffic, treading slowly through several blocks before turning off into a small, square asphalt lot. Parking and reaching over, I took Misty in my arms and pulled her to me across the car seat. I rubbed her back, whispered into her ear that she needed to be strong for Sonny, and let her kiss me lightly on my neck and chin.

Our chins weren't an inch apart now. "I ain't got drunk since I found the slips last week," she said, streaming stale Bubblicious into my nostrils. Tears were still flowing, but she was smiling. "He always told me to get right, and I never listened. When I thought he did himself . . . I got worse at first. I was high for days after the funeral. But when I realized he might not have done it—"

I pressed a finger to her lips and leaned into her. "He was a bright light, Misty," I whispered, over the thump of my heartbeat, "and so are you. You have to believe the best about him, and start believing the best about Misty now."

After a deep kiss, we raced toward Rock Creek Park in the SUV and talked about next steps. I insisted she not do anything else to confront Ike and Grady. There was no concrete proof that they'd a hand in Sonny's death, but once she passed the betting slips to the authorities, they were bound to take an interest in Grady's relationship with Sonny. Something like a dozen of Grady's customers had been murdered through the years; the problem was most had plenty of enemies or addictions just as culpable as their gambling debt. Not so with Sonny.

Minutes later we were parked in a remote, hilly section of the park. It was dark and there was no sign of imminent life, save the growing chirps of crickets. "I promise I'll stay out of their way," Misty said as she straddled me. Her eyes were aglow with newfound light, there was a smile in her voice, and her sweaty but sweet scent filled me with peace. "I'll call the authorities tomorrow," I said, my breath becoming shallow as she eased out of her sweat jacket, T-shirt, and bra. "You stay at your hotel and don't call me at the office. I'll call you. We need to wait a few days, see whether they're able to put heat on Grady and prove anything."

Rolling her tongue around inside her mouth, Misty unbuckled my belt and began to tug at my slacks. "What if they don't find anything, what if it just pisses Grady and Ike off? They might come after you."

My ability to think was slipping away. I gripped her hips and slid her sweats and thong underwear to her knees. "If we're wrong, none of this will matter. They were going to get rid of me at work eventually." With sudden grunts, Misty and I followed the push of passion and banged, rocked, and soiled the cabin of her Mercedes like two teenagers behind the football bleachers. I was the cynical, rusty student, she the young but seasoned veteran. I took my share but focused on giving her what I imagined any lovers she'd had since Sonny's funeral had not: patience, affection, affirmation, and as many peaks as she could take.

When we emerged from the shadows of the park, I was confident we'd avoided any prying eyes, and there had been no signs that Ike had followed us. We kissed desperately again and I hopped out several blocks from my office, sending Misty back to her hotel to await my update in the morning.

The office had been locked and shut down hours before, so I went straight to my minivan, ready to hit the Beltway. I needed to get the girls home, get them to bed and get some sleep myself. I was eager to plot how to approach the authorities, concerned for my safety, but confident it was worthwhile to see Sonny avenged. My proud, strong warrior had not sold out, had not abandoned the mission. He had been torn from it.

In the envelope of night, I didn't sense the intruder in my passenger seat until I had turned the ignition. I heard the labored breathing and smelled the pungent mix of cigarette smoke and beer. With a start, I flipped the overhead light. Grady Worrill sat next to me in a pinstriped three-piece suit, facing forward and chewing slowly on a circle of tobacco.

"You do good work, young blood," he said, turning toward me with eyes veiled by tinted glasses, "so I'ma try to make this quick and painless."

I leapt in my seat as he thrust a manila envelope into my chest. "You'll find this interesting." He yanked the shades from his face and looked at me with weathered, weary eyes. "My hands ain't clean, son. But I choose my battles. Some debts just have to be written off."

"Grady, I—" My voice caught in my throat as I wavered between anger and horror.

"I hate seeing what happened to the boy myself. I liked all those speeches he gave, the way he encouraged kids to overcome obstacles." Grady rose up in his seat, until his white Afro scraped the roof of my van. "Thought I helped him out with what I done, but you can't save people." He pointed a crooked, rugged finger toward the roof. "That's his job. You be easy."

Shaking in my seat, I grasped for air as Grady stepped from my car, slammed the door, and stepped into an idling late-model Buick that had pulled alongside me. As his ride zipped into the night, I ripped the envelope open. Inside was a copy of a handwritten letter addressed to Grady, a note filled with desperate words of thanks and signed, unmistakably, by Sonny. It was dated a full month before his death, before his wife's Jaguar was repossessed and he was served with an eviction notice. Before he was rejected for another sports announcing post, after stumbling through his audition. Before he was removed from the Right Guard commercial with Scottie Pippen, when he couldn't get his own name out. Before he figured out that his "way with words" meant the normal avenues for a retired NBA pro were closed to him. What had the suicide note, the one with the signature identical to the one on this letter, said?

> *To everyone I love: Deidre, my babies, Misty, and Lyle,*
>
> *This ain't your fault. I just can't do this no more. I've been lying to people from the 'hood to the White House, saying you can overcome every obstacle and right every wrong. I can't even make my mouth work long enough to keep food on my family's table.*
> *You're better off without me.*

I felt tears form as I accepted the truth for the last time. In an alternate universe, Grady Worrill would have popped me full of lead. I'd come face to face with him because I couldn't accept the truth; now I had no choice. If I went with the flow, I'd wind up soiling Sonny's memory with my own destruction. I knew he wouldn't want that; he had loved me and my girls too much.

Trudging from the car back into my locked office, I left the lights off except for the banker's lamp on my desk, where I sat and downed the rest of my secret stash—the beer as well as the vodka. As I swished the last bits of suds around in my mouth, I fished my schedule of AA meetings from the same drawer and stuffed them into my jacket pocket. Then I picked up the phone and dialed Misty's hotel room.

When she heard me, her voice brightened. "You ain't have no trouble?"

"Misty, listen," I said, before pausing and biting my lip. I wanted to keep her with me, but that would have been for my benefit and not hers. "I've already had a run-in with Grady. This thing could get hot. I don't think it's safe for you to stay out here."

We talked about friends, users, and others she could stay with in L.A. "I could stay with Truth Jackson. He sayin' he'll get me a part in his next movie." Truth was a rapper who'd used her for the occasional fling.

"Will Truth help you stay in school this time? I don't think so. Let me make some calls," I said, stuffing my bottles and flask into a plastic bag and flipping off the banker's lamp. "I've got friends from Maryland who can put you up for a few weeks. You go ahead and schedule yourself a flight first thing in the morning. Let me handle the police and this Grady thing."

I was surprised at her response. "I trust you, Lyle."

"Misty? You do realize there's no guarantee the cops can prove what happened to Sonny, no matter what we think?"

Misty sighed. "Lyle. I look like freaking Pippi Longstocking to you? I ain't expecting the police to solve a damn thing. I just want the truth known, that my brother didn't do himself. Any investigation, any rumor, will circulate on the street. That's all that matters."

My head feeling fizzy, I felt my lips spread in a weak smile. I'd have to make one last call to Grady. "You'll have that. I promise."

Có Mang

By
Corina Marie Ahn Knoll

Ma is cradling a bundle while crying and laughing at the same time. She reaches out to pat Selena's head, then pulls her close and pushes the blanket into her arms. She says something like, "you are first but he is first to you" only it is in Vietnamese and Selena is barely listening and only holding on tight but not too tight to a tiny baby that has Ma's eyes. Maybe it is instinct or maybe it is something she has seen others do, but she can't help but kiss his fuzzy patch of black hair and rub her cheek on his soft skin. And then Ma tires and leans back into the bed so Selena slowly moves toward a chair, sits down and continues to hold the boy who only blinks and sometimes moves his hand.

And then there is Ma twenty pounds and two shades lighter, lying on the couch in her yellow robe, too weak to move her head. She is trying to walk Selena through all the steps of preparing bún for Friday night's dinner. Her voice is hoarse and Selena can't understand her, but Selena responds from the kitchen saying, "okay, okay." She is 16 and already knows how to make bún, but she lets Ma instruct her. Suddenly it is quiet and so Selena runs into the living room to find Ma asleep. Kneeling on the floor, she strokes Ma's head.

The ringing of the telephone made Selena jerk her head up. She had been nodding off for half an hour, trying to fight the fatigue that kept urging her to drift away. Jumping up out of her chair, she grabbed the phone on the third ring.

"Hello?"

"Selena?" It was Tran.

"Hey."

"Whadup girl."

"Where you at?"

"I'm over at Hector's, we just trying to finish these flyers."

Selena sighed. "Well are you coming over beforehand still?"

"I dunno yet. Depends if we finish this in time."

"Well I planned on you for dinner, and I have all the stuff."

"I know Seal, but I gotta do this, we need to hand them out at the party tonight."

"Whatever—you always do this."

Tran groaned. "I'll try, okay?"

"Okay. Just try hard."

"Aight, I gotta go."

"Yeah." She clicked the phone off, tossed it back in its cradle and walked into her tiny kitchen where she began pulling out all the ingredients she would need for dinner. Rice noodles, shrimp, carrots, cucumbers, fish sauce, vinegar—she found herself slamming each one down on the counter. If Tran didn't show tonight, it would mean something. It would mean she'd been replaced. The notion had haunted her lately, especially as he became more consumed and passionate about his work. She couldn't remember the last time she and Tran had eaten it together.

Selena never saw her mother eat during the week. Ma would sit at the kitchen table and sip hot water while Selena and Tran ate cold cereal before school. At dinner she would always say she wasn't hungry and that she might have something later. It wasn't until Selena got older that she realized Ma probably never sat down to a full meal. Maybe that is what made her disappear. The absence of sustenance. Weren't women always doing this? Always starving themselves? To be thin, to be thinner, to be the thinnest. Mostly though just to have control. But it didn't make sense that they used this method to have power over their life, because all it did was make them weak. Maybe if Ma had just made time to eat, she would have been strong.

At least she had been beautiful. Selena had seen the envelope of photos Ma kept in her bottom drawer. Pictures of her as a teen in Vietnam, where her crooked smile was all your eyes wanted to see.

Being beautiful hadn't been enough. Ma shrank from the world and eventually withered away. Selena had her father's features. She always figured that meant something.

Selena sat across from Tran at her kitchen table, her hands cupped around a mug of hot tea.

"How's the biz?" she asked.

Tran was busy trying to shove as many noodles into his mouth at one time with his chopsticks.

"Hey—piggie . . ." Selena tapped on the table. "I asked you a question."

Tran took time to swallow. "It's all good. You know me and Hector are working with that girl Carla, you saw her at the last show, remember?"

Selena nodded.

"Man, girls got pipes, and then we found these three guys—get this, they're like a Vietnamese boy band."

Selena rolled her eyes.

"I know, shut up." Tran held a shrimp in his chopsticks and waved it around. "Two of them are Viet anyways, and then the third's a white boy—they're a little cheesy, but I got to admit they sound damn good. They're gonna sing a couple songs at tonight's party, we'll see if the crowd is feeling them. Anyways, we're still talking to Pablo in New York and he says he's found a bunch of people out there we could work with, he really wants us to come out there."

Selena snorted. "New York—yeah, right, it's like ten degrees there right now."

Tran looked at her. "Yeah . . . right." He slurped up a noodle. "Anyways, it's an idea. So how's Ryan?" he asked.

"Don't know really." Selena shrugged and took a sip of her hot tea.

"I was wondering how long he would last."

"Whatever."

"I gave him about a month—he lasted, what, four? Four and a half? That's pretty good."

Selena shook her head. "Don't wanna hear it."

"Seriously Seal—he was a good guy."

Selena shrugged. She could feel Tran's eyes on her.

"Are you okay?" he asked.

"Yeah. It's all good."

"Right."

"It is." Selena took another sip. She nodded toward his bowl. "How is it?"

Tran took a long slurp of the broth. "Tastes like shit."

Selena smiled. "I know—it's some good shit though."

He laughed and Selena flicked her tea at him.

"Why aren't you eating?" Tran pushed Selena's bowl toward her.

"I don't know. Not hungry I guess. Had a late lunch too." Selena touched her hand to her stomach.

A horn honked outside.

"That's Hector, I gots to go." Tran stood up.

"Finish your bún first."

"Seal, my stomach is going to bust open or I am going to vomit all over you if I eat anymore food."

She rolled her eyes again. "Fine, go."

He stood up and poured the remains in his bowl into the sink and then hurriedly washed his bowl and chopsticks. Selena watched him do this with a smile. He always did clean up after himself. Somebody taught that boy right.

"Aight Seal, gotta bounce. Get some sleep, you look like ass."

"Shit, you smell like ass," replied Selena.

Tran grinned at his sister and gave her a quick hug before rushing to the front door.

Selena watched him jog down the driveway and jump into Hector's truck. The kid had so much energy and was always running from one place to the next promoting the latest talent or hosting a gig. She went to the last event they held to promote some R&B singer. It had been in a tiny jazz club she'd never known existed, but it was really classy and everyone had a good time. She had been impressed by Tran working the room in a suit. So it was a good thing that he was busy and doing well.

There was still that tug inside of her though that wished he'd just sit still. There were things that needed to be said, conversations that needed to be had. Tran was her only confidant, especially now. Selena rubbed her stomach and went back to the kitchen to make a sandwich. She was hungry, but lately the taste of seafood made her gag, so the shrimp in bún made the whole dish unbearable. Craving peanut butter, she walked back into the kitchen and opened a cupboard. Grabbing the brown jar she suddenly felt queasy. Grimacing, she hurried to the bathroom where she immediately threw up. She had gotten so used to the act that it didn't gross her out anymore. She grabbed a washcloth and wiped her face. Sitting down on the tile floor, Selena leaned her head back against the wall. It was the same position her mother often sat in after chemotherapy made her sick and too weak to stand.

For a while, after Ma died, Selena would drive herself crazy wondering if cancer wasn't a made-up illness created by doctors around the world. She imagined them taking Ma and making her sicker by removing things they said were cancerous. It always seemed that it spread within the next two months. So every time she went back they would just shake their head and say that something new had to be taken out. Her ovaries, part of her liver, a kidney. Perhaps at one point the medical industry was failing and so they invented the idea of something that couldn't be cured, but that could slowly suck the life and money from thousands. It seemed to her a perfect ploy to give the medical and science world some sort of passion. A mission that made them appear credible and good, while really it was invented to keep them all in business.

It was a horrible thought for a 16-year-old to have running rampant through her brain. And when she got older she realized that such a thought discredited the unity that the disease brought to the world. Still, she wanted no part of a cause replete with pink ribbons and marathon runs and celebrity photo opportunities.

About a year after she was diagnosed, Selena's mother had gotten so weak that she was unable to stay at home anymore. They moved her into the hospital and there was talk of transferring her to the Mayo Clinic and trying some new treatments, but Selena knew no one took Ma seriously. She wasn't sure exactly how insurance worked, but she knew Ma had no money, which meant limited resources. When her mother was awake she was in so much pain that she only whispered in Vietnamese and her white nurses couldn't help but ignore her. There was no one to vouch for her, no husband to cry passionately at her bedside and plead with doctors to do everything they could for her. There were just two kids who visited every day after school and sat with their mother in silence. Words were harder to come by when they always had to be gentle or soothing. Besides, the communication lines between Tran and Selena with their mother had long since dilapidated. It was too much effort for their mother to speak English, while Vietnamese was forever foreign to their own tongues. The hour-long visit was always empty.

"Where the hell ya been? I've called you about ten times in the last hour. What good is a cell phone if you never pick up?"

"Sorry Seal—I'm working here. Besides, we was on a conference call with Pablo and his crew. Man, that cat is crazy! He was telling us about this one group he was promoting, he hooked them up with these dancers for their show, only he didn't know they were actually prostitutes and—"

"Tran, do I want to hear this story?"

"Probably not, but I could hear it a couple more times."

She laughed.

"Anyways," Tran continued, "Hector's gonna go meet up with Pablo in New York, you know, talk to him about some future business ideas and stuff."

"That's cool—maybe Pablo can hook Hector up with a nice girl, you know, one you don't pay for sex."

"You *do* wanna hear my story. I knew it," Tran laughed and then paused. "Man I wish I was going with him."

"With who?"

"With Hector—to New York."

"Oh, right. So it's almost ten, I take it you're not coming over tonight."

"I can't—but maybe tomorrow night—I dunno, I have to see."

"Okay." Selena breathed in. "I understand. Good luck." Her voice was strained.

"Thanks Seal, I'll call you mañana, okay?"

"Yeah. Okay."

"Aight, bye."

"Yeah. Wait —hey Tran?"

But he was gone.

When Selena's father officially left, neither she nor Tran really took notice. He had ebbed in and out of their life for so long that his presence didn't really matter. Well it did, but she tried not to let it.

When she was young, she saw her father several times a year. He'd stop by to say hi and bring her a dress or something girly. Her mother was always sent into a frenzy whenever he'd appear, cooking every traditional dish she could think of. Danny Rialto was Italian, but he sure did love Vietnamese food. He would sit at the kitchen table, and as he became more comfortable, he would make jokes, and Ma would sit there and beam at him. Selena begrudged him her laughter until she couldn't help it and would eventually giggle at his antics. He'd stay for a couple days, maybe five at the most.

His visits became less frequent as she got older. Selena became more wary of him and not as easily impressed. Tran barely knew him and hardly spoke of him.

Ma never explained her husband's absence, or even his occasional presence. She was only happy when Danny appeared.

It would have been so much easier for everyone if her father had been a bad man. If he had been horrible and evil and beat them. Then they could have hated him, they could have disowned him and felt good about it. But alcohol didn't make her father angry, it made him sad. And there was goodness in her father, which made Selena resent him more. She saw the kind of man he was capable of. Her mother seemed content with the man he chose to be.

Ma met Danny Rialto at his peak, when he was a missionary in Vietnam. Even then he had an affinity for hard liquor, but he had more control and faith in God, which somehow kept him focused. When they married and returned to the states, Danny's demise began.

Most people change their lives and become better people because they find God. Danny Rialto had to be original and somehow lose God. He stopped going to church, started spending more time in bars and would forget to come home.

When Selena's mother got sick he came more often, but never stayed long. He was so pathetic with his bloodshot eyes and sad attempts at conversation that Selena didn't want him around. After Ma died, Danny moved back in. Sort of. Basically his television was there which meant the courts could officially leave them alone about foster homes. Danny came home maybe once a week. After Selena turned 18 he left for good and took the television with him.

Selena sat hunched over her keyboard staring at her screen. She was supposed to be reconfiguring the new database, but she could only zone out and half-heartedly attempt to count all the lines in the figure eight of her screensaver.

Her phone rang and she grabbed for it eagerly.

"This is Selena."

"Seal."

"Hey!" Selena was surprised at Tran's voice. He hardly ever called her at work.

"You got a minute?"

"Yeah, what's going on?"

"I'm outside, you wanna go for coffee?"

"Uh, okay. Are you all right?"

"I'm cool, just come down, aight?"

"Just give me a couple seconds."

He was double-parked in front of her building listening to music with the windows rolled down.

"Tran, what the hell." She smiled as she walked toward him.

"Hey Seal," he smiled at her.

Selena stopped at the car door and cocked her head.

"If I'm not mistaken, that's a Vietnamese boy band."

Tran laughed. "Yeah, it's the demo we just made." He turned the music down.

"C'mon get in."

Selena looked at Tran suspiciously. "What's up with you?"

"Nothing, it's just—I just wanted to talk to you about something."

"Uh . . . okay . . . you crazy, but aight." Selena opened the door and hopped in.

She looked at him.

"Hey you want to get something to drink?" Tran was suddenly nervous. "We could go to that coffee shop you like."

"Naw, I'm straight . . . " She looked hard at him. "What the hell is up boy—you're spooking me. Is it Leia? You guys all right? She ain't pregnant is she?"

"Nah it ain't Leia—you know I'm smarter than that."

"Well sometimes things happen."

Tran looked at her sharply. Selena looked down.

"We on the outs anyways," Tran said.

"What? Since when?"

"Since like a week ago."

"Ha, and you giving me shit for Ryan—whatever man."

"It's different Seal—me and Leia . . . me and Leia on the outs 'cause . . . well 'cause we don't want to do that long distance thing."

Selena squinted. "Um, okay," she looked at him. "She moving or something?" Tran made no movement, his eyes focused on the steering wheel. Selena studied his face and began to feel her heart sinking.

"No," Tran said slowly, "she's not moving."

They said nothing and sat in silence.

"So." Selena's voice cut the air. "When and where?"

"Two weeks. New York." He said it quietly and slowly as if the words wouldn't hurt her as much that way.

"You decide this today?"

"I been thinking about it for a while—c'mon, you could tell that. Had to make a decision today though. Pablo's been holding spaces for me and Hector for a couple months now. He couldn't hold them any longer. Hector's been in for a while, they was just waiting on me."

Selena's face tightened. "Well then you gotta go."

"Yeah."

Selena smiled and looked out the window. She shook her head back and forth. "You out for yourself, my brother," she said slowly.

"What?"

"Nothing."

"Seal—"

"Nah, it's all good Tran. You do what you gotta do." She kept staring out the window, waiting for him to say something. When he didn't, she threw out the words that were playing in her head. "I just think you're pretty fucking selfish."

"What?"

"Nothing."

"Naw, you got something to say, just say it."

Selena said nothing.

"C'mon tough girl, you can't throw out that attitude and not follow that shit up. What do you got to say to me?"

Selena's head turned sharply at Tran's tone.

"Fine, you want to do this, do it. It's like it's all about you and what your plans are and how you can make it to the next step—I never even see you anymore. We supposed to be family, hell you know we're all each other's got—and then of course you wanna pull this shit. So go. Go to New York. Go do what you gotta do. Think about yourself, like you always been doing—"

Tran cut her off. "Do you hear yourself? Think about *myself*? God forbid I would think about anyone except you. Jesus, like you would ever let me forget. Don't do that shit to me—I don't deserve your random foul shit. You know you do that to anyone who crosses your path? They all get some sort of punishment—most of which they're never really sure about, but take anyway."

Selena cut her eyes at him.

Tran glared back. "You're just jealous."

"What?" She snorted. "Yeah—okay." She waved her hand.

"Admit it Seal, c'mon that's why you're so angry. What did I ever do to you? Just because I got other stuff to care about besides you, it's like you want to show me that makes me a bad person. It ain't my fault you're unhappy with your life. It ain't my fault that since the day I was born you been lording over me."

Selena felt her heart wrench at his words.

Tran noticed and he stopped. "Just let me have this Seal." His voice was quiet.

"I don't have to let you have anything Tran." She was looking at the floor. "And since I've been lording over you your whole life, well then I guess it's about time you stepped out from under my fucking regime and go do what you want."

A horn honked behind them. An oversized van was trying to make its way around Tran's car and was having difficulty.

"I gotta go," said Selena and with that she jumped out of the car, slammed the door and walked back into her building. She paused once she got inside and turned around to peer out the window. He was gone.

Selena touched her stomach. Her chest felt tight. If Tran wanted to leave her, well he had every right. It's not like he hadn't learned the art of leaving from the best.

When Tran was ten years old, his mother had been dead for two years and his father had officially left for good. He wanted to know things. He had questions and he wanted answers. Things that Selena pretended she couldn't remember.

"What did she say when I cried?" Tran would ask when Selena tucked him in bed.

She'd pull the covers up to his chin. "I don't know. You never cried. You were a good kid."

"I was?"

"Of course." Selena would kiss him on the forehead, which he hated and would always shake off.

"C'mon, Selena. Please?"

"It's late, you should be asleep already."

"I know she read us stories, Seal. I just want to know."

"I don't remember."

"Yes you do, cause I remember her. I remember her voice. She used to sing. There was that one song she sang all the time. It was Viet, though. I don't remember how to say the words. Do you remember?"

"No."

"She had black hair."

"Yeah."

"Like yours."

"Sort of."

"What else, Seal? I can't remember stuff. What else?"

"I don't know. I don't remember her at all."

"You're lying, Seal, you always lie."

She would say nothing and stroke his hair until she heard his breathing change and he was fast asleep. He always looked so peaceful, and she hoped he had good dreams. He didn't need to remember pain and she was afraid he'd see hers if she ever started talking about subjects like Ma. Tran needed to know his big sister was strong and unaffected. So she held back.

The box was kept in the back of her closet and only came out maybe once or twice a year. Selena found it in the weeks after her mother died. She was cleaning out the closet and there it was, a simple unassuming cardboard box. Inside was a mixture of Ma's things that she had never seen. Naturalization papers, letters in Vietnamese, pictures of an elderly couple that Selena could only assume were her grandparents. There had been a card with the words "Happy Mother's Day Ma" scrawled in the handwriting of a little kid. She couldn't remember if it was her or Tran that made it.

Selena sought the box now. She kicked aside a line of shoes and pulled it forward to the front of her closet. Carefully she began leafing through the papers. When her fingers found the bundle of old envelopes she pulled it out.

Selena and Tran had a grandfather that lived in New Jersey. Neither one of them knew him very well. Selena remembered meeting him on several awkward occasions when she was younger and Tran had only met him once.

Not until Ma died did Selena realize that this grandfather had been sending them money several times a year. For each check, Ma had kept the envelope it came in and had written the date and the amount on the outside of it. It appeared that she had been hoping to one day pay him back. With Ma's job at the supermarket, that seemed unlikely. Selena had been too naïve to wonder how they made it through each month on her mother's pay.

The name Anthony Rialto was typed in the left corner of each envelope along with his address. The address changed once, but the last eight said New Jersey. Selena stared at the bundle in her hands and chewed her lip.

The knocking on her door made Selena jump. It was after eleven. She put the bundle down, pushed her slippers on and walked cautiously downstairs. She flicked on the porch light and peered out the window next to the door.

Tran was standing there nervously shaking his leg.

Selena opened the door just as he was about to knock again.

He jumped. "Oh. Hey."

"Hey." Selena squinted at the car lights in her eyes. "You scared me."

"Sorry."

"You on your way?" Selena crossed her arms.

"Yeah, that's Hector," Tran motioned towards the car. "We're gonna crash at his aunt's and then she's gonna drive us to the airport tomorrow—we got a flight at seven in the morning."

"You got everything?"

"Yeah. I left a lot of stuff here—you know, at Leia's. We're gonna try to do this. She says after school she could maybe live in New York, so who knows."

"That's good. Leia's all right."

Tran laughed. "Whatever Seal, you hate her."

"I don't hate her—I just . . . she makes you happy."

The moment was awkward.

"You need anything?" she asked lamely.

"Yeah, maybe a couple thousand dollars and a lot of luck—you got any?"

"I got a ten in my wallet."

He smiled.

She made no movement, no expression.

"I made you this." Tran handed her a CD.

Selena took it, but didn't look at it.

"Thanks," she said quietly.

Tran searched Selena's face and then sighed. "I'm sorry Seal. I want us to be okay before I go. I don't need your approval, cause I'm still going no matter what—I just need . . . I just need to know you're gonna be okay."

Selena said nothing and only squinted.

"Selena. Are you hearing me?"

She breathed in to say something but nothing came out. She touched her stomach.

"Fine, you wanna pull that mime shit out of your ass now, that's cool too," said Tran.

Silence.

Tran sighed again. "Okay. Here's the deal." Tran's voice was quiet. "I'm gonna go now. If you won't talk to me, it makes it harder. You fucking frustrate me so much, but it don't make me love you any less. I get it. I get everything you've said and I get why me leaving means something bigger and I'm sorry I can't make it better for you. Jesus, Selena, I know you were my mom and dad—but I don't know that I owe the rest of my life to you."

Biting her lip, Selena looked up at Tran.

His eyes searched hers. "I want you to be happy. I think you should want the same for me," he said.

She felt cold and began to shiver.

"Fine. Now go," she said.

Tran stared at her for exactly five seconds. He looked up, bit his lip, then nodded his head. "Okay," he said.

As he walked down the driveway, Selena stood perfectly still as if moving her hand or blinking an eye would be a sign of weakness. There was a second when she nearly called out his name, but she swallowed the moment. It became safely packed into the thousands of other moments when she almost forgot her pride. Maybe they would all add up one day and form a solid rock inside of her to keep her from ever saying what she felt. At least it would be safer then. At least she would never have to worry about letting the moment win. It would just safely wither away inside of her.

Ma died at the hospital on a Wednesday. Selena and Tran had just taken the bus to see her, like they did every day after school. She had been dead for an hour or so, but the nurses had left her in her bed, because they knew her kids would be there soon.

Selena was old enough to understand and she had been expecting it anyway. She told Tran that Ma was sleeping, which made sense because she was always sleeping. Tran patted Ma's arm like he always did, but Selena just stared at her face. Her tired, worn-out face.

She resented her for being weak. For being that woman that would die looking so fragile. Typical. Typical female thing to do. Selena told herself that no matter what hardship ever came her way, she would survive it. But to be the kind of survivor that simply lived through it, not lived to talk about it on Oprah.

When Ma died so did Vietnam. Selena had never been able to speak Vietnamese and only understood a few things, but she had thought that one day she would really try to learn, although Ma had never encouraged her. Now, learning felt like it was only for those who already assumed she spoke the language.

Selena had always thought she and Ma would eventually visit Vietnam together. Ma would hold her own very nicely in a country that she understood and a language that she mastered. It would have been a good thing to see Ma in a position of power. Ever since she realized how awkward her mother's broken English sounded, Selena had felt smarter and stronger than Ma. And when her mother began to get sick and was always lying down or sleeping, she couldn't help but sense her mother's weakness.

Selena couldn't sleep. She kicked off her covers and sat up. The clock read 6:15. Pushing her hair back she got up, pulled her robe on and walked down to the kitchen. The tiles were cold on her bare feet and she walked on tiptoe to the cupboard. As she reached for a mug she noticed the CD Tran had given her lying on the table. She walked over and sat down and stared at it. She traced the design on the cover. It was a yellow star with the words "Soulful Sounds for Selena" written in curlicues over it. Tran would be on a plane in an hour. One more Rialto down. Soon she would be done with the entire lot of them. Surviving a family. Now there was an accomplishment.

In the quiet hour of the morning, Selena found herself wishing she wasn't so strong. She wished she was weak enough to run after Tran and tell him that yes, their mother did sing and yes she sang all the time and yes she loved music and yes that's where he got it from. But then, maybe it was weak to pretend to be so strong.

Clutching the CD, Selena walked back upstairs. She grabbed the handrail and paused for a second. She felt the nausea rising in her throat. The wave passed and she continued to her room. The bundle of envelopes with her grandfather's address was sitting on her bedside table. It would be almost 9:30 in Jersey.

"Hi, is this Anthony . . . Anthony Rialto?"

"Yes, who's this?"

"Uh, this is Selena . . . Selena Rialto . . . Danny is my father."

Silence.

"Do you know who I am?" Selena was standing in the middle of her room. She wanted to sit down, but she couldn't. She nervously stroked her stomach.

"How did you get this number?" The voice was cold.

"Um, Ma kept a lot of envelopes. Your address was on them. I called information to get your number."

It sounded like stalking. But maybe the definition was different for family.

The voice said nothing.

Selena continued. "I think the last time I saw you was . . . was maybe ten years ago. Well I mean I know exactly when it was. October 17. You know. The funeral."

Selena was dying and she knew it, so she paused and tried to will the other end to speak.

It stayed quiet for too long and Selena almost began to speak again.

Finally, there came a sigh. "Look, I sent those checks because of you kids."

"Oh—uh, I wasn't—"

"I figured it wouldn't be right to let kids starve—"

"I didn't even know until—"

"But you've been grown up for a while and I just don't think—"

"Look, really that's not why I'm calling, I don't need—"

"What is it that you want?" The voice was old and tired.

Selena took a breath.

"Look, I'm not trying to get in your business. I don't need money. See—Tran is moving, well he moved already—you know Tran, my brother? I uh, I thought you should know. He's going to be in New York. He's going to be near you. Uh, I'm not sure he remembers you, but do you remember him?"

Pause. "Yes."

"Well, he's only 18, I mean, he's pretty mature, but I thought—"

"You thought what?"

"I just thought maybe you should know he's there. He's a good kid."

The voice sighed. "I'm sure he is."

Silence.

"Look," came the voice. "I can't . . . I just can't. I am done with Danny."

Selena snorted. "I think we've all been done with Danny for a while."

"I don't think you understand. I know you're a good kid and I'm sure Tran has become one as well. I just—it's not my place anymore. Your mom needed help. So I did. But it's been ten years and now I am done."

Selena said nothing. She felt defeated before she even got to put in her best fight.

Finally she spoke. "I don't know why you came to the funeral. I think—I think maybe you came just to make sure she was dead."

The words hung in the air and she did nothing to ease them. It was a hateful thing to say and completely wrong and would only make Anthony Rialto become even more disgusted with Danny's family. But she couldn't help it.

She waited for a reaction. Nothing came.

So she laughed. "Okay. I hear you. Goodbye."

Selena clicked off the phone.

It hadn't been fair to expect anything from any of the Rialtos. She'd said goodbye to too many, she ought to have known better.

Who said a father had to stay? Who said a mother should survive? She guessed grandfathers were far enough removed that they only had to be a part of your life if they consciously chose to make the effort. And little brothers were meant to grow old and learn how to live on their own.

So she knew Tran would be okay. As much as she hated to admit it, he would be fine without her. He had probably stopped needing her years ago, but she had wanted to be his rock, the one thing that he could always depend on. Except Tran had always had lots of rocks. He was capable and smart and had friends and was happy and would probably end up married with three kids while running a successful business. He'd be fine.

So really, calling Anthony Rialto had been an excuse.

If their grandfather had been at all interested, it would have been a way to call Tran and tell him about the support system she'd set up for him on the East Coast. And then maybe she could have said nice things and talked about visiting. Or at least tell him that she was okay and she wanted him to be happy. That's all he had wanted and she should have been able to give him that. She had always tried to give him everything, so giving him peace of mind should have been natural.

And then maybe the subject of the baby would have worked its way into the conversation naturally.

But now a family member had rejected her once again and the thought of calling Tran pushed away.

She was going to do it alone then. She'd suck it up and she wouldn't feel sorry for herself and she'd stay as far away from being tragic as possible. Selena looked down at her stomach that barely showed three months of pregnancy. She remembered how excited Ma was when she was pregnant with Tran. She said she was going to raise a little gentleman. In a way Ma had thought it would be her way of answering Danny Rialto's demise. Raising a boy to be a real man.

Well Selena hoped to God she'd have a little girl, one who would be raised ten times stronger than Ma and who would know better than to always open her doors to a man who smelled of whiskey and vodka.

A baby would be like starting over. A clean slate, where her child would think that life began at her birth and everything she knew would be easy and good. If she had more children, she'd make for damn sure that they ate dinners together and knew how to act right as a family. It would be a new family and wouldn't include men that couldn't be fathers or grandfathers.

The newest Rialto was set to arrive in around six months. This one would be forced to stick close though, for a while at least. Maybe she'd start things off right by giving it a new last name. Family names did little for family ties. Selena had learned that much in ten years of three separate departures and one disowning from members of the Rialto clan. No, she definitely wouldn't give her child a last name riddled with sadness. Her baby would rise above and shake the family sorrow. Hopefully that included her own.

Friends of Distinction

By
Ian Edelman

Everything here is so clear you can see it.
And everything here is so near you can feel it.

"Hey beautiful, what's your name?" She barely spoke English and was freezing in her little dress. She was confused. Who was this dude driving a shiny new black Mercedes Benz S500 through Long Island City? He looked out of place.

"Hello," she replied. Louis had given her two pills earlier and she was feeling high.

Dude said, "you look hungry. Let me buy you some coffee and a pastrami sandwich," because that's what the prostitutes ate in the Iceberg Slim books.

"Yes, I'd like that."

But before Dude unlocked the door he inquired, "you don't have any crack on you, do you? I can't really have crack in the ride. So you know, I'm a cop." Dude wasn't a cop, but thought that way she would think twice before trying something.

Chick laughed and said, "no crack." She immediately found Dude quirky and amusing.

They drove off in an awkward silence over the 59th street bridge and south on the FDR drive to lower Manhattan, to Katz Deli, where Sally faked an orgasm for Harry. Where white kids with trust funds wear their thrift store finest and eat corn beef alongside Jewish retirees. Dude didn't particularly like the spot but Chick requested it by name. Dude thought it was dirty and also didn't want to run into any of his cop friends.

Dude had short, cropped brown hair, blue eyes and an otherwise nondescript face save the pencil thin mustache that his wife hated but he loved. He wasn't really good looking, but if he were famous, people would probably describe him as sexy.

Dude and his wife lived in a wealthy neighborhood on Long Island. He made a small fortune in the family business, South Shore Shower

Door, selling and installing high-end shower doors to luxury hotels all across the eastern seaboard, and most recently Las Vegas. Business was good, but Dude hated his job. He could give a fuck about shower doors. He wished his life were different. Dude had elaborate daydreams in which he was either an undercover cop or a high-ranking mafia general, or both, like Johnny Depp in "Donnie Brasco." But most of all, Dude wanted a big family.

Dude and his wife had no children because she was unable to conceive. She blamed it on him, and in couples therapy would always scream, "he just doesn't know how to fuck me right!" Dude hated her when she said that. What does that mean? Is there somebody out there who does fuck her right?

Since Dude was unable to get his wife pregnant, she decided to cut out sex entirely. She had always hated sex anyway. It had been six weeks since she slept in bed with Dude and longer since they had done it. On his birthday Dude paid his wife $2,000 to have sex with him and that was too much. Dude needed to find a more cost efficient alternative to fucking his wife.

Chick had a booming body and spoke with a thick Russian accent. She was wearing a tight lime green lycra dress that hugged her curves. She had a weathered face and runny eye make up. Her nose was big and her front teeth were kind of jacked. And while her thighs were chubby "cottage cheese thighs"—all things considered, she had definite sex appeal.

Chick ordered hot pastrami on rye, black coffee and a Dr. Brown's Black Cherry soda. Dude ordered the same exact thing and also requested some fresh pickles for the table. Chick got up to go to the bathroom. When she left, Dude noticed an old man starring at Chick's ass. The old man looked at Dude and said, "if I was thirty years younger, you'd be in trouble," and then burst into a hysterical hacking laugh.

Dude cut him off, "it's not what you think. I'm a cop."

The food arrived and Chick returned shortly thereafter. She looked better. She sat down and ate a pickle.

Dude felt awkward. "This is weird, right?"

Chick shrugged and took a big bite of her sandwich. When her mouth was full, she said, "why you think this is so weird?"

"It's cool, I guess," Dude conceded.

Chick offered, "you're cool guy."

"You're cool girl," Dude said in a fake Russian accent.

"You are my friend."

They both ate half a sandwich. Dude looked around the room then leaned in and whispered, "so do you just love fucking? Are you a nympho?"

Chick repeated him and tried to sound sexy. She said, "I love fucking," but didn't sound very convincing.

"C'mon. For real, are you a freak? Have you been dying to have my cock in your mouth since I picked you up?"

Chick licked her lips and said, "oh yes, baby." Then giggled and took a sip of coffee.

"C'mon, seriously."

"Serious. I serious."

"C'mon, be honest."

"You're funny man."

"C'mon, tell me. I want to hear you tell me what a freak you are."

"I'm a freak."

Dude was getting frustrated. "What? C'mon. That wasn't very convincing. Don't bullshit me here."

"I think you are playing a joke," Chick retorted.

"What!? I'm not joking with you. This is total bullshit. You don't even crave dick!"

Chick giggled and looked confused. She thought it best to not say anything. Dude was getting worked up. "I mean, really. How many times did you get fucked tonight?"

Chick hated that Dude was so loud. She lost her appetite. She didn't want to be at Katz Deli anymore. She wanted to get away from Dude. She wasn't really that scarred of him, she just found him annoying.

"Huh? How many times?"

Chick got up to leave. Dude grabbed her by the arm, "oh you're going to leave now. Fine. But you don't know who the fuck I am. I'm on television. You know cable television. You know HBO? The Sopranos? Huh? Ever heard of it? You know the guys with the pinky rings and the pasta, the fancy cars. All that's me. Okay? So you can go back to sucking cock, or not sucking cock in your case, and I'll go back to my big house and my hot fucking wife, okay? Is that what you want? You don't want to make no money tonight?"

Chick could only say, "I love Sopranos."

"Okay. See, now we're communicating. Listen, sit down, finish you're sandwich and I'll drive you back."

They finished their snacks and drove back over the bridge to Queens, Chick chewing on some gum. On a deserted side street, Dude pulled over.

"How much is a blowjob?"

"45."

"How much to fuck you?"

"90."

"How much is it if I jerk myself off and cum on your face?"

"No!"

"What about on your tits?"

"45."

"What! That's the same as a blow. I could get a blow job for that and not even have to do no work."

Chick suddenly cracked her gum as she chewed it. Dude was confused.

"Alright, I guess I'll just fuck you then."

Chick rose up on her feet, arched her back and removed her underwear.

"What's that, a thong? Nice."

Chick handed dude a condom from her purse. Dude took the condom and slowly ran his hand up Chick's leg. Chick closed her eyes as Dude's hand caressed her inner thigh. He was more gentle than she thought he'd be. Slowly Dude reached his hand between Chick's legs. As soon as he felt the stubble of her pubic hair he immediately jerked his hand away. A lost looking police car slowly crept around the corner. Dude's heart started to thump. Chick opened her eyes. As the cop car rolled down the street, Chick pulled her breasts out of her dress and crawled on top of dude.

"What are you doing?"

Chick didn't answer, instead she unfastened dude's belt and reached into his pants.

"I can't be having my fellow officers see me with no whore, you know?"

With the cop car on the next block, Chick took dude's joint in her hand. He was erect. Chick began to position herself for sex.

"Fuck are you doing?"

Dude strong-armed Chick off his lap. She fell onto the floor. The emergency brake caught her dress. Dude could see scratches on her ass. It turned him off.

"Oh fuck. Are you OK?"

Dude reached over to help her back onto her seat. Unexpectedly, he felt horrible for this woman and her battered ass. Dude wondered how she got the marks on her ass and how old she was. Dude wondered what her name was and if she had parents. Dude thought how miserable her pops would feel if he could see his chubby daughter laying half-naked on the floor of his Benz. Chick climbed back into her seat and crossed her arms. She was getting a little frustrated.

"What's your name?"

Chick didn't answer. The pills that Louis gave her were beginning to wear off. She no longer found Dude's insecurities amusing. She thought he was annoying and possibly a virgin.

"You want to fuck or no?"

"What? Do I want to fuck? Do you?"

"Yes."

"Well, what's up with those scratches on your ass?"

Chick had enough. She put her breasts back into her dress, grabbed her thong off the floor and started to exit the car, but her door would not open. Dude had the child proof locks on.

"Where are you rushing off to? You got a date?"

Chick ignored the question and turned on the radio. The Jamming Oldies station came on. Phil Collins sang, "I can feel it coming in the air tonight." Chick quickly hit the scan button and after some searching, finally settled on something by Usher.

"You like to dance?" Dude asked.

Chick rolled her eyes.

"Maybe one time I'll take you out dancing."

Chick kept her eyes fixed out the window. It would be light out soon. Dude wanted so desperately for Chick to like him, but it just wasn't happening. He wanted to find the nymphomaniac prostitute with a heart of gold who got gangbanged on her days off. He wanted to save somebody. But Chick wasn't for the saving. Chick wanted to get paid, get up with Louis, cop some pills, take a bath, light her vanilla scented candle, and listen to her new Faith Hill CD until she fell asleep. She ignored Dude.

"Okay, sure that makes sense to me—you'll put a stranger's cock in your mouth for forty five fucking dollars, but you won't let me take you out dancing. Fuck is wrong with you?"

Chick kept Pepper Spray in her bag. She'd used it once before in a similar situation, but wasn't sure if Dude might still want to fuck or not. The last thing Chick wanted to do was lose the money. The weather had been shitty and the streets had been slow. Chick reached in her bag and took the safety off her pepper spray.

"Listen. This is weird, right? This is weird to me. I should probably just take you back to your home. You live alone?"

"No."

"Yeah, that's good. It's good you're not alone. You got a roommate? A boyfriend or something?"

"I have roommate, a Russian girl."

The way she said Russian girl aroused him. Dude imagined she had a beautiful roommate, and that they slept in the same bed, had pillow fights in their panties and showered together to save water. This turned dude on. He reached over and felt Chick's breast. She reluctantly turned to look at him. He smiled revealing a chipped front tooth she hadn't noticed before. He looked horny and pathetic. Chick was glad she hadn't pepper sprayed him earlier. Dude took out his erect penis and put on the condom.

They fucked.

It was over in less than a minute. Chick didn't even have time to make him think he did a good job, which was her usual tactic. Chick climbed off Dude, who was still breathing heavy. Dude started the car and peeled out. He was taking her back to the corner where he had picked her up.

"It's extra because you take so long, okay?" Dude nodded in agreement.

"Listen, I know you probably think I'm a scum bag, but for whatever its worth, I want you to know that I think you're a beautiful girl and if you want to ever get together I'd love to take you out. I'm a real nice guy, you could ask anybody."

Dude slowed down as he approached Chick's corner. Louis was there looking pissed off.

"You're in America now; this is the best fucking country in the world. You can have a better life than this. You're not in Russia no more. You can do anything here. Look at me. This is a $90,000 car. You understand what that means?"

Dude pulled up to the curb, put the car in park, popped open the locks and continued, "this is the land of opportunity. You could be anything you want to. You got to get off the drugs though, okay? I'm going to help you. Do you have any dreams? Maybe I'll come by tomorrow and we could talk about it. Even like doing porno movies might be good for you."

Dude pulled out a large wad of cash and peeled off three $100 bills for Chick. Chick snatched the bills from Dude and quickly exited the car. Dude watched as Chick hurried down the block toward Louis. She never once looked back.

Dude drove around the corner and pulled the car over. He turned the radio back to the Jamming Oldies station, hummed along to Friend's Of Distinctions' "Grazing In The Grass"—then located his police issue .38-

caliber revolver from under the driver's seat, and took his life. "Everything here is so clear you can see it. And everything here is so near you can feel it. And it's real. So real. So real. So real. Can you dig it?"

Faithful Afflictions

By
Anthony B. Pinn

FATHER FORD stared nervously into the small mirror on the wall of his room. He looked down at his note cards and them back up at himself. He sighed, "your children have been baptized here and have come to know the grace of God in this church. We have cried together, laughed together, and fellowshiped within these walls. But, the connections we have made as a church family are not defined by our limited physical building. God's church is more than this. We are stronger than these bricks. We are more than this space, and the Gospel message will have meaning after this building no longer exists."

Father Ford stood there for a moment in silence before looking down at his outfit—his best black suit and newest collar. This was going to be a special Sunday; in fact, it would be the church's last meeting. The Bishop had made a decision to streamline. All congregations that could not support themselves would be forced to close, and Ford's church—St. Barbara—was the first to implement this change in policy. This small parish in the middle of a transitional neighborhood was about to be destroyed. Stores that once sold pig's feet to blacks, now sell Korean goods. Store signs once written in English are now written in four or five languages. Even ATM machines—the few that remain in place—are bilingual. Street sounds change too. New voices are heard and new music echoes through the neighborhood. The neighborhood was changing, but Father Ford never imagined that the last sign of this change would be the disappearance of his church.

Ford looked over his note cards and awkwardly pushed his hand through what remained of his hair, "I don't even buy this shit."

Ford put his cards in his pocket and slowly walked out the door of his room, down the hall. He had taken more time to prepare than usual, but this wasn't a usual day. After today, everything would be different. He continued to walk through the office that connected to the sanctuary and took his position in the pulpit to begin church service. After the songs were song and the prayers rendered, Father Ford took a deep breath and started his last sermon in front of the people he had grown to love over the course of ten years. Ford looked around the sanctuary for the last time and reluctantly began, “your children have been baptized here and have come to know the grace of God . . . ”

Ford fought his way through the sermon, smiling, gesturing, and attempting to speak with an energy that would—hopefully—suggest confidence. He was almost able to convince himself that things would be fine; parishioners would find new church homes and he, of course, would be assigned to another church where he would work to increase the size of God’s kingdom on earth. He continued to speak, to preach the closing of his church, and as he attempted to convince parishioners and himself of the ultimate purpose of this plan, its fit with God’s grace, he punctuated his words with volume and passion. “God’s hand is on even this plan! Some times the faithful experience afflictions, situations that are difficult to understand and accept; but God’s presence is real and we will survive the closing of this place.”

After the sermon, Ford moved to the back of the church to shake hands with his members for the last time. “Father Ford, why? Why our church?” Jane Johnson asked. With a forced smile and gentle pat on her back, he responded like he responded to the twenty who asked the same question before her, “the Bishop thinks it is best.”

Ford made it through the service and walked back to his office, removed his vestments, and continued the lonely walk back to his small room. He’d made this transition as easy as he could, considering the fact that he had not mentioned what the church building would soon house. Father Ford left out details. He didn’t tell of his disappointment in the Bishop. Or about the poor decisions being made. Or the fact that the Bishop sold the building to the state for use as a new prison! A prison? A church to a penitentiary? How could Ford explain this to his congregation? The police had never been much of a positive presence in the community, and he’d spent too many Saturday’s visiting relatives of parishioners who were in the local jail for one reason or another. Now, their church was going to be turned into a prison. Ford sat in his room, thinking about the paradox: God’s house, the church, meant to free souls and uplift spirits would now storehouse bodies and limit the hope that feeds the character.

It wasn’t his normal practice, but during times like this, Ford indulged in a bit of scotch. He sat there, with his collar still on and his best suit hanging off his limp body, sipping his scotch and hoping he’d never have to share the full story. Slumping further into his chair, he imagined alternatives—baked good sells, auctions, a bank loan, tapping into the rich citizens who might need a tax break. But he knew these things wouldn't change anything. The church was as good as gone. Thinking these thoughts, and holding his glass of scotch, Ford fell asleep and dreamed of better days.

ಌ ಌ ಌ

He awoke the next morning feeling no better but with an added pain in his neck from his awkward sleeping position. His pants were wet and sticky from the scotch that slowly leaked onto him during the night. Ford put the empty glass on the table next to his chair, stood up and tried to stretch out his aching body. It was going to be another difficult day. His congregation had the evening to think about the loss of their church and he just knew confessions would be particularly difficult to hear this morning.

After morning mass, Farther Ford sat in the darkness of the confessional. Dark wooden walls, a red curtain that had seen better days separated his space from the space where parishioners came to confess. It had always been an odd situation for Ford, perhaps for most priests. He would find himself thinking, over and over again—*What the hell do I say about things my religious life is supposed to exclude*? This was his mantra, used in most cases regarding sex stuff, acts that he wasn't supposed to even think about. But today was different, he was certain they would come, one after the other wanting answers, wanting him to say a prayer or proscribe some action that would allow parishioners to keep their church.

"Forgive me Father for I have sinned. It's been months since my last confession," said Michael sitting down and making himself comfortable.

He'd been attending the church for a few years now, but was an unassuming figure, one who came across as the type wanting a contained and manageable spiritual experience—service on Sunday and a few community service programs when his work schedule allowed. Michael, who usually dressed in a conservative suit and wing-tips, was the type of guy who came to mind when the term "yuppie" was mentioned, but with a twist. There was something those who met Michael, heard him talk and watched his eyes, could not fully understand or explain.

"I usually depend on my wife to take care of this for me, let her handle her sins and mine during one session," Michael continued. "But not this one."

"What do you mean?" Ford replied.

"Well, Father. It's not really a sin, at least I don't think so. I'm planning on following the Bible on this issue, so it can't be a sin, can it?"

Wondering what Michael could be referring to, Ford shifted his weight, steadied himself, "you'll need to explain before I can answer that question."

"I heard your sermon about plans to close this church, and I'm going to do something about it . . . at least that's my hope. I've been reading the Bible and I've come across a solution to my problem . . . or, uh . . . I should say our problem."

Ford was anxious and curious. He'd wanted a solution, had hoped the scotch and deep thinking the night before would have produced some possibilities rather than just a pain in his back. He wanted to know more, but was cautious, even guarded in his response. "I'm not certain I know what you're talking about." It was a noncommittal response, but one Ford hoped would entice Michael to say more.

"OK, Father," Michael continued, "I've been reading the book of Matthew, and I can't get pass Jesus and the money changers. You know this story? Of course you do. You preached about it. The story where Jesus punished the greedy. Well, I'd like to follow that model."

Father Ford's anxiety increased. He could feel his heart beginning to beat faster and his throat became dry. He thought to himself, *this is just what I need. Random quoting of the Bible. What the hell is this guy talking about?* But he kept this thought to himself and instead replied with as much control as his stressed body could muster up, "please, I'll need to hear details. Vagueness won't help."

"Well, Father, it's simple. You know . . . word gets around and I know what they plan on doing with this church. Middle management has its benefits. Information, Father. Information."

"Please get on with it," Ford responded, raising his voice above the usual whisper.

"I know that the church is becoming a prison," says Michael boldly. "And I think I know a way to stop it."

The verbal dance was over. Michael had Ford's full attention now. He began to explain that he had once considered the priesthood, going so far as to start seminary training. He decided the religious life was not for him, too confined, too distant from what he admired most about the world. He hadn't had a real opportunity to apply his perspective until now, when he felt there was something really at stake. Michael believed that there was a beauty in Jesus' violent attack on the money changers who polluted the temple. On the surface, it might appear to be an act of vandalism, but that's not the message, Michael argued, we are supposed to get from it. It's a justified action because it maintains the values and concerns that should motivate our existence, our reason for being. Jesus's vandalism was righteous because it maintained the purity of God's relationship with humanity and it kept sacred the space marking that relationship.

Michael wanted desperately to follow this example—to strike out for a righteous cause. And what better cause than this one, the welfare of his church home and all it represented? And what better way than to take violent action? He'd left behind the idea of religious life years ago, but he was certain about this: he wouldn't sit by and allow this to happen. Protest, Michael was certain, would prove useless. Who pays attention to signs and catchy slogans shouted by a faceless crowd? What had to happen was clear, and so Michael tightened every muscle that covered his small, pale frame and said it, "Father, the Bible teaches us that money is the root of evil and we have an obligation to prevent this from contaminating the Church. Turn this church into a prison, the temple into a den of thieves? They've got to be kidding . . . Isn't this why Jesus punished the money changers? The same should be done now."

Ford was chilled by what Michael suggested. How far was Michael willing to take this? "What are you planning? What are you talking about?" Ford asked, his heart beating even faster, his body beginning to tense up.

"Father, it's simple . . . I'm going to destroy the church, set it on fire."

" . . . What?"

"I'm going to save it by destroying it," continued Michael, feeling more comfortable having finally spoken the words for the first time to any one. "Don't you see the beauty in my plan?"

"You can't be serious!" screamed Father Ford. The conversation's location no longer mattered. Michael was talking about a crime—wasn't he? —committing an evil act under the illusion that it was actually beneficial and righteous.

"Please, Father, keep your voice down. And try to understand the poetry in my plan. Don't you see? It's the only way. There's nothing left to do but this."

Trying to collect himself, to speak as calmly as possible, hoping it might help Michael see the danger in his plan, Father Ford responded. "That plan is a mistake. If you can't see the uselessness in destroying property, think about the children, the families. What about them? How can this possibly help them?"

"Father," Michael said moving closer to the curtain that separated them, "don't be a hypocrite. Really. I expect more from a man of God. You said in one of your sermons that the true church is not confined to a physical space. It's a community of like-minded people committed to God. Did you mean it? Or was it just meant to make us feel good as the prisoners are unloaded into the church . . . uh, I mean, prison?"

These words hit Ford hard. A truth ran through them, but it was a harsh and clumsy truth, one he could not easily embrace. There was a fine line between righteous action and criminal behavior; he knew this, had been taught it throughout his years of study and ministry. But didn't this push it too far, cross the line? Michael spoke of an action that Ford found hard to reconcile with the actions of Jesus, the Christ who rebuilt lives and morals; created hope and enlivened possibilities. Didn't Jesus preach peace to a troubled time? To give more of one's self in the aid of others? Yet, when he opened the inner doors to his desires and sensibilities, this was worryingly attractive to Ford. Why allow the loss of his church? Why replace prayer with prison conversation? Why substitute the Stations of the Cross for prison politics? But couldn't this be God's will? Perhaps this was just a time of tribulation out of which God would bring about ultimate good—make them more faithful, bring them greater comfort and closeness to the faith. Was this the season of pain that led to the budding of renewed commitment to God, to a deeper understanding of Christ's sacrifice through a sacrifice of one's own? Ford desperately wanted to believe that the surrender of this earthly temple was not the end of the story, but rather removed obstacles that prevented a deeper connection with God.

"You can't burn the church. There's got to be another way," said Ford eventually. "God works in mysterious ways to bring into our historical moment, our limited time on this earth, a richness that is beyond our imagination. We must be open to God's hand in even the most distressing event." He wanted to believe this, but did he really have a choice? The decision had been made without his input and he was left to explain it to his congregation, and help them live through it. Ford understood that he lived between two worlds—the church and its vision of life and the historical moment and problems that confront those to whom he ministers. Hadn't he always been taught to believe that God's purpose is worked out in unlikely ways, through improbable events? And wasn't it true that God's plan for those who have faith is found in events that, with our limited knowledge, appear tragic? Recognizing this requires a willingness to venture forth with faith, to challenge the obvious and uncover its glorious potential.

"God always works through confrontation, Father," Michael responded. "Think about those who got in the way of God's chosen children of Israel. Didn't they die? Didn't God demand violence? Why not now? Why not, Father?"

"That's enough!" screamed Father Ford. Michael's questions and persistence clearly getting to him. "We're done here." In an instant, Ford left the confessional, clumsily navigating the elaborately craved interior, leaving Michael behind.

ꕤ ꕤ ꕤ

Ford tried to carry on with his other obligations for the day, tried to escape Michael's voice and its haunting message. Ford wanted to forget the conversation in the confessional; he fought to remove the images from his mind, images of a church destroyed, a ministry perverted, and a community left in chaos. But he couldn't shake it; not even more of the scotch that helped on those other painful occasions helped now. He kept hearing the voice from the confessional: *There's nothing left to do but this . . .* Ford wanted to know who that was on the other side of the curtain, but more importantly he wanted to quiet the voice, to keep the plan it suggested from echoing through his mind.

Sleep caught Father Ford, sitting at his desk, in his small room, still dressed in his clothing from the confessional. But this didn't happen before Ford pulled himself up, reached for his Bible, and read the passage the voice spoke about: Matthew 21:12:

> And Jesus entered the temple of God and drove out all who sold and bought in the temple, and he overturned the tables of the moneychangers and the seats of those who sold pigeons. He said to them, it is written, My house shall be called a house of prayer'; but you make it a den of robbers.

Shit, Ford thought, *what do I do with this? Jesus rides into Jerusalem, preparing for his crucifixion and glory, but first . . . the temple must be cleansed.*

ꕤ ꕤ ꕤ

It was Tuesday, the next morning, when Ford awoke with that familiar pain in his back, a headache from the scotch, and the faceless voice's proposition. Again he was running late, but he was in no rush to return to the confessional.

He went into his bathroom, splashed water on his face, and brushed his teeth. Too tired and emotionally drained to worry too much about his appearance, such concerns had never played well with him as friends were want to say, he pushed his thin, pale hand along his skinny, narrow face, shook his slight frame as if to dislodge his troubles. He slowly walked out of his room and back to the confessional resolved to make the best of the day, and to better handle his responsibilities before church and city officials turned the building over to the prison industry.

"Hello, Father." Father Ford slowly sank into his seat.

"I've been waiting here. I skipped work again today, but . . . this is important business isn't it, Father?"

"Please forget this plan of yours. It's not God's way."

"But it is," Michael responded, "it is God's way. You should have read the passage in Matthew I mentioned."

Ford moved closer to the curtain, so close that his lips touched it and his words caused the red curtain to shift and move like a gentle flame. "I know the passage, and you're wrong." He hoped moving closer to the voice and making this statement with passion might emphasize his point, change Michael's mind and end this plan. But he also knew, deep within, that this wouldn't be the outcome. Ford sat there, speaking these words, knowing the response would only push him deeper into violent possibilities.

"I'm just an instrument, one who has finally come to realize the risk involved in devotion. For too long, Father, and listen carefully, I've been content to pretend. I've come on Sundays, sure, and I've given some money, no problem. But nothing about this relationship with the Church entailed risk, the type of risk that Jesus encountered and his disciples embraced . . . not the kind of risk that Jesus showed dealing with the money changers," says Michael, pausing to catch his breath. "What's wrong Father, afraid to be like Jesus?"

Ford refused to take the bate; he wouldn't respond to Michael's question. He'd pose one instead. "So, you are holding on to this plan to destroy this Church?" Ford realized this was a weak question. Here's someone planning to burn down the church, and he can only muster a ridiculous grasp of the obvious. So he quickly tried again, before the voice could respond. "Uh . . . you think destroying the building will prevent the dismantling of the congregation, the end of church? You can't really believe that."

Michael was beginning to sense an openness in Ford, a flirtation with the idea of destruction as regeneration. "Sounds like you're looking for me to convince you," Michael responded sarcastically. "It shouldn't be necessary for me to play that role with a man of God, but hey, I'm willing." Michael explained his perception of the required action with a calmness and assertion not as present earlier in the conversation. God did not merely condone this violence; God required it. God is far from squeamish when it comes to destruction of peoples and property.

Ford couldn't take this calmly; he couldn't sit and be lectured on the merits of violence. Yet, it was oddly attractive to him. This was the problem. "How can you be so certain about this?" Ford asked. "The consequences are staggering. What if you're wrong?"

It was clear to Michael that he had the upper hand, and so he replied to Ford's frantic questions with an ever growing sense of certainty, not only that he was right but that the Priest could be convinced to participate as a new dimension of his religious life. "Relax, Father, relax. It's got to be done and in the end we'll know we were right."

"We?" Ford asked. "What do you mean we? This is your madness, your plan! Whose the we?"

Ford tried, but he couldn't put his finger on the moment when it became plausible. All Ford knew for certain was that it didn't seem as offensive today; actually, it was rather sensible. He could appreciate the biblical irony involved—perhaps God could work even through this. Hadn't he always believed and preached that God's grace and will could be manifest in the most unlikely ways? He told his congregation to be open to the possibilities, so could he close off this option? No matter how much he wanted to dismiss this conversation, to forget about it and make the most of the remaining days before the closing of the church and his transfer, it grasped him and teased his religious imagination and political sensibilities. Perhaps because Ford couldn't explain his growing attraction to this plan, he started to think, it's a plan from God. It's the voice of God or it's madness. A link or dependency between destruction and construction, between virtue and violence was becoming undeniable.

"Isn't it obvious to you? I'm here for your help, Father. You and I . . . we. And," Michael continued, "by the way, Father, you might as well use my name; I think this conversation blows away illusions of indifference and distance. The name's Michael."

Michael knew he had to get a commitment from Ford now. Time was running out and the plans had to be made, the work completed. He needed Ford's participation not just because Ford knew the layout of the church, nor because it was a plan that required four hands. No, he wanted Ford's participation because it would signal a much stronger relationship between the deed and religious life; it would make Michael more comfortable with the idea that God was working through this because a man of God was involved. He was certain enough to bring the plan to Ford, but carrying it out required Ford's presence as the physical representative of God. "So, Father . . . what do you say? Are you willing to risk God's work?"

Ford thought for a minute. Time for debate was quickly coming to an end. Decisions had to be made. In or out. "My name's James . . . James Ford."

Still maintaining some doubt, Ford was prepared to do something, even something that seemed so very outside his understanding of God's will and movement in human history. But he'd take a chance and destroy the building to save the Church. Was it the righteous thing to do, a part of God's will? Perhaps yes, perhaps no; but one thing was increasingly certain for Ford, standing still couldn't be God's way. The church would not be turned into a den of thieves, and he'd risk doing the wrong thing in order to prevent it.

"I have it worked out, James. It's amazing what information you can get off the Internet."

"Not too fast," Ford cautioned, "I'm still making the mental adjustment."

"O.K. Fine. Meet me here tomorrow. What time do you lock the door?"

"Shortly before dark," Ford replied."

"So, I'll be sitting in the last pew with all the supplies, around nine. I'll tell my wife I need to go to the office to take care of something."

❧ ❧ ❧

Michael left the confessional. Ford sat there for a few minutes, thinking through what had just occurred. It was too late to change his mind, so he slowly lifted himself off the seat and made his way through the assignments and tasks for that day. All but one. There was no need to pack up his books and the church items that were to be moved to another location. The fire would take care of those things. Instead of packing, Ford spent the hours before Michael's return thumbing through the Bible, looking for nothing in particular but everything that might give him that deep sense of comfort with the decision he'd made.

Michael spent the time with his wife, showing her tenderness that hadn't defined their relationship for a long time. They talked, held each other, and shared a connection that pleased and troubled his wife. She was left with a sense that something was wrong, but why disrupt a closeness that was so pleasing and so long in the making with questions for which she really didn't believe she could withstand the answers? She decided to just enjoy it.

Evenings usually move quickly for Ford, so many small things to accomplish for a priest without an assistant, whose parish couldn't afford a housekeeper or church clerk for that matter. But this day seemed to last forever. For Michael, the hours didn't matter any more; hours were no longer the way to measure time for him. As of this evening, he would measure time in terms of risk taken and deeds done, and clocks couldn't capture such moments. After this evening, he would measure time by memories of flickering flames.

ଓ ଓ ଓ

It was shortly before nine o'clock. Ford locked the door and looked around the sanctuary to see Michael's outline on the last pew on the right said of the sanctuary, not far from the depiction of one of the Stations of the Cross; but Ford couldn't make it out and his mind was too full of what was about to happen to remember which station. *Did it really matter, anyway,* he thought as he moved toward Michael. Hearing the footsteps moving toward him, Michael turned around. He couldn't make out Ford's expression; it was too dark for that.

"Father . . . I mean James . . . are you ready?"

"As ready as I can be to commit an act I'm not certain about," Ford responded finally reaching Michael and seeing his face clearly for the first time. He thought back as he looked at Michael, trying to place him in the context of worship, church meetings, church events but he couldn't. It really didn't matter; Ford understood. Their bond was an odd one; both seeking to save a church through the destruction of a building, saving it from what it would become otherwise. They were chasing their own money changers out, preserving God's temple from a use that would only soil it. Past connections, a handshake, a pleasant word, prior to this moment mattered little. Ford wanted to believe they were disciples of Christ in committing this act, and the prior lives of the disciples were overshadowed by the task before them. Wasn't this the case?

Anyway, it was too late for entertaining doubt.

"James, this may sound odd," Michael said with a meekness that startled Ford, "but can we have communion before doing this?"

"Uh, I imagine so," Ford said a little confused and wanting to move through the deed as quickly as possible, "but why?"

"It's a closeness to Jesus, isn't it? I mean it is taking in his body and blood and in a way becoming one with Christ, isn't it? A kind of taking Jesus in before the fire consumes him."

"A bit more complicated than that, but I get the point," said Ford as he moved to the room where the elements were kept. Pushing past the vestments, he gathered the wine and wafers and headed back to the sanctuary where he found Michael at the altar, next to him a container of gasoline and rags.

"This is the body of our Lord and Savior Jesus Christ broken for you and for many . . . " The wafer dropped out of Michael's hand, but he picked it off the red carpet and ate it. Ford took a wafer, paused, and ate it.

He knelt in front of Michael and handed him the cup of wine. "This is the blood of our Lord and Savior Jesus Christ shed for our sins," said Ford, watching Michael drink from the cup.

"Thank you," Michael whispered before standing and gathering his supplies.

Ford, not knowing exactly what he should be doing, walked toward the altar and collected the sacred items, kissing them and putting them on one of the pews. *It's too late to turn back. Lord, I hope this is right,* he thought as he walked back toward the altar. By this time, Michael had poured gasoline from the large container over the altar and along the carpet and choir pews, with gasoline soaked rags strategically placed.

Michael handed Ford a box of matches. As the priest lit the match Michael whispered to him, "and Jesus chased the money changers out of the temple, saying this temple will not be turned into a den of thieves." Ford looked around at the stained glass windows only dimly lit by the moon. He looked at the pews that once held members of the community who came to this church for guidance and comfort. Thinking about the children who had been baptized and the couples married in this sanctuary, Ford looked at the wooden crucifix on the pew and touched the match to the gasoline that bathed the altar.

The flames jumped, quickly caressing the base of the altar. The two men ran through the supply room to the back of the church, through an exit that would allow them to remain covered by the night.

"It's done," Ford said, out of breath and not knowing whether to celebrate or mourn. Michael didn't reply. He didn't know what to say. Instead he looked at Ford and motioned for him to follow. Michael led him through a hole in the back fence. Looking around, they cautiously walked to Michael's car and climbed inside. The smell of smoke and gasoline quickly filled the car. It was now ten o'clock and, although it seemed to take forever, the process had gone fast. Just the way Ford hoped it would.

"Look," Michael said, "you can see the flames through the windows. It's spreading." Ford turned his head slowly afraid to look, but needing to see the outcome of the risk they had taken.

Slowly and deliberately, Ford spoke. "And Jesus went into the temple of God, and cast out all them that sold and bought in the temple, and overthrew the tables of the money changers, and the seats of them that sold doves." He pauses as the flames begin to break through the building and lick the sky. "It is written, my house shall be called the house of prayer; but ye have made it a den of thieves."

"That's the scripture," Michael said interrupting Ford. "That's the call to action, the demand for people like us to do something." They sat there looking at the church burn.

The sound of fire trucks broke the silence and people began to look out their windows and step unto the street; but Ford and Michael were far enough away and the flames too engaging for anyone to take note of them.

The church begins to collapse, sending flames high into the air. Ford and Michael sat in the car, watching the flames and the fire fighters, wanting to be certain that they'd done the right thing. But neither man could think of anything to say, no words of comfort, no clichés. They sat there waiting for someone to speak wisdom, but the silence continued and was consumed only by the sounds of fire fighting. Both sat there in silence, thinking about a passage of scripture, and an act that had changed everything, while somehow leaving everything much too familiar.

The Journey

Indira Shaves Her Legs

By
Faynessa Armand

THE DOCTORS told Indira nothing but pelted her with questions. "Where are you hurting today? Did you eat breakfast? Are you allergic to any medications, do you want another blanket, did you order breakfast, do you want to see the chaplain, does this hurt, did that hurt, *that* hurt?" The *experts* asked *her* questions for hours and still told her nothing. Indira was pissed and afraid.

They lied to her too. Sometimes they said, "this won't hurt at all."

When the nurses and orderlies would ask, "what do you have?" Indira would say, "I'll take suggestions. And another pain killer please."

ေ ေ ေ

Friends and family visited. Indira hadn't been diagnosed so people came near but not too close. Their eyes were soulful, Disney-sized, swallowing their faces. "What happened, girl? Why didn't you tell us you were having trouble? What can I do? Anything?"

What Indira wanted them to do was take away the fists of pain that pummeled her flesh and bones but she couldn't say that to them. That would not be gracious and the sick, especially those who are hospitalized, are supposed to be demure. The friends and family wanted to hear how wonderful they were for taking time out of their busy schedules to visit a colleague, a lunch mate, a daughter. They wanted to hear about her becoming helpless and riding in an ambulance at four in the morning. They wanted to hear her story—but not its ugly parts. Indira had to make them feel good. And usually she was medicated enough not to mind, to play her part.

Oh yes, yes, it was the worst moment of my life. When the doctors told me how close I came to dying . . .

No really. I got to the point where I couldn't pick up my goose down pillow. My hands were that bad.

I know you prayed for me, child. I felt every prayer.

Because her nights were so long and sleep would only come with the right combination of medicine, sedatives, boredom, and exhaustion, Indira spent long, pre-dawn hours investigating her body. Smelling her shoulders, shifting, having Cynthia, the nurse, position pillows under her legs and arms. Trying to simulate painlessness, to recall a body that wasn't an enemy. She labored through three days of IV drips, miniature paper cups of multi-shaped, multi-colored, hard to swallow pills (yes, Indira's jaws were swollen—cheeks the size of navel oranges), and three days of nurses coming as soon as she buzzed the buzzer (Indira was in a special ward with three other people). There had been six but two code blues the night before reduced their number. The nurses always responded promptly to the buzzes; after three days, Indira could draw her knees up and she felt her legs. Hair! Some stubbly, some silky straight. But hair. She was hirsute. The word sounded ugly to her and the picture it conjured up was worse. Were they that bad? When was the last time she shaved her legs?

Her hands were too weak to hold a razor but Indira wanted to shave her legs.

At first, it was just a passing thought. All thoughts were. Each one had to age, to be savored. Sometimes, when Indira was in the middle of thinking, the drugs would take her away and she'd find herself waking up, drooling, with an orderly noiselessly mopping the floor. Indira really hated how everyone felt free to go in and out of the room whenever they liked. The only time the door was closed was during the code blues and then it closed automatically. Once, when Indira woke up, she found a nun in full habit next to her bed saying a rosary, watching Jerry Springer.

ೞ ೞ ೞ

The same day that Indira thought to shave, she learned that she was generating a lot of interest. The doctors stopped asking questions and started saying, "well, ahem, it could be this, that, this or probably that." Dr. Specialist Number One told her he had reversed one of her more serious conditions even though her problem was unknown. Dr. Specialist Two said, "I'm presenting a paper on you today." Beaming. Proud of himself, proud of Indira's disease. Indira congratulated him and asked for a razor. Dr. Specialist Three laughed and said, "your blood isn't clotting . . . You'd have smooth legs, young lady (he was younger than Indira), but you could bleed to death." Indira chuckled with him and pressed the button and begged Cynthia for more drugs.

ও ও ও

Indira still had insomnia, still searched her body at night. Her skin was so dry it felt as if it was flaking away when she rubbed it. She shouldn't have rubbed but her skin was the only thing immediate to her. She rubbed it as a meditation and all she could do in that bed was ache and cry and medicate. She didn't understand her body raging against her but she did understand what her hands felt. Dry, flaky skin and hairy. Head partially bald, Indira could braid the hair on her legs.

Maybe Indira was exaggerating. She told Anita, the best friend.

I know I'm crazy. I should be worried about other stuff but . . .

But my legs feel like bottlebrushes.

I am grateful that I'm alive and I love you too. But, Anita, this hair harasses me at night.

When the morning shift came on, the nurses drew blood, gave her a bedpan, gave her the breakfast menu of no choices. Exhausted and full of pain killers, Indira slept. They took her temperature, counted her white cells, counted her red cells, turned her urine into a chemical equation, sucked marrow from her bones in long needles. In the evening, when the night shift came on, they drew blood, gave her a bedpan, gave her the breakfast menu disguised as dinner. She slept while they took her temperature, counted her white cells, counted her red cells, turned her urine into a chemical equation, sucked marrow from her bones in long needles.

During a sponge bath, Indira wondered aloud if Cynthia could get her some things. Cynthia said, "you're not slick, young lady (Indira was old enough to be her mother). Dr. Specialist wrote it in your chart—no shaving your legs."

ও ও ও

A full week now, other visitors. Indira was ready.

Don't feel bad for me. I've learned so much getting through this. This was an opportunity to learn.

I am thankful that it happened. I've learned to appreciate what I have. I'm thankful for this wakeup call.

Let me introduce you to Preston, the orderly. He's treating me like I'm his own child. I can't even ask for something before Preston's handing me socks or tea or another pillow.

It's okay that Lena hasn't visited me. She can't handle sick people. That's just who she is.

When they left, Indira trembled and cried with fatigue.

ꕥ ꕥ ꕥ

Pilar, the second best friend, came to visit every day. Indira begged her to shave her legs. Instead, Pilar made the nurse call Dr. Primary Care for permission to give Indira a wheelchair ride. A ride with a rolling IV. Permission granted. "Let's cruise," Pilar said.

Indira got dizzy getting out of bed and fell into the chair. Pilar wrapped her in four blankets and put her feet into two pair of twenty-dollar hospital socks so her teeth would stop chattering. "Don't worry about the cost of the socks," Preston said. "Insurance companies expect to overpay." Patsy, the supervising nurse, watched suspiciously but Pilar said, "ready, set, go!" and she pushed Indira, shaking and nauseous, through the doors of the ward. Away from people who died in the night, away from people who didn't have to ask to come into her room, away from the skill and safety of the obliging nurses. Indira threw up on the sidewalk near the main door.

Pilar pulled out a joint. "Want some?"

"Yes. More than almost anything."

"What more than a joint?"

"I want to shave my legs."

"I can't do that. If I cut you, if you bleed . . . What if you get some kind of infection? I've got a J right here. Herb *is* medicine."

"Pilar, they look hideous. Shave me."

"If I shave you, you'll miss the rubbing. You like being obsessive. I'm not going to create some medical emergency because you need to have slick legs under those funky hospital sheets." Pilar rolled the chair into the sun and watched for signs of nausea. "What about Nair?"

"Not the same. I need to feel a blade."

Indira wanted to be hairless. *She* wanted to choose to be hairless. *She* wanted to choose.

ꕥ ꕥ ꕥ

Indira asked Preston the orderly to help her. That disturbed him.

"Don't get me wrong. I wouldn't mind seeing those fine legs up close, but I need this job more than I need to make you happy."

Indira promised to buy stuff from the gift shop that Preston planned to open once he got a settlement check he'd been waiting for for four years.

"I'll get you the stuff," Preston whispered, "if you don't say it was me."

He was really helpful. Clever. That's what Indira told Preston they'd be. Discreet. Circumspect.

More days passed. Fewer drugs, more tests. Less pain. Preston brought a pink razor and blue shaving gel. Indira hid them in a drawer.

The night Preston made good on his promise, there was another code blue. Indira smoothed blue shaving gel on her legs when the doors shut but before she could get the razor, a nurse, radiant and competent, popped in. Indira pulled the sheets over her legs. "We saved this one," the nurse said. She didn't notice the sheets turning blue. Embarrassed, Indira wiped her legs clean.

❧ ❧ ❧

Another week passes, fewer drugs, more tests. Only Anita and Pilar visit now. And Preston.

Doctors Specialists One and Two come to say they wish Indira well and they won't be back. Dr. Specialist Three says everything is fine now and the medicine will make Indira better.

"Better from what," Indira asks.

"Better from being sick," Doctor Specialist says.

Tearing sheets from his prescription pad, Dr. Primary Care says Indira can go home.

Preston says, "Praise the Lord!" Indira says, "He might not come when you call Him, but He's always right on time."

❧ ❧ ❧

Pilar and Anita help her into a silk sarong, into her own bed at last. As soon as they leave her, Indira gets up and sits on the edge of the bathtub, wondering if she will fall and shaves her legs with Preston's pink razor. She has just the right combination of medicine, sedatives and marijuana to do an excellent job.

Loaded, with legs as smooth as a baby's bottom, Indira dreams of pain.

The Inner Harbor

By
Stanley N. Bernard

"Gonna be, gonna be . . . a lovely day . . ." The radio blared loudly . . . in Larry's sleeping ears. Reaching over from his prone position, he slapped the snooze button and fell back to sleep.

Three minutes later the radio blared again, ". . . a lovely dayyy . . . gonna be, gonna be . . ."

Larry hated the song. And it wasn't because the radio station played it over and over again in the early mornings, either. It was because Larry knew that no day that he had to wake before noon was a lovely day.

He raised himself up onto his elbows and sat up on the bed, the sheet strewn over his bottom half. Summoning all his will, Larry forced his feet to the floor. He looked at the clock radio and turned it off this time. He stared at the time for five minutes before his brain came to life.

"This organism is on line," he said to himself as he scratched his head and rose to his feet. Walking shakily into the bathroom, Larry started his morning ritual: a shit, a shower, and a shave, not necessarily in that order. After the ritual, he stepped out of the shower and dried his soaking body. He looked in the mirror and wiped the fog away. He frowned at the hazy reflection of himself and hissed his teeth like a West Indian.

"Lawrence Stanley Dunbar, you're a fucking bore!" he said evenly, pointing to himself in the mirror. He walked out of the bathroom, a stream of fog following close behind. He began to dry himself when the phone rang.

"Hello, Veronica," Larry said in a cheerful voice. "What's up, Baby?"

"How did you know it was me?" Veronica answered.

"I can sense you," Larry replied. *Because you call me every two freaking minutes*, he thought to himself.

"That is so sweet," Veronica said sincerely. Larry could almost hear her smiling across the line. He rolled his eyes.

"Larry, are you going to pick me up from work tonight?" she asked.

"Haven't I picked you up every day for the last two years? Eight or nine tonight?"

"Eight. And please don't let me have to wait too long. A girl was mugged here last week in the parking lot."

"Then don't wait in the parking lot."

There was silence on the other end of the phone and Larry knew he had messed up. *Girl's are so sensitive.* He sighed and began damage control, "No, see? What I meant was, if you wait in the parking lot, then some unpleasant stuff could happen. Then I'd have to track down the guy. Then I'd have to kill him and be tried for murder. But because it'd be so chivalrous, there'd be a bunch of media coverage about it. Al Sharpton would show up. MTV would sign me to a reality show. Oprah would have me on. I'll be forced to become famous and then we'd never have time to see each other. I'd rather you just stay safe and wait inside."

Veronica laughed, "then pick me up on time, for once."

"Of course. Eight o'clock. Can't wait."

"Bye. I love you."

"Yeah. Me too. Bye."

Larry hung up and fell into the leather couch by the phone. The soft leather expelled air as it sank to accommodate his weight. He spread the towel across his naked lap and folded his hands behind his head. He loved Veronica, but the emptiness and ambivalence he was feeling for her confused him. It was as if something was missing, unfinished. He grabbed a comic book from the rack near the couch and began flipping though it. *I bet superheroes never have this type of confusion.*

The phone rang again. "Hello," he said sternly, hoping it wasn't Veronica again. He had had his quota of her for the morning.

"H-hello," a timid female voice spoke with a slight Caribbean accent, "c-can I speak to Larry, please?"

Larry pulled the receiver away from his ear and stared at the thing like it was an alien artifact. He stood up, the towel falling to the floor. Goose bumps ran up his back across his wet, naked skin. *No way . . .*

He put the receiver back to his ear. "This is Larry. Who am I speaking to?"

"Hey, Larry. Guess who this is?" the woman's voice said.

Larry's mind went red with anger. He couldn't say the name.

". . . Who is this?" Larry said finally after a long silence.

"Take a wild guess," the woman answered back.

The happy, mocking tone in the voice of the woman at the other end made Larry even angrier. "Who is it," he yelled.

"It's me, Sharon!"

Sommabitch . . .

"Sharon Byrum! Don't you remember!?"

Larry began to tremble, more from having his suspicion confirmed than from the cold water on his back. It was her. The sweet Trinidadian voice twanged with a singsong English accent. It was Sharon, no doubt.

"Sharon Byrum. Well, I'll be damned."

"I hope not."

"What?"

"Nothing, I was making . . . I'm unfunny," she laughed with her sexy accent. "How are you, Larry?"

"I'm good. I'm . . . a little startled. How are things with you?"

"Fine."

"How is married life treating you?" He smiled when he said this. He had heard from friends that Sharon's marriage was on the rocks. He couldn't help jabbing it at her since . . . well, she deserved it.

"Oh, my marriage? As good as can be expected," Sharon countered.

"How good is good?" Larry parried.

"Good as good gets." Sharon jabbed back.

Larry considered saying "good isn't great," but couldn't decide if that was clever or just stupid. Probably stupid.

"Larry," she said after a long silence that hinted something bold, "I need to see you. There's a lot of unfinished business between us and I need to finish it."

"Five years is a long time to wait to finish a book," Larry retorted. "My chapter with you is long done, Sharon."

"Larry. I'm serious."

"I am too. You call me out of the clear blue after five years and you expect me to jump?"

What a bitch. Sharon Byrum is a bitch! Larry wasn't used to this kind of conversation. Not with Sharon. Not when they dated for almost all of college. In college, it was all about passion. Sharon was beautiful. Beautiful and curvy. She was his black queen to be praised and held above all things. In fact, Sharon was held so high, Larry wrote poetry about her—about her hair, her smell, her smile. She was his flower and he was the world's greatest gardener.

What balls on this woman! I'm finally almost satisfied with my life and now she wants to see me? Larry was angry and he had every right to be. But he also had memories. Vivid ones. His thoughts drifted to how it would be to kiss Sharon's lips again, to hold her hand, to make passionate love to her. Before his male instincts got the better of him, Larry pushed it out of his mind. He shook off the urge to let his little head out-think his big one. *That bitch. That unmitigated bitch.*

"I had hoped you would be civil about this, but . . ."

"No, wait," said Larry, realizing the moment could be over if he continued to be difficult. "I want to talk to you too. Face to face. I still have a lot of questions. Tell you what, I'll meet you for lunch this Saturday at the Inner Harbor."

ဢ ဢ ဢ

The sun was high in the sky and a brisk ocean breeze blew through the Inner Harbor. Larry's nostrils flared as he waited for Sharon. She was late as usual. She was driving from Northern Virginia, but he drove in from Delaware. It was about the same distance, and he felt like a fool waiting there now for almost an hour. His knees were shaking more from the overall excitement than from the cool fall breeze. He had thought about staying in bed and standing Sharon up. But curiosity got the better of him—it had been five years, after all.

"Hi, Larry," came a voice from behind him.

Larry tried to remain calm as he turned to see Sharon standing there in a pair of pleated blue jeans, ankle boots, and a lithe silk shirt with African print, covered by a brown leather bomber.

He took in everything. Her hair was cut short with budding Rastafarian locks just reaching her temples and the nape of her neck. Her lips were the same red, wet, kissable things he remembered them to be. Her smile was the same quiet excitement he saw in his dreams for the last five years. And her body—fatter, but a healthy "phat," with her butt peeking out from under the bomber. She looked good. Damn good.

"Don't I get a hug?" Sharon asked with that quiet, excited smile.

"Of course," Larry replied wrapping his arms around her, hating himself for enjoying the feel of her.

"You still give that bear hug, I see." Sharon pulled away slowly, wiping a smear of lipstick off Larry's cheek.

"I see you're still slim and good looking as ever."

"Liar. But I'll take it. You'll still tell me anything, huh?"

"No. I will tell you those dread locks aren't extensions this time, though," Larry said sarcastically. He forced himself to smile despite the ambivalence he was feeling for her right now.

"No, not this time," Sharon answered touching her hair. "You never got over my braids in college being extensions, did you? I never said they were real."

"You never said they weren't. And I wrote so many poems about them. My sister had to tell me your hair was fake. I felt like an idiot."

"But you kept writing the poems."

"True. But then it was fiction—not about my ideal African princess."

"Well, these aren't fiction," Sharon said with a smile, "touch them and see."

Larry reached out and touched her thick hair and laughed. They were real. He resisted yanking them at the roots.

"Let's take a walk," he said, coming back to reality, "I know a nice restaurant around here that sells Caribbean food."

ᔓ ᔓ ᔓ

Sharon sipped her hot tea and nibbled at her crumb cakes. "That's all you're going to eat?"

"Yeah, I'm not that hungry. I've been having trouble keeping food—"

"So, to what do I owe this untimely visit," Larry said abruptly.

"Oh, don't you want to finish your chicken first?"

"No, I think you should tell me now."

"It looks really good," she replied.

"I'm fine. Sharon, enough already. Why are we here?"

Sharon paused and bit her lip, "Larry, I need you to tell me to leave Norris."

In his belly, Larry's stomach exploded with laughter. Bill Cosby take notes, this was the greatest joke he'd ever heard. This gave poetic justice new meaning. She wanted *him* to tell her to leave Norris? Norris. Good old Norris.

Larry and Norris used to be good friends. Best friends actually. In fact, they were roommates for two years in college. But that was before the girl. Before the conflict of interest. Before Sharon decided to leave Larry and sleep with Norris. *Dumb bitch, you made your bed, now sleep in it.*

"Why do you think I would tell you to leave Norris?" Larry said after a moment of silence. "Divorce or separation is a cruel thing. I wouldn't want to be the person to tell you to do it if I wasn't sure it was the right thing for you." *Dumb bitch.*

"You're right," Sharon retorted, "I shouldn't have imposed on you like that. That's not fair."

Larry watched Sharon take a sip of her tea. Her throat gulped as she swallowed. "Can I explain why I did what I did back in school then?"

"I'm listening." Larry answered in an emotionless tone.

"I loved you, Larry."

"Of course," said Larry, still unmoved by Sharon's emotional plea.

"But I didn't know you felt the same way. You were so . . . so . . . moody."

"Moody? What the fuck do you mean by moody?" Larry craned his neck around to stare at her angrily.

"Ambivalent," Sharon answered, not meeting his gaze. "Ambivalent would probably be the better word. When I met you, Larry, I was a little girl. I was a freshman, a baby, I had no idea what I was doing. I hardly dated in high school. I had only one friend, and my parents would never let me go to parties. I loved you because you gave me an identity. I was 'Larry's girl.'"

"I never called you that."

"No, I'm not saying you did. And I'm not saying it was a bad thing. I liked being Larry's girl. I loved being with you. It just wasn't about me," Sharon shrugs. "And then when we hung out with Norris, he made me feel so different. Like maybe there was life outside your shadow. So I left you to find out. It wasn't supposed to be long, only until I found out what was right for me. I was so young and stupid."

You got that right. Larry looked at her and saw a tear roll down her cheek.

"Unlike you," Sharon continued, "Norris forced me to get my own personality, no matter what the consequences. I fell in love with the idea of being 'me' for the first time in my life, more than I fell in love with Norris. But you never allowed me that and he did."

Larry sat there for a minute, letting it sink in. "You should have told me, Sharon. I didn't know that . . ."

"You never noticed that I changed my major six times before finally settling on nursing?"

"I did, but how was I supposed to know that was about my approval?"

"I wasn't trying to get your approval; I was trying to get my own. That was really hard for me. You were so strong-willed and confident. I was never able to make any decisions for myself. You were my first boyfriend, you could have asked me to pose nude for Playboy and I probably would have done it."

There was truth to what she was saying. He obviously didn't know it at the time, but as Larry thought back to college, he could see what she meant. She never did have a personality, at least not in the conventional sense. She always seemed to just "fit in" with him and his friends. She was always willing to go along with the group as long as they made the decisions for her. He realized that she was only following his lead and she couldn't create any leads for herself. Larry felt sorry for her.

"Now that you mention it, I know exactly how you must have felt," said Larry with more emotion in his tone. "Lately, I don't feel much like myself. I don't feel like anybody at all. In the past five years, I've changed jobs about five times and gotten two Masters Degrees in things that won't help me get anywhere in life. It's a really fucked up feeling."

Sharon looked over at Larry with glazed eyes. Larry had never sworn in front of her without apologizing. He always swore to his other friends, male and female, and never apologized. Some would tell him not to swear and some would laugh it off, but at least they had the chance to tell him their feelings on the matter. She was never given a chance to share her feelings. Larry never really accepted her feelings as legitimate. She took it as a show of contempt for her. She waited, but there was no apology. She smiled.

Larry smiled too. Not because of the cursing, but because he felt more comfortable now than ever. Information that was missing for five years was now being downloaded to his memory banks. The story was now complete. Sharon left him to stand on her own—to become her own person. To . . . go off and marry Norris?

"Wait a minute," said Larry. "This doesn't make sense. If Norris was such a better fit for you than me, then why are you trying to leave him? What's wrong with him?"

"There's nothing wrong with him."

"He doesn't beat you, does he?"

"No, of course not."

"He's gay?"

"Larry, just stop, okay?" she said. "For a long time, Norris was exactly what I needed. I knew he wasn't half the man you were, but there was no shadow. He allowed me to be me. But now that's changed. For whatever reason, he's not the man I used to know. He's always off doing God-knows-what and I'm all alone. I can't trust him and now I'm—" She takes a moment to catch her breathe, " . . . well, I'm stuck. But that's my problem, not yours."

Larry touched her hand across the table and smiled. He felt he understood her now. He understood the years of torment that he inflicted upon her and the years of torment that she now endured with Norris. But, like many men, his emotions misguided him. He did not see her as the long-suffering hero returning from a perilous journey down the marred road of life. Instead, he pitied her. His next words would forever cripple their relationship.

"I'm sorry," he said with a heavy sigh and an embarrassed smile on his face. Sharon raised her head and looked at the man seated across from her. She had opened all the doors to her mind and heart to him and he was sorry; like he had stepped on a dog's tail or had accidentally kicked the cat. He was sorry. And she would use that.

"Larry," Sharon said decidedly, "I want to make love to you."

❧ ❧ ❧

Sharon sat on top of him fully nude. Her round breasts heaved with asthmatic excitement. She bounced on him hard, trying to pound him into the bed. She would make him pay for his pity back at the restaurant.

Larry was in the moment; enjoying Sharon, not caring that at that moment her body was a weapon of mass destruction and she was a warrior seeking vengeance. He closed his eyes, his mouth curled into a smile as his hands reached behind her and squeezed the soft flesh of her buttocks. Sharon's new aggression was stimulating him. It never crossed his mind that Sharon was not experiencing the same ecstasy he felt now. He never noticed that she was biting her lips with her eyes wide open, her upper body like a statue, transfixed on his ecstatic face and the tense musculature of his body. It was, after all, her idea to make love to her ex-boy friend. She was the married one, not him. Veronica did not matter. The only thing that mattered was the soft flesh on top of him bringing him closer to climax; closer, and closer, and—

Suddenly, Sharon grasped her stomach; her eyes still fixed on the man beneath her, and threw up.

"Shit!" Larry exclaimed as the lunch he had bought spilled unto his face. "What the fuck is wrong with you?"

"I'm sorry. Oh shit, Larry. I didn't mean to do that."

Larry brushed Sharon off his lap and ran to the hotel bathroom, ignoring her plea for forgiveness. He jumped into the shower as he went flaccid and began to wash himself. As the shower ran the warm water on his body, Larry heard Sharon's footsteps creep into the bathroom and she proceeded to expel more of the contents of her stomach into the toilet.

"Thank God they have mouthwash in these rooms," Sharon said penitently from outside the shower. "Can I join you in there? I feel all dirty."

"Whatever you want," Larry said nonchalantly as the lower half of his body saluted Sharon's proposal.

After a brief joust in the shower and quickly pulling the top sheet off the bed, the two resumed their lovemaking. This time, it was a thing of vengeance for both of them. After some grappling, Larry managed to position himself on top. His weapon at the ready, he prepared to get back at Sharon for all the lost time they should have spent together. His lovemaking became a violent expression of his feelings for her. His love, hate, disgust, desire, and lust were in his every thrust. He wanted her to remember him forever. So much so, he didn't even care they weren't using protection.

It was soon over. They both lay there with eyes closed, flesh enjoying the ecstasy, and minds wishing to be elsewhere. Larry moved first. He rolled off of Sharon, his body still excited from the experience.

"I loved you," Larry started, "but that was then. I'm here because I'm thinking about then."

Sharon caught her breath and looked over at Larry. Her eyes glazed over and she began to stare at the ceiling. "I loved you too."

"But you left me."

"Because you deserved more. I just wanted you to have the chance to get it."

"Thanks," Larry retorted sarcastically.

"I know you must think I have a self-esteem problem, but it's not like that anymore."

"Really? We're in a hotel."

"We're here," Sharon started, "because I want to be here. Nobody forced me here. This is my choice."

"Good choice."

"No, you don't understand, Larry. This is just fun for you. I am so tired of doing the right thing all the time. It's never for me; it's always about somebody else. And I don't want to be like that anymore. Right or wrong, I need to make the best decision for me."

They both lay there for a quiet moment. Then Sharon sat up quickly, "oh shit, look at the time. Norris will be home from soccer in a half hour."

Sharon grabbed her clothes and headed for the bathroom. In moments, she was dressed.

"Larry, I'll call you. Um . . . thanks for a wonderful time."

Larry sat up, "damn. What's this, slam, bam, thank you Stan?"

"What am I supposed to say? You know I've never done anything like this before. Shit, Larry, I have to go. Bye."

Then she was gone.

ꕤ ꕤ ꕤ

Sharon held the key at the door when the phone rang. It was Larry.

"Sharon, that was just wrong." Larry said, clearly almost in tears. "I was thinking of Veronica."

"Who?"

"My girlfriend, Veronica. If she did what you did today, I would fucking kill her. I was just thinking about that. The good part about seeing you is that it made me realize that I don't have to worry about that. Veronica has her quirks, but she could never do what you did. I'm not getting caught in this type of confusion again, though. That was a mistake. Bye."

"Wait, Larry, you must know that I never planned to . . . wait, hold on a second," said Sharon lowering the phone and entering the house. Softly, she entered the kitchen expecting Norris to be there, jealousy burning his eyes and knotting his stomach, wondering where she was or at least pissed because dinner wasn't ready.

She was wrong. Norris had not been home. Even his dish from breakfast was still on the table unmoved. She lifted the phone. "Hello, Larry?"

"Yeah, I'm still here."

"I was saying that I never meant for this to happen. Not this way."

"Me neither," Larry retorted, "I have to go." He hung up abruptly.

Sharon hung up as well, her lips curling into a smile. After hanging up her coat, she grabbed a knife, a cutting board, and an onion from the refrigerator. She began to slice it. The smile grew into a low giggle, and then laughter as tears welled in her eyes.

ꕤ ꕤ ꕤ

When dinner was a cold memory, Norris walked in, his shorts hanging off his rear, his soccer cleats scraping the tiles on the kitchen floor. If he had gotten home three hours earlier he would have seen his wife packing her clothes. He would have heard her phone call to her parents. He might even have heard her car leaving the driveway. Instead, when he opened the refrigerator he saw the note Sharon left for him. It said simply:

"I'm tired of being you. I got another me inside me. Don't call me, I'll call you."

Circus

By
Matt Rhodes

When I was 12 years old the circus came to town. Though I now admit my petulance, at the time I refused to go. I hated the smell of animal shit, I was in the middle of Sartre's *Being and Nothingness,* and earlier that day at a local record store my mother had refused to purchase for me Black Sabbath's *Live Evil* album. I was angry, and I wasn't going anywhere, damn them all.

But my mother and father were in the midst of a phase, the crux of which was getting me to do things that normal 12-year-olds do. They encouraged video games, organized sports, and heaping amounts of ice cream. I preferred chess, chaos theory, and heaping amounts of Joyce, though I must admit I did enjoy the Dairy Queen banana split that my mother used to pry me out of my second deconstruction of *Ulysses*. I'm not inhuman.

But the circus came to town, and I was going whether I liked it or not. I implored my parents to put away the money they planned to spend on admission and peanuts and cotton candy so that I might stand a chance of attending Exeter as opposed to some ragtag Iowa public school full of yokels. I was bombarded by the usual fare: they appreciated my genius and hard work but they felt I needed to expand my horizons and make some friends. In their eyes, if I played some baseball or went to the circus perhaps I could wash my hands of phenomenology and that silly Chomsky fellow I was always carrying on about at dinner. I reminded them that they could do whatever they wanted but that if they forced me to do something so beneath me I might just run off and join the goddamn circus to escape the iron grip of their parenting. Per the norm, they looked at each other, thoroughly befuddled, and it was decided that if I went to the circus I would be rewarded with the live Black Sabbath double album. I once read *The Art of War* three times during a week-long period when I had been grounded for peering across a wheat field and into Jenny Landsman's bedroom window using my trusty Celestron refractor. A gem came to mind:

> Disciplined and calm, to await the appearance of disorder and hubbub amongst the enemy: this is the art of retaining self-possession.

My mother was the daughter of an alcoholic farmer who was blind in his left eye from birth. He championed Helen Keller and W. C. Fields, though my mother was hardly influenced by his eccentricities, too often forced out of the house by her mother, a few coins placed in her hand. She would run like a gazelle to the end of the quarter-mile-long dirt driveway and wait there next to the mailbox for Zip Neederson. The curmudgeonly Zip would slow down just enough for my young mother to hop aboard his three-speed Ford pickup, and the two would bounce violently in silence in the cab, down unpaved Route 43 for about four miles until they hit town. She'd run off to the movies while Zip got farm supplies and whiskey and cigarettes for her father, and more of the same for himself. When the necessary sundries had all been collected, Zip would patiently wait outside the theater for her, shaking his head at the newly installed parking meters. She'd get in with a smile the size of Dubuque painting her seraphic face, and then Zip would ask how the movie was, only thing he'd say all day. On the way back my mother would recount the entire plot, share her multitudinous opinions of the various cast members, and deliver a cogent plea for another ride when the next feature would be showing. Zip always smiled but never said another word. Then he'd pull all the way up her driveway and she'd run out and dart at her mother's legs. Zip would unload the goods in the front yard and decline her mother's money. She usually had a black eye, and the house was always dead quiet. He'd tip his straw cap and get back in the truck. In the back of the pickup truck were always a rotary-blade lawn mower and a little boy. He was my father.

Eventually these two youngsters gained in years and began the cursory breeding rituals associated with being human. I am the sole glorious result, without siblings due to an odd infection that led my mother to infertility. My genius seems rather unexplainable on the surface, but I argue that it in fact can be traced directly to the two georgic figures that once inhabited the upstairs master bedroom at 1412 Farmdale Lane. While neither progenitor of mine could be accurately described as brainy, each possessed peculiar mental talents, the genes for which must have dementedly reconnoitered in the cloisters of their loins and spliced to formulate the code that expanded into the skin and bones of my existence. My father was highly regarded in Wayne County for his mastery of the calculated vagaries of chaos theory. My mother was able to recite the entire script from beginning to end, with proper animated inflections, characterizations, and gesticulations, of *Casablanca*, including Sam's score, played note for note on our aging Steinway. She also did a mean *Breakfast at Tiffany's*, especially on the rare occasion when she had her dainty hand wrapped around the requisite Hepburn highball.

In an agitated state, I called Dr. Clem McMasters to collect his opinion on the matter of my going to the circus. It was Dr. Clem, an hoary chain-smoking retired mathematics professor at Iowa State University, who inspired me to strive for my current life as the reigning international policy pundit of the cable news circuit. Dr. Clem became a Wayne County legend thanks to his weekly spot on the Channel 7 news. No matter what the *sujet du jour* happened to be, Dr. Clem would coolly explain why and how it was happening, all the while establishing incredible ethos with a mere tug of his bow tie or adjustment of his wire-rim specs. He once used the Pythagorean theorem to show why a farmer's current system of fences was hopeless to defend against chicken-devouring wolves. He took his city-slicker knowledge and clearly related it in a country dialect alongside big colorful charts and pictures. In my own work, I struggle to establish this level of accessibility to my fomenting ideas. Dr. Clem could do it naturally; with little effort, he could get a sixth-grade dropout watching a 13-inch black-and-white Zenith in his unheated trailer to grasp the frivolities of the Doppler effect. He showed me that encyclopedic knowledge of everything and a few fancy degrees weren't enough to earn the respect of the huddled masses—you need a catch phrase. Accordingly, Dr. Clem engendered a cottage industry of producers of T-shirts, mugs, and bumper stickers inscribed with his famous closing line, "This Is the Way Things Work."

My father first encountered this gentleman during his brief time in Ames on a baseball scholarship, a time when nothing meant anything to him was it not emblazoned with the Rawlings logo and full of the summer dust. Though he found all other classes prohibitively unpassable, to which his transcript and expulsion certainly attest, father was able to call to attention a brain cell or two whenever young Dr. Clem spoke. The two developed a strong relationship based on their shared passions of baseball, Budweiser, and of course, chaos theory. As the story goes, on one damp fall afternoon when I was four years old, the two of them were carrying on in lucid slurs about the possibility of Ted Williams meeting Edward Lorenz in a small tavern in Pocadello, Idaho. Out of the corner of his steel-gray right eye, Dr. Clem noticed that I had my own Mortimer Marker, the wacky writing instrument popularized by Bill Cosby's *Picture Pages* TV program, and he came over to the patio table to see what I was up to. All parties agree that he spilled his Budweiser on the head of our yelping

Labrador when he came to discover that I was quietly proofing the quadratic formula in effusive, gangly handwriting.

Dr. Clem said that he would be thrilled to attend the circus with us and that it would be in my best interest to loosen up.

Early on the day of the show Dr. Clem came by for breakfast. My mother was at the stove preparing a feast of Spam, buttermilk biscuits, sausage gravy, bacon, and eggs. (Despite my intricate knowledge of the cardiovascular system and its sworn enemies, I am still fond of these large, dense breakfast spreads, particularly the canned, sodium-rich rectangles that my mother so naively served me on a regular basis.) My father and Dr. Clem were enjoying a cold Pabst on the porch, and Dr. Clem let me have a sip. My father gently admonished him, and I remember an incurable feeling of want all through breakfast. My father was especially jovial that day, for earlier that week his mathematical acumen had earned him yet another promotion within Charlie's Cement Company, the original reason he ended up out in Wayne County. (My granddaddy Zip had convinced Charlie himself that though my father had managed to get himself tossed out of Iowa State due to poor grades, he was no dummy. Though he started at the bottom, actually pouring cement at various construction sites around the county, he quickly moved into managerial roles that exploited his ability to perfectly calculate the proper mixtures and quantities needed to fill cavities of all sizes. As much as I've learned in my life, I still don't know a damn thing about cement.)

My mother, however, was wound tight that morning, babbling madly about going to the lake instead of the circus. She couldn't go there, she realized, she just couldn't. When she got so worked up that she began to cry, Dr. Clem stood up and put his arm around her and then retrieved two more Pabsts from the refrigerator, which would assist him and my father in the considerable task of ignoring my frenzied mother. He could see that I was desirous of another swill of the fabulous liquid, but his eyes told me clear enough that he just couldn't. My mother began imbibing highball glasses full of screwdrivers at an unrelenting clip.

We took our seats in the fourth row under the big top, where beneath the pulsing gray skies of an Iowa summer the heat was stifling. I remembered a picture of my grandfather hoisting a large barbell above his head, his muscles rippling like the waters of a tanned muddy creek, the perspiration on his waxed moustache vaguely noticeable. My mother was sobbing, her head against my father's shoulder. Dr. Clem quickly produced a pint of Jack Daniels and offered my mother a nip, knowing full well that she would refuse, for it was not in a glass. "I'se Hoolly Goolightly, seez here," she burped into father's blue Izod. Dr. Clem enjoyed a monumental swill and my father followed suit, and in a fit of absentminded compassion, he passed the pint to me.

I woke up in Topeka, a menagerie of deformities hovering above me, the prairie winds roaring and reminding me that I was alive. I imagined that this must have been how Alice felt, though I wouldn't exactly know since I'd never deigned to read that particular yarn. I studied the lines on the face of a porcelain doll of a woman as she held my head and poured water through my desert lips. I gagged slightly and then appreciated the cool rush that momentarily assuaged the nightmare nausea I was experiencing. A large bald man with a waxed mustache effortlessly lifted me to my feet and led me to a red trailer, where he forced me to eat plain oatmeal, insisting that this was a fantastic short-term solution to the myriad problems that I was facing that blazing summer day.

After much debate, it was discovered that I had taken certain liberties with the frail wench alcohol and surreptitiously gone to sleep beneath the cot in that very red trailer. My parents and Dr. Clem were derided by local authorities who discovered them in ramshackle disarray, frantically screaming my name in the area where the large main tent of the circus had been. They convinced the inebriated adults to have a seat and some coffee, assuring them that they would find me in no time. But no time had passed, the circus was packed up and ready to move down the road, and I was absolutely nowhere to be found. I imagine that Kafka was madly searching the interior of his coffin for a pen when he caught sight of hundreds of ragged Iowans and a handful of dawdling circus freaks scouring the grounds for a boy who had absconded with a bottle of hard liquor, a vast collection of indentured animals leaping and neighing in the background, desperately attempting to be as successful at escape as I had managed to be.

A man called Hairlip, no doubt because of a singularly overpowering characteristic that conquered his satirical face, told me that I should not be worried, that he had contacted my parents and they were on their way down to procure me. I could not stifle my laughter in reaction to the sound of his voice, identical to that of a boy at my school that we also called Hairlip. I may have been a future Rhodes Scholar, but I was not above a slightly malicious, childish giggle at the misfortune of others. I asked him for a pen and paper and quickly set about outlining my demands. It wasn't until my second year at Harvard that I discovered the proper spelling for the alternate name for a cleft lip is "harelip."

My parents and Dr. Clem piled out of our maroon Buick early that next afternoon. They looked entirely frazzled, and upon spotting me attempting to juggle rings with an exhaustingly slender man wearing a top hat and lacking a shirt, mother kicked off her sandals and dashed at me, engulfing me in a farcical shower of hugs and kisses. The men of my tribe and the men of the circus convened and discussed matters, and my father offered cash to the manager of the troupe, who graciously accepted his remuneration. My mother spewed forth a jumbled string of thanks to those around me and tugged at my arm without results. Her grip slipped, and she fumbled a few feet away from me as I solidly stood my ground. She approached me warily, and I handed her a piece of paper. She began to laugh and showed the note to my father and Dr. Clem, who joined her in robust amusement.

First and foremost, I required the immediate gift of the Black Sabbath album. Were it such an hour that all record stores were closed, I would be allowed to sleep in a tent in the backyard until the purchase could be made. I had to have a Les Paul autographed by Ozzy Osbourne and a Marshall stack amplifier through which I could nimbly acquire the skills of a veteran rock god. I wanted an indefinite subscription to the *Utne Reader* and the prohibitively expensive G.I. Joe fortress. And I demanded an Exeter education.

Though my parents snickered viciously upon reading this list of childish wants, Dr. Clem bore a visage of absolute seriousness after his initial chuckle. He solemnly let them know that I was finally attempting to be normal. My father gravely noted that for all the times he had yearned for this moment, he had never once knocked on wood.

Looking at her grave, I have a hard time comprehending what my mother must now look like beneath the grim damp earth. I'm sure that on her worst dead day she could still outshine Bergman or Hepburn. I will not accept the standard elementary school theory that the worms go in, the worms go out, ad nauseam. Streaming through the headphones of my Sony Walkman is a taped version of that very vinyl that I had once demanded with such ignorant temerity. The song is "Children of the Grave," and the sour purple sky belches loud flashes of light just before the rain begins to cascade and make the ground so soft as I might fall through and see her once more, smiling radiantly as she belts out a chesty "As Time Goes By." I have to be back in New York in the studio tonight to explain to a worldwide audience why people of different religions hate each other and wish to blow each other up. There was nothing in my Ph.D. program at Yale that even came close to explaining why this might be. I do not have an umbrella, but I have an excellent education, a pint of Jack Daniels producing the butterfly effect in my head, and one dead beautiful mother. This Is the Way Things Work.

The Darkness Away

By
Michael Gavin

SCOOTER CLAPPED the door to his car shut. He walked through the cold night, a night that threatened snow despite the late season, and without looking up to where he was going, as if a blind man walking to the mailbox just on the corner from his home, he found his way into Max's.

Smoke hung like silk in the bar and neon light from the Pabst Blue Ribbon sign shined through the smoke and rested on Scooter's cheek. He watched Sammy and his three brothers slam poker chips down on the green felt table and fill glasses with beer from a pitcher.

Scooter counted cards so well that the only people that knew he counted cards were the ones he told. Long before Jimmy died, long before Scooter threw away the night light he slept with—a light that made him feel secure as he fell through the utter black and uncertainty of sleep—long before Angela pinched his heart with the fingers of love and responsibility, long before the snow began mesmerizing Scooter and drawing him out to the winter night, Scooter was forbidden to play cards in the bar. Max never took his eyes from Scooter, who had his eyes on the poker game.

Max made sure there was no cheating, that there were no fights.

Scooter stood behind Sammy and watched each raise being made, shaking his head and making a clicking sound with his tongue when poor decisions were made. He did this to spite the men he perceived spiting him for his part in Jimmy's death.

These nights, tension manifests its ugly head because card players would rather pretend that they were unlucky than know that they were wrong. That was the thing with counting cards: Scooter always knew when he, or others, made a mistake. Always.

Scooter found pleasure in watching a game of stud poker because he could still know that he was better than others by watching; and that was why Scooter played, to know that he was better than others. And the converse of this was also true in other times in his life: The certainty that he had done wrong with Jimmy in the tunnel, with Angela in her trust, and with so many other people in his life created in him a deep sadness; and he knew its depth would increase as time and regret increased.

It was for this knowledge of being right, though, that Scooter would stay in the bar until the end of the night, perhaps beyond the night if poker was played.

Occasionally, Max would jerk his head in Scooter's direction to ask, "you need anything, Scoot? Hate to see you standing there with nothing to do," and Scooter would shake his head slightly.

"How about a drink on the house, Scoot?"

"I don't need anything from you just because you feel sorry for me. You wanna pay me back, you get Pilate to apologize for its wrongdoings."

"Scooter, there ain't anybody here that knew Jimmy would die. Nobody here can bring him back neither."

Sammy turned in his seat, and with his cards in hand, motioned for Scooter to listen. "When you gonna see that the things this town does to be this town are what makes men men and women women? Nobody wanted nothing bad to happen. They just happen. Been happening since Eve bit into the apple. Been happening since Adam was stupid enough to follow her. The thing about paradise is that nobody is satisfied. When you gonna see that, Scooter? Everybody needs to move on. Things just happen and we have to get through."

Sammy's brother Graham, whom they called "The Scholar" behind his back because he was the only digger in town to take courses at Harrington University, said, "it's not about all that, Sammy. You were there. And now you know what's happened because of the death. Our wives look at us longer in the mornings, scared we won't come home. They love us harder for fear they'd have love left over for us when there wasn't any of us left to love. That's the truth."

Scooter smirked, realizing he was preaching to a group of drunken card players without enough sense to play well. "But there isn't anything heroic about digging rock. It's a job and that's all there is to it."

Now Max leaned over the bar and tapped Scooter on the shoulder. "Your cousin dying didn't change the way we look at digging. Jimmy's death changed the way we look at the men who do it. Don't be starting in with all these fellas. They work just as hard as you and I don't want no trouble between you all tonight."

"But we ain't changed," said Scooter. "You all have."

"That's right. Even I didn't think the way I do now. I realized how hard it is for you all."

"That's right," Graham said. "Before Jimmy, Max used to say the job is something bigger than life. But men make the job work. Used to be I'd leave to go to work and give my wife a hug. Said goodbye to the children while they still slept. Now, even if I go on an errand my wife wakes all the kids up and they all say good bye to me when I leave. Little Harold won't let go of my leg some days. Gotta shake him off when I get to the car."

"The way people see it, the job has done changed."

"Like shit it has, Scooter. You're just now realizing that all men are not the same. Not all men are like Jimmy."

"He and I are a lot more alike than you all would like to know," Scooter said.

"Come on, Scooter. Jimmy and you?"

Scooter turned around and leaned over the bar, scowling at Max. "What's that supposed to mean?"

Max picked up a glass and began buffing it with a washcloth. "People talk, Scooter. That's all."

"What's that supposed to mean?"

"Nothing except . . . " But before Max could finish, a woman walked through the door, all bundled up so that nobody could see her face, only that she was a woman by the red pants rolled up to her pale white calves.

Paying no mind to her as she unsheathed her arms from her coat, walked to the bar, ordered and received a beer, and then walked alone to a booth in the back, Scooter continued, "you know how we take pride in what we do?"

Sammy spun back around in his seat and laid his queen of hearts down. Scooter smirked, "well the longer we work for a company that told us it's all right to pick up the same tools that killed Jimmy, the more we are the ones that killed him. I don't want that blame. That's why come spring, I may quit." There was a pause. "Queen's no good when the ace is still out there, Sammy. Shouldn't be raising everybody so much."

Sammy dealt out the last round of cards to the men and Graham received the ace, snuffing out Sammy's queen.

Without looking up from the card game, Sammy's voice came booming and cold, "damn it, Scooter, people will still pick up those tools. It don't matter how much you protest, somebody will always fill the place you leave empty. In life. Love. Work. People take your place in the things you devote your life to quicker than any of the other things in this world."

"There isn't one damn reason that should be how it is!" shouts Scooter. "That isn't supposed to be how the world works."

"Scooter," Max placed a glass on the woodsurfaced bar, "why don't you have a drink. Relax. Forget about what's done. Forget about the death, the poker. Just let things be. You can't change the way things are."

Scooter pulled a stool out, sat, and drank. The sounds in the bar were as if it was hollow—men around the table only murmured when they spoke and Max was afraid to look at Scooter for more than a second at a time which made conversation, if it occurred between the two, intense and short. The only indication that Thelma was in the back was that she set her beer glass down on her table just loud enough for it to echo in the dark. If Max wanted to tell Scooter that Thelma had been trying to escape from Allan's grasp for three weeks he did not show it; and if the other boys wanted to tell Scooter that a man trying to honor another like Jimmy Chrisman would not fall from his marriage, they did not say that.

Scooter leaned back on his stool to catch a glimpse of her, and Max leaned back against the ledge that held the hard liquor, shaking his head. "How long has it been since you kept your eyes where they were supposed to be?"

"This stuff don't mean nothing."

"Seems to me if you spend enough time doing anything, it begins to mean something."

Scooter held a hand up and bobbed his head to let Max know to let well enough alone. But Max would not, "Angela deserves to have you where you're supposed to be."

"She's the one who kept me from being where I was supposed to be the day Jimmy died. I wasn't where I was supposed to be then."

"You know Jimmy's death and your marriage have nothing to do with each other."

Scooter wrapped both his hands around his beer and slouched over, "they do, though. I could have been in that tunnel with him, like I always had been before. I would have noticed the dynamite dragging, that it was unsafe to explode the rock. I would have kept him safe."

"You can't change what's done."

"It's not my aim to."

"Angela's the one who kept you safe that day. She watched after you. You're a lucky sum buck if you ask me."

"She's the one who made me lose my way. Telling me not to go up in that tunnel with him was the same as killing me and him at the same time."

"That Thelma," Max placed his hand atop Scooter's, "that's Allan's. She's Allan's woman."

"I don't see no ring on her finger."

"She's staying with him, Scoot. In his home. You know that isn't something to be taken lightly. You mess with her, you're messing with more than just your marriage."

Thelma's cheeks were the white snow outside and her lips were full and red like the skin of an apple. Her face looked like the pulp of an apple with only a sliver of skin left at its center. When she stood, glass in hand, she straightened her blouse and then smoothed over the wrinkles in her pants with her hand. Walking over to the bar, she set her glass down, signaled to Max to fill it up again, and swayed with the confidence of a serpent deciding whether or not it will attack—her smile indicated knowledge and Scooter's blank eyes indicated a lack of it.

She leaned on the bar with her elbows and the rounded bottom of her breasts nestled against the bar's surface. Scooter peeked at her and she saw this; but she made no attempt to hide the carnal and casual lust that beamed in her eyes. She slithered her hand around Scooter's waist and Scooter trembled, ensnared. He lost words. There was a brief silence filled with a desperate need to know one another and so the anticipation of a question whose weight in the meaning of things was minute, but for the moment was everything.

"Heard about Allan and you that day at the quarry weeks back," she said.

Scooter did not look up from his hands that were wrapped around the bottom of his beer mug the same way hers were wrapped around him. His voice trembled, "it was my fault. All of it. It was my fault. All I had to do was do what Jimmy asked, think for myself. He would have been safe. Allan and I would never have been in that scuffle." She looked up to Max, then tilted her head of stark black hair away from Max to signify for him to leave. She said, "sometimes things happen because they do. I can hear you from back there, you know." She ran her nose along the nape of his neck and whispered to him, "you can't bring Jimmy back by adopting his philosophies, trying to fill the space he left empty in his death. He's gone."

"Never tried nothing of the sort. I just wanna make things right. Like they were."

"See what I mean? From the way Allan described you, this is not what I would've expected of you. You're a sad man and you're trying to remain sad."

"Nobody expects you to be perfect when you mourn."

"How long will you mourn?"

"Long as I feel it. Long as I remember that look in his face when I told him I wasn't going to explode with him."

"You couldn't have known he would die."

"He expected me to be there with him. I always had been before. It was the end of his being able to count on me to make him safe."

"Some things are worth forgetting."

"Some things can't be."

"Forget about that moment. You're not the one that died."

"I was one of them."

Thelma looked directly into Scooter's eyes and the dark in her eyes was the void of a rattlesnake's. She told him that things would get better and the pain would dissolve so that he could be himself again, but only if he came home with her. "Sensations let us live, Scooter." She squeezed him tighter, "I can help you live."

Thelma reached in her pocket to pay for her tab, but before she pulled out a single bill, Scooter laid two bits on the bar that Max slid back to Scooter.

Scooter looked down at the bill then up at Max, "I'll pay for her, Max."

"The money you save me by not playing cards covers your tab in here just fine, Scoot."

Scooter nodded and Thelma jerked her head for him to come join her in the back of the bar for another drink. Max shook his head slowly, warning Scooter of the dangers lurking back there, near the bright, neon signs. But Scooter grabbed his beer and joined Thelma.

Before Scooter was in his seat, Thelma was already refilling his glass. They drank heavily, finishing off three pitchers, and then a fourth. Scooter poured Thelma a glass and then he poured one for himself, not once looking at her, but instead at the splash of the amber liquid. While he poured, he searched for things to say to Thelma, things that would make her love him, things that would make him forget pain for the moment. But nothing came to mind.

At the same time, Thelma sipped her beer in a way that she thought was seductive, but the way her eyebrows raised confused Scooter, making him think there was somebody behind him; when he looked, there was only the inauthentic light of the juke box in the otherwise gaping dark of the bar.

Thelma leaned forward, cupping one of Scooter's hands in both of hers, smiling, and said, "Allan's out of town tonight, on a trip to play in the band. Some bar called Wilsons. In Harrington. You come back with me, and everything will be better tomorrow. For both of us. Things will be different for both of us."

Scooter took another sip and looked up at Thelma, pleading with her as if she had a power not to be resisted by men, a power not to be known by those for whom the wretched ways of the world—whose defining characteristic was that it spun in a field of darkness, approaching light only to recede into the same darkness from which it sought to escape—was still foreign.

"Allan was the one who went and saved Jimmy's body. He's why nobody else got hurt out there. Why I didn't shoot anybody in the face. It wasn't peacemaking he did. It was making us realize we all were there together."

"All you quarry men are alike." Thelma reached for her purse and shimmied the strap up around her shoulder. "You think that doing the job you do and speaking like you are now makes you heroes. You think you make each other safe and so you are something better than simple men. You all think that enduring pain is being brave."

"Nobody thinks that."

"You all think that a man who can hide his pain and has a good work ethic can be at peace." She leaned in close and whispered, "but let me share something with you. There ain't nobody outside of Westbend that thinks like that anymore."

"It's the way men act. The world out there forgets that."

"Being a man is an idea. The way everything people work for is. Allan is more concerned with ideas than what's real. Don't worry about him. Or you. Just come on home with me." She cocked her head and pursed her lips, "come home with me, Scooter. Allan won't be home until tomorrow. Come on home."

Scooter fidgeted with his fingers. His hands fretted over each other. "I don't suppose that would be right. People would think things." He shook his head, thinking he was whispering softly enough that Thelma would not hear him, "I've tried to become the man Angela thinks I am. And Allan. He's the reason things in Westbend didn't get worse when Jimmy died."

Thelma responded: "That's how you got in this rut in the first place, isn't it? Trying to be the man Angela wanted you to be? Not going up there in the tunnel because she asked you not to?"

"Lay off. I could've gone up in the cave with Jimmy if I wanted. I have my own mind. She don't tell me what to do."

"Exactly. Start using your mind the way you know you want to." Thelma now stood over Scooter and teased his hair, "just for the night. Nobody would know. You pull your truck in your driveway, say good night to your Angela. Tell her you're going to see Isabel. Tell her you're going ice fishing. It doesn't matter. I'll be outside waiting for you. Tomorrow you'll be home before she knows you were gone. And if not, let her forgive you." She nestled into him and lowered her voice in what she imagined was a seductive tone. "Scooter, that first night I was in Westbend, three weeks back, I saw it in the way you watched me play pool right over there," she pointed to the pool tables in the front of the bar. "You were already thinking of making me your own. Your eyes following each movement of my body. Allan just got to me first. I would have gone back with you then. We can make up for what we lost that night."

Scooter's skin flushed. He picked up his glass of beer and in slow, long pulls that made the liquid gush forward then back, he swallowed the remainder of his drink. In a single motion, he set the glass down on the table slant wise so that it twirled around before settling. He peered beyond the booth to see the men playing cards and Max who was now smoking a cigarillo, hand rolled by Franklin Jones, the first man to retire from Pilate with enough in his account to live comfortably, and he saw that they had little interest in the doings of Scooter Chrisman. So he got up from his seat and nodded and walked as if in a trance behind Thelma.

They pulled up to Scooter's house, one after the other, and Scooter pulled into the driveway. As he walked through the cold dark, he clenched the flaps on either side of his unzipped coat and winced as if he could warm himself that way. In the car, as she waited, Thelma lighted cigarette after cigarette and when she exhaled, the stream of smoke leaking out from her cracked window spun through the same colored snowflakes and spiraled upwards so that, momentarily, she thought she could replace with her breath whatever the dark night lost by snowing flakes. That is why she lighted another cigarette when she finished the first and that is why she did not notice Scooter knocking on the passenger window of her red pickup; he had to come around to her side to get her to unlock the door. She rolled down the window and blew a last stream of smoke beyond Scooter's head and watched it disappear through the bands of flakes and stars and smiled at Scooter. Her teeth were white in the shade of the truck. "Well, you coming in or what?"

He made the sound of shivering. "Yeah," he nodded. "Yeah."

Without looking at him, she lunged over to the passenger side and pried the lock open. When Scooter got in, he stomped snow off his boots onto the floor, and Thelma thought about scolding him, but decided not to.

The whole ride up Elm Street to Bluegrass and down Cedar Road was silent. Scooter was drunk and he was thinking drunk thoughts of the woman next to him and shaking those thoughts of his beautiful wife from his impure head: His wife who was at home in his oversized shirt that she wore to bed; and her ivory skin that rivaled the color of a moon in a dark night and demanded the same awe.

He kept looking up and down Thelma's body.

Allan's bedroom was lavender. In it, there were pictures of friends from little league teams Allan played on, and those same friends from little league now worked with Scooter and Allan in the quarry. Framed embroidery pieces done by Allan's mother Shirley that said "Home is Where the Heart Is" and "God Bless this Home" hung on the walls.

When she lay on the bed, it was not graceful and when she giggled at how drunk she was, it was not endearing. She had already changed into silk lingerie which was the red of love but in the dark it looked black, like a cancer suffocating Thelma's white skin; Thelma's body an apple and the infectious tree she was born from had roots extending to the core of the earth which itself was the core of another apple of the same infection, only made for bigger mouths. The Earth an apple, was but one of many apples disguised as planets, all hanging from a tree infinitely dark whose spoiled nectar secreted into not only towns and cities bigger than Westbend.

Though Scooter and Thelma were microcosms of this cancerous system, none of these things occurred to Scooter who was merely a man not so much seduced as he was human and Thelma, the seductress, was not so much the evil, but naive because she believed in the healing power of love; the power of love to suppress hatred from being born from adultery if love be born from the act. And there was yet the innocence of Angela, alone, at home, asleep, whose despair, if she knew of Scooter with Thelma, would be a rot deteriorating the universe to complete darkness, borne from an apple eaten.

Thelma extended her hand for Scooter to take. And he did. He nestled in close to her. As snowflakes tumbled outside to the white ground, Scooter held close to Thelma, then traced the slick curves of her body with an index finger.

She whispered to him in a lustful, drunken, panting, "slow down. Be quiet."

Scooter unbuttoned her garter belt. Before either was aroused though, Scooter rolled off of her so that he lay on the bed next to her and placed his palms to his eyes, saying in a quick-paced breath, "this is too much. Too far. I can't do this."

Thelma, now propped on her elbows so that her shoulders arched in the air, looked at him with pupils deep and dark, scowling.

A senseless laugh escaped from her and she rolled over to reach around her leg to snap her stocking in place. Without looking at him, and with a sharp voice, she said, "stopping like that, after a night like we had. That's not how people do things. You can't turn back now."

"It'll save us both from guilt. From wondering why we went astray and feeling bad about it every time we see each other."

"All you damn men from down there, it's like you have these morals that can't be broken. But damn it, Scooter. I swear in the short time I've been here, I've heard that you leave Max's later than this with women fatter, uglier, drunker, and further away from the image you have of your wife than me."

"I never said that I was above doing things the wrong way."

"Just above doing them with me?"

Scooter did not reply.

"Scooter, you've already done wrong by coming here. It never mattered whether we did it or not. Not inside. You cheated on Angela soon as you got in my truck."

"Sometimes you need to see what's been going wrong before you can right yourself."

"What?"

"Sometimes you don't know you're lost when you are. And you just need someone to show you that you are lost. I'm like that. I'm lost."

"If Angela ever knew that you came here, she'd be hurt."

"She knows things aren't right with us. She knows I'm trying, though."

"What if I told her about you here with me? What if she knew?"

"She'd forgive me."

"Forgiveness is divine. But things are divine only because people can't do them."

Scooter had not moved and this encouraged Thelma so she inched over on the bed and placed her cheek on his shoulder. She stroked his hair. "Listen, Scooter. I got this theory." She took a deep breath and shifted so that her legs coiled around his waist. "There's so little love in this world, but you can create it and distribute it by making it. You make love, the world becomes better. It may be just a small amount, but it's a happier place. You can change the world."

Scooter wanted to leave, but Thelma was tempting, so lovely. So he said, "it'd make a nice motto."

"Believe what you want. But that's why they call it making love, Scooter. You make love for the world to have. It's an offering."

"You're just trying to feel like you belong. You don't love me the way you're saying you do."

She shook her head, "I believe in this, Scooter. It's something I believe in."

He wrestled to unwrap her legs. "It's silly, Thelma. Silly. It doesn't make no sense. If you could make love, people would sell it. And what about Allan and Angela. We can't do this. Not now."

Thelma told him that Allan would not be angry because she would love Scooter forever if they made love. She said that people can't get mad at others for loving each other. She also said that the greatest thing about love was that it was a commodity that was free to make and that its resources were limited only by those who rejected theories like hers. "It's not fair to the world for us not to have sex," she said.

"That's not how the world works, Thelma. People kill each other over things like we're doing. Your theory is nothing but a bunch of words." There was a pause, then Scooter got up from the bed and faced Thelma and added, "we wouldn't love each other beyond tonight nohow."

"Even if we didn't we could give this world something it's never had before. Our love."

"And break Angela's heart."

There was a moment where man and woman stood up in silence. There was another moment where man and woman seemed to lunge at each other, but that moment fell into a space that never would again be acknowledged, so they dressed. And when Scooter finished he pulled the door to a gentle click, not saying goodbye or parting in any pleasantry, merely leaving Thelma alone in the lavender and dark room; a beacon of white so that the dark itself would not be afraid that it had no salvation. For in the darkest of times, there is always hope, and in this room, it was apparent that after the most hopeful of times, there despair always lurks. And now it did. Yes, and now it did.

Even from the top floor, she heard Scooter gently shutting the front door. She imagined him trudging through the snow, the snow that was a deep purple beneath the oil-slick sky. He held both hands out, extending them like a scale, as if to measure the worth of his life in relation to his cousin's. Thelma crossed her arms in front of her stomach as she sat on Allan's bed. She squinted, thinking of Scooter out in the night, alone. She knew that somehow, the hand that weighed his own worth would find its way to being even with the one of his cousin's worth, despite that the love Jimmy Chrisman gave was more than Westbend could keep within its boundaries and the love that Scooter gave was nothing but an empty promise.

And this was enough to make Thelma reach over to the phone on the bed stand and dial Angela.

On the other end of the receiver was a voice, tired and misloved. The raspy "hello" hung in the air unanswered for a moment while Thelma collected herself, now realizing the extent of her drunkenness, now realizing that any story she told Angela of Scooter would have to account for her devotion to Allan and Scooter's to Angela, because the story that she was going to begin with—the truth of it all—failed to preserve love, would admit that each had fallen away.

"Angela?"

"This is Angela."

"I wanted you to know I saw Scooter walking home tonight. It's cold out and I wanted you to know he was out alone. In the dark and in the cold."

"He does that."

"Do you love him?"

"What?"

"Do you love him?"

"What kind of a question is that?" There was a pause that took away the tire from her voice. "Who is this?"

And now Thelma bit her lip. "Thelma. Allan's . . . Allan's. Well, it's Thelma. I'm new in town."

"I know who you are."

"You do?"

"Small towns."

"Yes."

"Well?"

"Just wanted you to know I saw him coming home. He'll soon be with you, home from the cold and the dark."

"He's been out there a long time. Hasn't he?"

"Maybe you would know better."

"You would think so. He's been so distant. So detached. I just let him. He's been so sad."

"Things aren't the way you would have them be. Ever."

"I'm not sure what you mean."

"Well."

"Well. Thanks."

When they hung up, Angela gathered the blankets from the bed and moved to the downstairs couch. She lay there, waiting for her husband to come home. She couldn't remember whether he came in earlier in the evening to tell her good night or not. He must not have, she thought. Things just wouldn't make sense if he had.

Out there, in the night, Scooter held the two flaps of his jacket together to keep the cold from getting to him, but he couldn't stop it. "Damn cold," he said, "damn night." By the time he could see the small windows puncturing light in the dark from his house, he was sober. He was unsatiated. "That's what you get. That's what you get for going away from your wife. Losing your way home."

He stomped the snow off his boots immediately after walking into the three bedroom company-built house, then hung his coat on a rack they kept near the door. Easing forward heel to toe so as not to make noise, Scooter looked over to the couch and there in the lighted room, was Angela with skin of porcelain, near enough to sleep that he could have sneaked up to the room, but he did not.

Scooter sat beside her, in the curve of her torso and stroked her hair. He whispered to wake and she did.

The smile on her face was enough to make him feel that he was safe. That he was home. That he was loved.

She reached his cheek. "Where have you been, baby?"

"Nowhere. Just out."

"Thelma called."

Scooter straightened and silenced.

"She told me you were out. Where were you?"

"You know where I was."

"I don't. Since Jimmy, I don't ever know where you are. Do you know where you've been?"

Scooter could feel a vice-like tension squeezing his stomach. He looked at the wall across the room, turning his back to her. "You want me to say it?"

"What, baby?"

"You want me to tell you what I was doing tonight? You want me to suffer through telling you?"

"Baby. It's just a question. I just want to know."

"Men act like men do because they are men."

"What is this, Scooter?" She pulled herself up from her position on the couch and held herself up by wrapping her arms around her knees. "You don't have to tell me things you don't want to. I just thought we would be able to talk."

Scooter looked at Angela's face. She wore a shirt of his to bed that was so big it looked like she had wings tucked behind her. He exhaled through pursed lips and the stream of air that came from his mouth wisped against her forehead, flailing her hair up. He was silent.

"Where have you been going when you go out at night?"

"I just go."

"It's always at night. Is there something you need to tell me?"

"There's something out there."

"Where?"

"Out there. A feeling I get when the night comes. Like somewhere out there is the reason that I've done the things I've done. And if I could just get beyond that part of the night, I could be the man my cousin was, the man everyone wants me to be. But it seems like the horizon. When you think you're there, you turn, and it's further away than it was at first."

"Scooter, how did Thelma see you in the dark?"

"What do you mean?"

"She said she saw you on your way home and that you would be cold and alone."

"I don't know. Maybe it's dark enough out there to see anything that isn't night."

Angela reached around her husband's stomach and brought his head to her bosom. She rested her cheek on the top of his head and whispered to him. "Honey, there are things that are always going to hurt. Jimmy's death is one of them. You can't let that get you down. You can't."

"It was my fault."

"No it wasn't, Scooter. You're the only man that feels that weight on his shoulders. There's no reason for you to feel that."

There was a whimper. As if guilt itself could speak or release or transform despair to hope or love.

Angela stroked his scalp. As his hair sprawled between her fingers, he felt her compassion. But there was something more. Yes, he anticipated despair. He knew that the one who would demolish the feeling of this moment was him, not God, not love, not jealousy, not his wife. It would be Scooter lost in the world that betrayed him; but he knew that he was the one that betrayed the world, for the world was set in its ways of work and hope and despair. Betrayal, he knew, was left to him, which always led to his despair.

His wife kissed his head. She told him things would get better because they always do if you stick them out.

Scooter welled with tears.

Without taking his head from his hands, he asked her, "how do you know how to love?"

"I don't, sweetheart. I've just figured out who to love and how to act. How to forgive."

"It's dark out there. Away from home. It's dark and cold. It's so easy to be lost. So easy to lose your way."

Angela held his head closer to her until she squeezed darkness from him and she again asked him where he was tonight and before he could reply, there was a deep, pitying cry that exuded from the cavern dark in his deflating body. He clenched onto the too big shirt she wore.

There was a moment where all fell silent in the house and in Westbend. In that moment, Scooter thought of his love, his wife, of Thelma alone, and he said to his wife, "I had things to figure out tonight."

Angela rocked back and forth with him. "There aren't answers to the things you want to know."

"How do you know what it is I need?"

"I know that you want to know what to do now; that you feel the guilt of this county's men. I know that you think things here don't matter any more because of what happened to Jimmy. I know that you struggle with things since the death. I know you don't know anything about love. I know that there is no answer to struggle. There are only ways to get over it and ways to get through sadness."

Scooter lifted his head and stared at the hazing eyes of Angela. "I want to get rid of all our pain."

"I know. Just tell me where you go at night."

Scooter hesitated. He looked beyond his wife's head to a picture of the two on their wedding day. She was happy in that picture and so was he. There were people in the background laughing. "I've been wanting to find something to hold onto."

They each looked down. Scooter's hands were yet clenched to Angela's shirt.

Scooter smiled. Angela wrapped her arms around her husband's neck.

Old Friends and New Lovers

By
Annette B. Almazan

". . . I'm getting married," he said casually, after calling me out of the blue, six months after the last time we talked.

> What the fuck?!?! What does he mean he's getting married? That's not right. *I'm* the one who's supposed to get married first. I mean, I knew he was dating someone pretty seriously, but shit, marriage? That's forever, and he's never stayed faithful to any of the women he dated after we broke up. What am I so bent out of shape about? I know it never would have worked out between us no matter how much we loved each other.

"I'm so happy for you! She's really good for you. And it's about time you settled down," I said in response.

> I had never lied to him before about anything, so why now? I'm not really happy for him. Call me a hater, but I'm not. And it's not because I'm not married and my own life feels so unsettled. Okay, I'm lying again. It is. So? At least I'm being honest. And really, weren't we supposed to end up together? Granted, we were young and totally unprepared to be married, but we grew up together, we used to take baths together. I saw his "weewee" when it was no bigger than a baby toe. When we broke up, I knew it would be for good. I knew we wouldn't end up together, but I didn't think he would still have such a strong presence in my life. Besides, if she's the one, why do you still come to my bed? Why do I still get calls out of the blue? Shouldn't she be the one you call?

"So what about you, are you seeing anyone?" he asked hopefully, as if my being in a great relationship would make his announcement any less difficult.

"No one serious. Just having fun," I answered, a little too happily.

> I don't know why I keep playing this game. I need to stop. But what am I supposed to do; I really can't imagine him not being part of my life. Part of it is that we still have great chemistry, and

part of it is that I'm scared of getting hurt again by letting someone else really know me. So, in some warped way, my limited, reduce, reuse, recycle policy doesn't seem so bad. But now, he's engaged and I really don't want to be that kind of woman. Right?

"Come on, there's probably someone with potential?" he presses.

"You know how busy my schedule is. I can't imagine juggling my schedule with someone else's. Besides, my attention span is definitely getting shorter and shorter," I rationalize.

I know he wants me to say it. Why would I say it, though? Why would I admit that I haven't had a decent relationship since we broke up? That just makes me sound lame. I'm not lame, I just . . . haven't let myself trust anyone. I can't say I haven't met good men, but I usually jump ship before it really gets started. There is this one guy, but . . . whatever. It's none of his business.

"I know you. If you found the right person, nothing would get in your way," he states matter-of-factly.

"You know me too well. So have you set a date?"

What is wrong with me? Why did I admit that he still knows me so well? We'll go for months at a time without speaking, and then as if he knows I'm about to cut him out of my life, he calls me and sucks me back in.

And, what do I care if they've set a date? It's not like I'm going to be invited, and even if I was, there's no way in hell that I would go. I imagine that experience would go something like, "*'Are you friends of the bride or the groom?'* Groom. *'Oh, how do you know him?'* I was his high school and college sweetheart . . . We used to fuck . . . Um, I mean, we grew up together . . . That would go over really well.

"We're aiming for a mid-summer wedding," he replied.

Great. Good for you.

ಌ ಌ ಌ

"He's getting married," she manages to blurt out before bursting into tears.

Girlfriend doesn't need to tell me who "he" is. There's only ever going to be one "he" that matters, no matter how many men (and better ones) have come in and out of her life. What can I say to convince her that she's better off without him? It's not that I don't like him. He's good on paper—charming, intelligent, good-looking—but their connection is too much. Too intense, too passionate? And after they broke up, their relationship took on epic proportions, as if she's erased all the bad things that happened, all the shitty things he did. Now that he's actually engaged maybe she won't talk to him anymore, or have dinner with him anymore. She damn sure can't sleep with him anymore. Maybe Catholic guilt will finally kick in. Keep her away this time.

"Girl, are you surprised? You told me when they first started dating that you thought she was the one he would marry. They've been together a long time. It's about time he stepped up. Hopefully, he'll grow up and start acting right," I said.

I hate having to be so honest with her. I love this girl like family.

"I know, I know. I had that feeling. I just, maybe, I hate to admit this, but . . . part of me held out hope that something would happen, and we would end up together," she said with a heavy sigh.

No fucking kidding that's what she's been holding out for. If the two of them were to give it another try, fine. But they would have to do it all the way, not the half-assed shit they've been doing for years, which she thinks she's been hiding from me. But I can always tell when he's in the picture. Suddenly she stops talking about the guy she's been seeing, and she doesn't go out as often.

"You know that was just the part of you that will always love him, no matter what. Do you really think you'd be happy together?" I asked.

I have made it clear that I think she should've cut him out of her life a long time ago. Their relationship is completely self-destructive. Granted, she's dated some "special" guys—like the guy who talked about himself in third person, or the dude who, no matter where they were, or what they were doing, would put his hand down his pants. But there have also been some great guys that she really cared for and just wouldn't take the risk. Always some excuse.

"No . . . I don't know . . . who knows? I'm just freaking out, again. I know that everyone thinks I'm so strong, but all I want is for someone to take care of me once in a while. Great role model for my students, huh? I'm setting back the women's movement 200 years," she says guiltily.

Sometimes it is hard to be her friend. I hate when she gets this way. Everything is a disaster. She can't do anything right. The weight of the entire world is on her shoulders. Shit, she even feels bad about feeling bad!

"You are way too hard on yourself. You have a right to rely on other people, and they'd gladly be there for you if you let them. You have so many great things going for you; a job you love, a city you adore living in, and friends that love you. Not many people are as lucky as you to have a best friend like me. I'm the shit," I say.

Ah, a chuckle. That's a step in the right direction. If I can get her to laugh more, then I know she's over the worst.

"I know you're right, but the thing I want most is something I can't really plan or work on, which kills me. You know how I am," she states.

Miss Control Freak. The girl cannot take having anything unsettled in her life. She works hard and knows exactly what she wants, so she's not so good at taking uncalculated chances, especially when it comes to men who don't fit into her idea of who she should be with.

"I know, honey. But I know that you're going to meet the right person," I respond and immediately regret saying.

"It's easy for you to say that, you've got the world's greatest husband! He cooks, and still let's you blow up at him all the time. He even does the dishes!" she says, pausing to laugh. "The older I get, the harder it seems to meet a decent guy, who's even halfway interesting. I don't want to settle for someone who's just my friend. I want everything. And I don't think that's too much to ask! I don't know, maybe this isn't even about marriage. Maybe it's about kids. Women's fertility starts to drop off at 27. *I'm* 27! Technically, I'm closer to 28. My birthday's in five months!"

Listen to that tirade.

"Girl, you have got to stop watching Oprah and listening to the news. There is no magic age for getting married and having kids. There is no perfect plan. Our friends who are already married probably feel too young to be so settled, and our friends who are single feel too old to be unattached. We always want what we don't have."

Wow, I sounded kind of smart. And I can't believe she didn't interrupt me? Normally, she would stop me halfway and tell me she knows what I'm going to say. Her stubborn streak runs deep. Maybe she's really ready to hear what I have to say to her.

"I know, I know. God, why is it that every time I talk to him I start doubting my entire life?" she laments.

Amen to that.

The last time this happened she stopped going to church for months. Angry at God for not giving her a sign that her personal life was headed in the right direction. "If God has a plan for everyone," she said, "then am I supposed to be a nun or something? But if I'm supposed to be a nun, then He should never have let me fall in love or have so much incredible sex. I can't imagine giving up the possibility of ever experiencing either again!"

There's only so much that God or fate can do for anyone. Once the opportunity presents itself, it's up to each person. She knows that her biggest obstacle to falling in love is herself.

"Well, maybe it's time that the two of you finally stop talking altogether," I conclude.

I said it. Again. Even when they were thousands of miles from each other, one of them draws the other back in. I should put a taser on her phone so every time she talks to him she's shocked. Aversion therapy.

"Yeah, but I just don't want to say I'm never going to talk to him again and end up not being able to follow through. He's like my eternal broken New Year's resolution," she admits.

"You don't have to promise anything to me . . . Look, let's stop talking about him, okay? Tell me something else. Oh, tell me about what's his name? That's definitely more interesting . . ."

❧ ❧ ❧

". . . You don't know what you're getting into with me," she says for the umpteenth time.

When we met, she thought I was a cocky asshole, which is not completely untrue, and I thought she was uptight and bossy, which is flat out true. I know she didn't know what to think when I asked her out, but why wouldn't I? She's cute, has a great ass, and she called me on my shit. She intrigued me. Surprised me, too. Especially after our first dinner when she told me she was a card-carrying liberal, party girl. I'm a Republican, I'd rather watch football and reruns of SportsCenter on the couch. But now that it's

> been a few months, she's definitely backing off. Jesus, this is going to end up in a "talk." I must really be crazy about her to initiate a state-of-the-relationship talk. Either that or I'm a masochist. Yeah, probably a masochist.

"I know exactly what I'm getting into with you, which is why I want to be with you. Why don't you let me worry about me, and you worry about you. The real question is, do you want to be with me?" I ask.

> When we were first getting to know each other, and we weren't physical, she talked to me about the things that worried her - were her students actually learning anything, did she need to be spending more time with her parents now that they're getting older, and, of course, whether she would meet someone who'd make her happy. Now she's definitely keeping stuff from me. I'm not exactly sure what, but she's not letting me in. All she wants to do is talk about work and Georgetown basketball. The Georgetown part I like because not many women are even interested in sports, let alone are real fans, but even I'm smart enough to recognize when it's for show.

"I'm sorry. I do want to be with you, but I'm scared of risking our friendship. Don't get me wrong, being more than friends, has been awesome. But I can't remember the last time I've been in a real relationship, and I don't know if I can share my life with anyone again," she worries.

> I don't know who did this to her. She never talks about the guys she used to date, but there was definitely someone who fucked her up. I know I should be worried about trying to get serious with someone with this kind of baggage, but there is just something about this girl. I dig her.

"That's some bullshit. You, what, want me to be at your wedding if I'm not going to be in it? Can't you give us—give ME—half a chance? Look, I know it's not perfect. You like fancy restaurants; I'd prefer Burger King. You like to go dancing; I have two left feet. You love museums; I'm . . . less enthusiastic about them. But what about everything else? We could both eat pizza and ice cream everyday. We both love sitting in a coffee shop just to people watch. Who else would watch animated movies with you? And, I'll even go shopping with you even though you drag me to every shoe store you pass by! I know that you don't trust being happy, but I'm not going to let you walk away!" I argued.

> The truth is we're not going to be friends if we break up now. We can't pretend that there isn't something between us. I've been

through this before and so has she. It'll be fine at first. Maybe it'll even seem like things are back to normal, whatever that means. But then one or both of us will want something more so we'll pull away. Seeing each other less, definitely talking less, until we aren't friends anymore.

So really what's the point in that? Let's take the risk. I'm down. It's not that I don't care about her friendship, but being her friend and wondering what more we could've been would be worse. I can't stand what ifs. I'm not going to let her fear get in the way of finding out how good we could really be together.

"I don't know why you're trying so hard to be with me. You're so stubborn," she finally says.

"Look who's talking. I'm not the one having a full on battle in my head ALL BY MYSELF! Stop thinking so much. We're gonna be great. Rock Stars even. We'll be giving people whiplash because we look so good together. You know it, too. So seriously, why keep fighting me?"

She's laughing. It was the Rock Star part for sure.

"Fine. I got nothing, OK? Satisfied, now?" she relents. "I can't promise you anything, but I'm tired of fighting with you. You win. Now can I please come over?"

ꕤ ꕤ ꕤ

There's already a message on my cell phone? It's kind of early. It's probably my mom, she never sleeps.

"Hey, it's me. I know we haven't talked in a while, but I need some advice, and you were the first person I thought of. Call me when you get a minute."

Lost Your Way to Heaven

By
Edwardo Jackson

"YEAH, I fucked him."

I blinked twice. She didn't blink at all. I went ahead with my question. "When did you first meet him?"

"Last night." Took a drag on her cigarette. "I was at the bar downstairs. He came onto me like an unspayed dog. Got me hammered on Jack and Coke, then took me up to his room and *really* hammered me."

Her words popped like firecrackers. I was a writer. I could appreciate that. Verbal grenades.

"He didn't need to juice me up with all that Jack and Coke." A bemused smile. "I woulda fucked him for free."

"Because he's a movie star?"

"No. Because he's *Mark Frasier.* I mean look at him! He's so gorgeous, I'd screw his bodyguard just to have the chance to suck his pinky toe."

Damn. That's *gorgeous.* "How did he approach you?"

She snorted. "Like the sun revolves around the earth. Walked right up and sat at the bar next to me. Didn't say a word, just kept staring at me in the eyes, daring me—no, baiting me—to recognize him."

"What did you say?"

"I said, 'I don't give a damn who you are, staring isn't for free.'"

Sure ain't. "What did he say?"

"He said some shit like, 'I don't buy drinks for women. They buy drinks for me.'"

Bold little sucker.

"After I turned my back on him, he said, 'But I do buy drinks for dates.'" Her nose crinkled, as if she were remembering the part of a story that makes a story. "'What makes you think this is a date?' 'Because after I buy you a few drinks, we're going up to my suite and having sex.'"

"This is his idea of a date?" I asked incredulously. This guy needed a script doctor for life.

"Men like him don't date," she observed wryly. "They don't have to."

She paused, absently playing with the ends of her hair. "And that's exactly how it happened. Just that fucking easy."

"Any regrets?" I asked.

"I shouldn't have any, but I do." Her face clouded over like a solar eclipse of the soul. "He wasn't at all what I expected. Wasn't at all."

I let her thought gain weight. "So he's an arrogant asshole?"

"No," she said, her fire rekindling. "He's Mark Frasier."

EMMA.

ॐ ॐ ॐ

"Whoa, Mark Frasier? That dude is like a god or something! He's gotta have the best job in the world! Who wouldn't want to be that guy? Dude is rich, famous, good-looking—well, he ain't as pretty as *myself*, but he's not bad . . . Bro! That guy is living The Life! I saw his house on TV one time, I mean it friggin' blew my mind! I ain't got no problem with him. Shoot, I wish I had Mark Frasier's kinda problems! Fuckin' A!"

ॐ ॐ ॐ

"I'm sick and tired of talking about Mark Frasier."

Yet she was here. "Then why did you agree to be interviewed?"

She tried not to roll her eyes. "Because my last two films tanked, I don't have another major film coming for the next fifteen months, and it's for *Vanity Fair*. I could use a little publicity."

Movie stars. They could be as pretentious as they were honest.

"Well tell me something you haven't already said before about Mark Frasier."

"Like how he has a mole on the tip of his dick?"

That got my attention. "He does?"

"No. It was just a catty thing to say." Took a swig of water and popped a Percoset. Or was it Vicadin? "What would you like to know?"

"Did you love him?"

"You waste no time, do you?" Sarcasm flowed like the Nile—filled with blood.

"Look, this isn't a puff piece for his latest action film/cottage industry/pop cultural extravaganza. This is an in-depth exposé of the real man inside Mark Frasier."

"If such a thing exists." Snapped at her water like trying to snatch at fog. "It started off sweetly enough. Well, as sweetly as Hollywood gets."

"Met him backstage at the Emmys, right?" I consulted my notes.

"So the fairy tale goes." She shook her head. "At first, it was like two whales mating. My camp would contact his camp, my person called his . . . After the end of the first month, we missed connections with each other so much, our *assistants* had their first date before we did."

I raised an eyebrow at her.

"When you really want to get in touch with somebody, you can get in touch with them. But, sometimes, there are channels that need to be followed. Just to protect yourself."

I had to keep her talking. The more she talked, the more her distant, Hollywood façade seemed to drift away. "From what?"

She bent forward with interest. Dry, wry interest. "Believe it or not, a lot of men will try to date you because it raises their profile, enhances their career. Shocking, I know," she quipped. She knew that I knew the deal in this town. "A lot of times it's not even their own idea. An ambitious publicist, a buddy of theirs from their infamous past maybe, even their own movie star male friends will suggest it. Hell, I even do it on set sometimes. Talking to my co-stars or makeup people, playing Movie Star Rotisserie Baseball and matching up who we think would look good together."

"Who you got at third?"

"Huh?" was her response. She missed the joke like the Bulls missed Jordan.

She continued. "Some people even get married that way, and it's all a sham. But their careers take off. I'd already been through one of those type of relationships. I didn't want to go through another."

"So his status as a peer, multi-million dollar movie star, and *People*'s Sexiest Man Alive two years ago had nothing to do with it?"

"It didn't hurt," she admitted. "It gave him access. Being in the same business, that is. I meet beautiful men all the time. I don't call all of them."

"So what was it like when these two 'whales' finally met? Did you find him arrogant?" I baited her.

"No. Well, not at first." She blended back in her chair, reconciling a memorable past with a far distant present. Off camera, a lot of these film types never matched their glow onscreen. She didn't just match her glow, she defined it—especially during moments of introspection. "Remember this was over a year ago. Mark was coming off of his first real bomb with *The Chicagoland Murders*. At the time I met him, he had reason to be real humble."

"So money and success gives you the power to be an ass?" I translated.

"No. Just success. At least in Hollywood, anyway." A smile. "He was charming at first. Mark had real moments of chivalry, gallantry even."

I didn't believe her. "Give me an example."

She exhaled away all reticence, diving into her story. "For my birthday last year, only about a month into our dating, he picked me up from the set himself after I was wrapped that night. Usually, I'd just go home or he would send a driver when he wanted to see me or I'd have my driver take me over to his place. But he showed up himself, which was unusual, but nice. Unusually nice.

"He kissed me hello and then blindfolded me. I couldn't see *anything*. When I asked him where we were going, he said, 'The rabbit hole never tells Alice about Wonderland. Patience.' I was real curious and real excited. Like a kid on Christmas Eve.

"He helps me into a Gulfstream—one that I learned later he borrowed from the president of Warner Brothers—and we were in the air for about an hour, maybe two. Mark escorts me off the plane and into a limo where we're riding for about half an hour. When the car stops, we get out, and he finally takes the blindfold off, but only after two minutes. I hear waves crashing. I open my eyes and we're on a private, moonlit, Mexican beach, without a soul in sight.

"He asks me, 'What time were you born today, thirty-one years ago?' I said, 'Eleven-thirteen PM' He said, 'Happy birthday, sweetheart.' I looked at my watch and it said nine-thirteen. 'That's so sweet, Mark, but you know you're two hours early, right?' He said, 'That's Pacific time. You were born at eleven-thirteen Central time. Happy birthday, sweetheart.'"

She took a moment to soak in the entire memory, moved as the Red Sea was after Moses parted it. "That was Mark, right there. When he wanted to, he never missed a detail. That night we had dinner on the beach at a table he had already set up. And for dessert, I made love to him right there on the sand."

"You made love to him?"

"He didn't want our first time to be his 'taking advantage' of me on my birthday." She grinned. "So I had to seduce him."

"That must have been hard."

"Yeah, it was. I had to seduce him over and over and over again." She rested her chin in her palm. "And that's when I knew he had me."

"Did you love him?"

She blew right by my question. "You know, he was always a confident guy. After *Ripcord* took off, his confidence became cockiness. Cockiness gave way to arrogance. He became totally self-absorbed."

Her jaw set bitterly, Jell-o hardening in its mold. "It was as if the movie's success—career success—validated him. Mark became so emotionally aloof after awhile . . . I couldn't reach him. The him I met at the Emmys. The him who took me to the beach. The him who got her. Who got me."

I had no more questions to ask, except for the one she refused to answer.

"It's like loving God," she said finally. "You just have to have faith that he loves you back."

CYNTHIA. CYNTHIA STEELE.

ଓ ଓ ଓ

"Mark Frasier? Yeah, I've seen *all* of his movies. He's charismatic, you know? Sexy, sweet. Kinda has a real believable persona. He's the kinda guy you automatically trust, who's handsome and trustworthy in that Harrison Ford, Robert De Niro, Denzel Washington kinda way. He's not snarky and smug like Brad Pitt or Tom Cruise. He's just *real.* When he had to save his daughter and he had that monologue in . . . in . . . what was the name of that movie? Oh yeah, in *When Doves Cry*, I bawled like a baby. I wish all men were as sensitive as Mark Frasier. I wish all men *were* Mark Frasier."

ଓ ଓ ଓ

"I should be asking you. Who *is* Mark Frasier?"

I was prepared for what could easily be the most vacuous interview of the bunch. She flicked her hair the way supermodels did because, well, she was one. Hair down to her ass and legs as long as a Steven King novel. For a guy who had graduated summa cum laude from Stanford, Mark Frasier didn't seem like the type to end up with a glory girl like her.

Playing my part I said, "I was hoping you could shed some light on that for me."

"I don't know the guy on the billboards and in the movies. I don't know 'Mark Frasier.' I only know Mark from the second floor who used to 'borrow' toilet paper from me and try to pay it back with sex."

Good God, was this guy just some walking erection? Who hadn't he slept with? "So you two were more than just 'good friends.'"

She smiled perfectly, transcendently. Now I see why Revlon hired her. "Of course. We dated. I mean he was a good looking guy, we found each other attractive, and we were only one flight away. This had to have been at least five years ago. We were both new to L. A. Had been here less than a year. It helped to have someone who was . . . close."

"What did you think of him then? How did you perceive him?"

"Hungry. Ambitious. Always had his eye out for something more."

I took inventory of her flawless body. Curves and swerves Rand McNally couldn't chart. After a former *Baywatch* star and a certain young coquettish singer-cum-softcore porn star, hers was the most downloaded image on the Internet. Okay, maybe just after Anna Kournikova. As much as I hated to admit it, she wasn't as airbrushed as I thought she would be. "I can't believe he could want more than you."

She could have turned smug, but didn't. A hint of sadness lived in those eyes. "I was an arm charm. I was only with him for the status of being a beautiful woman. Mark was . . . emotionally unsettled. It wasn't his fault."

With my eyes, I prodded for more.

"I was a transitional woman. I guess right before he moved to L. A., he had broken up with someone. Someone he loved very much." A moment. "Someone who broke his heart."

I was fascinated. There was once a time when Mark Frasier was vulnerable to a woman. "Did he talk much about it?"

"No. And he won't either. It took a year of us dating to even get that much out of him," she said gently. "By the way, none of this is your business. I'm not telling you any of this for you. I'm telling you this for him. People can say a lot of things about the man they think they know is Mark Frasier. I want to make sure you say things right."

This was a woman who was wholly comfortable in her own skin. Each word came out measured, calm, as if predestined to exist before she ever spoke it. I envied her self-assuredness, her emotional feng shui. She was more than just a successful model and singer—she was a nice person. Even after the three or so years they had been out of touch with each other, she still cared, if not for him, for the time period she had known him. She was protecting him as if she were protecting the memory.

I instantly felt bad for having judged her.

"Do you ever remember him being arrogant or full of himself?"

"No," she answered. "Just on occasion when he would be at an Industry event with me. He liked being with me but, I think even more so, he liked being *seen* with me. Mark was a puppy. He would poke his chest out to cover up his pain, but I knew it was there. On the inside, he was just this wounded little puppy, too insecure to deal with his broken heart but smart enough to conceal it from the world."

Even though this was all being recorded, I scribbled furiously on my notepad, feeling the beginning of the Lewis and Clark Trail to Mark Frasier. This only elicited a bemused smile from her.

"If you think you're going to find out who Mark Frasier is, think again." Protective, confident, yet totally at ease. "Mark is an actor now, just as he was an actor then."

AUBREY.

ᏡᏅ ᏡᏅ ᏡᏅ

"Mark Frasier has had quite an interesting career. Six years ago, he got his start in a small role as a scientist in *Armageddon*, in a scene that was eventually cut. Several guest appearances on TV that followed include two junkies, a pimp, one pusher, and a male nurse on *ER*. Then an independent film he starred in directed by a recently graduated USC film school student garnered him rave reviews at Cannes, Sundance, and Toronto in the title role of *Antonio.* Bursting on the scene with eleven movies in the next four years, Mark Frasier's movies have grossed $2.5 billion worldwide. His current asking fee is $17 million, up from the $15 million he received for *When Doves Cry* and *Triple Z II.* His box office appeal has been tied to a relentlessly volatile off-camera persona, one involving brawls, an ever-changing cast of celebrity women, and a notorious inaccessibility to the media. He is one of the hardest interviews to get in the business. A versatile actor for dramatic, action, or light comedy roles, Mark Frasier has also been nominated for an Academy award for *writing. The Reality Factor* was nominated for Best Original Screenplay, as was his performance as the lead, for his only Oscar nomination for acting. He is one of the most charismatic, talented, and bankable movie stars in film today. And he's only 28."

ᏡᏅ ᏡᏅ ᏡᏅ

"Mark."

She lingered on the word like the Bible did the Old Testament.

So did my eyes on her. Short, turned out hair in a layered flip. Deep, sensitive, chocolate eyes that could melt just as easily. Three cornrows of wrinkles in her forehead. An unforgiving mouth. That hardened jaw. When this woman did something, it was done. Beyond a doubt.

"You used to date Mark about six years ago, correct?"

"That's when it ended. We dated for over two years," she said plainly.

She shifted uncomfortably in the hotel chair. For the first time, I was interviewing someone unused to the interview process. She wasn't a wannabe model barfly, an actress, nor a supermodel/singer. She was middle management for a bank in Barstow, California. Despite her self-possessed sense of style and general self-awareness, nothing about her screamed anything else but ordinary girl. But it was this ordinary girl who had done the extraordinary. "Were you in love?"

She eyed the tape recorder on the table next to me as if it captured more than just words, as if it would steal her soul. With an exhale, she stood, paced a bit until she could proceed. "Yeah. We were in love."

"What was it like?"

She stopped pacing. This was the part that came naturally to her. "It was wonderful. Like being on the road to Heaven, Mark used to say. For awhile, it was all I needed. We had totally complementary personalities, you know? He was artistic and creative, I was logical and practical. We were lovers and we were friends. We saw each other every day. Spent every other weekend entirely together. It was college. We were inseparable. I never wanted for anything."

I let those words float and blend into the air like a gentle morning mist. I kind of envied her. No one had made me feel like that in a long time. "What was he like?"

She sat down, clearly enticed into a comfort zone. "Smart. Sweet. Gentle. Sensitive. So very sensitive. Romantic. He was all those things a boy in love is before he becomes a man."

That answer intrigued me. "How so?"

Those eyes were melting like I knew they could. "Men don't love like that. He was so unconditionally loving, trusting, and giving, it was almost . . . naïve. Sure I loved him, but he loved me like there was no tomorrow. He used to tell me that."

"A man will say anything in the middle of orgasm."

That mouth of hers conveyed its disapproval, jaw hardening. "That's just it. He would tell me that *all* the time. I'm telling you, he was an entirely different person when I knew him."

"Why did you consider his love naïve?" That was the $64,000 question.

She shook her head sadly. "He loved me like we would last forever. Hell, he thought we *would* last forever. Mark invested everything into me. He couldn't see past me."

"But you could?" I tried to stifle the accusation in my voice.

"It was *college*, you know? I was 21. As wonderful as our relationship was, I wasn't naïve enough to think it would last forever. Nothing lasts forever. Not even love. Especially not love."

"So you broke his heart."

"I broke his heart," she stated in a clipped, "there, I said it" sort of tone.

Gingerly, I asked, "what happened?"

"It was stupid, I'll be the first to admit," she conceded. "But I was beginning to feel trapped, you know? He graduated a year ahead of me, hung around Palo Alto temping and working retail, just to be around me. Sure he was doing local theater and got a bit part in some Hollywood movie, but I felt like I was holding him back. Like he was betting his entire future on me, on us. That's a lot of responsibility for a 21 year old Finance major who's more concerned about her finals and job placement than whether she's going to marry her boyfriend after graduation, you know?"

I nodded my head, but only to keep her talking. I had no idea. I didn't think men like that existed, much less in Mark Frasier.

She managed a meager laugh. "Judging by that blank look in your eyes, you don't know. I know, it must sound like a trip. Little old me broke *Mark Frasier's* heart."

"For *loving* you too much. It's a lot to wrap my mind around."

Prideful. "I don't regret it, either. We do things in life, we make choices. Those choices affect our actions and reactions, and those of people around us. I made a decision based on how I felt at the time and I was being true to myself. I don't begrudge the success Mark has had, nor do I feel left out of it. If anything, I feel responsible for it. Had I not let him go, he wouldn't have been free to become the man he is today."

"And what do you think of the man he is today?" Subtext: Do you think your breaking his heart turned him bitter?

"I don't want him back. I can see the subtle arrogance in his interviews. I heard about his fight with Russell Crowe. The models, the strippers, the hos. He's not the boy I fell in love with."

But he's the man you always thought he would be.

<u>ALEJANDRA.</u>

ᔓᔕ ᔓᔕ ᔓᔕ

"Mark Frasier was horrible. Granted, he was a sixteen year old sophomore when I had him, but he was not good at all. He had trouble with basic beats, breath control, intention, throughline . . . You name it, he was not good at it. Mark also did not take the class very seriously. I think he was forced to take an acting class for his arts requirement when Woodworking was full. But, I have to admit, he always had a little something. Charisma, you could call it. He may not have been the best actor in the class but he always had your attention. Am I surprised to see how well he's done with acting? Absolutely. I guess the acting bug finally got him in college and he took it seriously. It is amazing what happens to someone when they fall in love with something. You can tell that, on screen, Mark is a man in love."

❧ ❧ ❧

"Mark Frasier used to ride my bus to school."

This one was a bit of a stretch, I know, but I had to try it. Something about going all the way back to his roots intrigued me. There was something about the interviewer being one part dime store psychologist that fed my ego to go off on this route. I craved more. The pieces were coming together, but very tessellation-like. No matter which end you looked at it, each piece fit the same but still did not complete a whole picture.

"When was the last time you saw him?"

"We were fourteen. Eighth grade. Mark ended up going to a different high school." She sighed. Her large frame seemed to ripple and then settle, like satin bed sheets. "If only he had gone to Lincoln or I had gone to Washington . . ."

I smiled. "You had a crush on him?"

Her bright, dark eyes turned shy. "Sure did. We were friends, rode the 989 bus route to school, sitting in the back, and talked a lot. He wasn't as handsome as he is today, hiding behind a pair of glasses before changing into contacts his last semester in eighth grade, but he looked good to me."

"What was he like back then?" I think I had an idea but I wanted her to confirm it.

"He was such an idealist, a romantic, a big dreamer. Had a heart as big as the whole wide world."

"Wow."

"I know, right? No kidding. He was so purely sweet, innocent, naïve. Nothing like the guy they make him out to be on TV. I don't know him."

"So you think he's getting a bum rap?" I leaned forward.

She matched me. "Sure. My grandmama always said 'Believe none of what you hear and half of what you see.' I don't believe that's the same guy they're talking about with the fights and the temper and all those women. There was nothing in life he wanted more than love, that boy. He talked so much about it, about the purity of love and how he would be the perfect boyfriend if given the chance, I mean he practically breathed and existed for it . . . Is it any wonder why I had a crush on him?"

I smiled widely. Who wouldn't have a crush on *that* guy?

"If you see him, could you please tell him I said hi?" The large, somewhat shy woman became as beautiful as a shrinking violet.

I closed my notebook, nodding. "Sure."

"I always knew he would be a star," she added. "He dreamed so big, he had no other choice."

SHAY.

∽ ∽ ∽

"Mark Frasier saved my life. I was sick, stuck in the hospital with brain cancer. I was always going in and out for operations and all that. The doctors gave me six months to live. Well, one night, I decided I wasn't going to take it anymore. I was so sick from the chemo and different drugs they were pumping into me that I was puking out, I thought I would just OD the medication in my IV once the nurse shift changed. But my nurse just would not leave, sitting in one of those crummy plastic hospital chairs watching *When Doves Cry* on the TV. I had to wait so damn long, I started to watch with her. It was amazing. The way Mark looked his wife goodbye before sacrificing his life for his daughter's . . . Powerful is an understatement. I know it's just acting and all but . . . I swear . . . that look in his eyes came from somewhere real. Somewhere of love. That man really knows what love is all about. He loved her so much, he traded his life for their daughter's . . . I tear up every time I think about it." Sniffles. "I decided to stick it out and not kill myself. Two months later, my cancer went into remission and now I'm living completely cancer-free. I saw the power of love in his eyes that night, and it gave me something to live for. Now, I'm engaged to a wonderful man and I owe everything to having watched that movie, to having watched him. Mark Frasier saved my life."

∽ ∽ ∽

"I don't give interviews."

"Good, because this isn't gonna be one."

As far as scenes go, this was a good one. We were essentially on my home turf, the same hotel suite I had rented out the past couple of weeks while researching the Mark Frasier article. I sucked down half of a bottled water in an effort to calm my nerves. Soothing Angie Stone music played in the periphery. But nothing could stop my heart from marching.

I was a journalist, an entertainment journalist at that. I didn't get excited or flustered by movie stars. Shoot, it's how I made my living by interviewing them. The only time I had been this nervous was when I had gone skydiving with Ben Affleck just to show him I wasn't a wussy. And I got the interview done, too.

But here I was. Six feet away from him. The man. The subject. Two weeks' worth of professional and personal obsession.

I had over prepared, for sure. I had enough to write a book on him, let alone a featured cover article. There was a reason why I was nervous. I was curious to see if he would find out the reason, too.

"Then why are you here?" asked the cocky, affected Mark Frasier. He looked like he had stepped right off the screen of the Mann's Chinese Theater in Hollywood. I envied and hated his perfection.

"To find the impossible," I said, turning my tape recorder on. "To find out what makes you tick. Or tock. Which is it, Mr. Frasier?"

"Tock," he grinned. "Definitely tock. And good luck."

The way he kind of tossed off that last comment pissed me off. "You kind of like being an asshole, don't you?"

That slapped him in the face. "Look, woman, you called me."

"Is this all part of the dog and pony show? Fronting like a hardass, limiting information, creating some sort of 'aura' that is to become Mark Frasier?" I accused. I downshifted into blasé. "I'm not impressed."

He, however, was. "Call me Mark."

A silent, internal fist pump as I watched him break into a smile and then immediately try to stifle it. This wasn't going to hurt one bit . . .

"Okay, Mark, first things first," I announced formally. A dramatic pause. "Shay says hi."

Another unauthorized smile. "Shay? Shay-from-the-989-Shay?"

"That's her," I verified. "She said she had a crush on you, even back in the eighth grade."

"Wow. That really takes me back."

"Aubrey says that I'll never find out who the real Mark Frasier is."

"Aubrey's right. An interview with me is like trying to see a Lakers game from the 300 level in Staples Center."

I grinned. "I'm in the room, but still a mile away from the action."

"You catch on quick." Another oppressed smile. I would have to find a way to liberate that region.

"Good thing this isn't an interview," I reminded him.

With a charming, devilish gleam in his eye, Mark leaned forward to engage me, visually seducing me as I'm sure he had done many a journalist. "Let's quit dancing and get down to the real deal here. You need to talk to me in an attempt to balance out your story, so it's not just some hack hatchet job by a relatively obscure reporter trying to make a name for herself by bringing down a celebrity. And I need to talk to you because I'm opening the biggest film of my career next month and a *Vanity Fair* cover is invaluable publicity that I couldn't even buy if I tried. So let's quit dicking around and get this over with."

People make life a lot harder than it needs to be. The answers to the most complex situations in life are so astonishingly simple, they defy conventional logic.

"We will never be that naïve again."

Mark's face drained down an imaginary gutter. "What did you say?"

Almost in a trance, staring sharply into his eyes, I repeated, "we will never be that naïve again."

It was so true. As long as I could remember, I had always wanted to be a writer. Writing was the one thing that would make me happy, that would never fail me, that would rarely disappoint me. So what if love had avoided me like a panhandler? I never sacrificed career for love; I focused on career because love wasn't coming. And it still wasn't coming. Until today.

I smiled. "This is all an act. I could know you, I could not know you, it still wouldn't matter. You act just like everyone else in this world, everyone else who has gotten hurt. You hide behind your status, your money, and a badass arrogant demeanor just to avoid the simple fact that you can't bear to reconcile with yourself, that we will never be that naïve again."

He glared a hole through me, but I continued. "You're nothing special, Mark. We've all been hurt. What makes your pain any more special than anyone else's?"

"Because it happened to me," he growled.

"Right. And that's fine. I feel that," I agreed. "We all feel that. But we can't turn back the clock. You can't recapture that lost innocence that spoiled devotion to someone any more than I can squeeze into my high school cheerleading outfit. You have to make a new outfit, one that fits you."

"Who are y—"

"This doesn't *fit you*, Mark! I may not know who you are but I certainly know what you're about. You're about commitment. Honesty.

Romanticism. Communication. *Love.* I'm a writer, too, Mark. I know what you're about."

"Why are you saying all this to me?" He was clearly disturbed, if not frightened. "What are you trying to prove?"

I sighed a little exasperatedly, mentally breaking down the simplicity to its atomic structure. "Don't you ever feel like you want to be with someone you don't have to work so hard to be around? Someone who *gets* you?"

Mark nodded, protons and neutrons flying.

"I mean you meet some of the most amazing and beautiful women, but don't you ever feel like there's something missing from your relationships? Something you can't name, can't quite put your finger on, but is still there, nagging at you like a scratch in the back of the throat?"

"Absolutely." Positives and negatives were attracting.

"Everything is in place, damn near perfect even. Yet you still want more." I let that settle. "It's because they don't 'get' you—and you don't get them."

Silence.

"I *get* you, Mark."

Mark got up and walked out to the balcony. I watched him go, sitting alone in my stupidity and foolish pride. Had I said too much? Did I get too close? Big sigh. *Go get the boy.*

I found him at the railing, leaning over, being absorbed by the sounds of the city at night. I had come this far; I had to finish the job.

"I know what it's like to love someone, just to lose them," I said softly. He turned to face me and my quiet, pensive eyes. "I know what it's like to invest everything into them. To love them more than they deserve to be loved. To love them more than you love yourself.

"I know what it's like to hurt, to feel that dull throbbing in your stomach that feels like it will never go away. I know what it's like to never want to open up to anyone, for fear of opening yourself up to pain. I know what you feel like, Mark.

"But a funny thing happened on the way to writing my 'hack hatchet job.' I was exposed to this guy who reminded me what it was like to be me again. This guy was everything I was and still could be—romantic, honest, sincere. Naïve. If it's naïve to believe that all you need is honesty and expression then, yes, I am naïve. We all are. Deep down in our hearts, we all want to be able to trust and fall in love, to completely devote ourselves to someone who is doing the same for you—someone who will take care of you when you are old and crotchety and having a bad hair decade.

Hearing about this guy made me believe again that all this was possible. He made the naïve not so naïve."

I could sense Mark's mood shift—for the better, I don't know—but something reached him.

"Mark, through you, through hearing about you, how you are and used to be, I understand completely. I understand what happened and it scared me enough to see that it had happened to me, too. It scared me but it affirmed me. I once believed like you did. I think, at one point or another, we are all Mark Frasier. I think that I *can* believe like that again. But it's not naïve to believe—it's brave. To do something as simple as love someone is to be courageous in a world of cowards."

His coal black eyes shimmered their approval.

I sighed. "Life doesn't have to be that hard. Life *isn't* that hard. But being yourself, your romantic, idealistic, *naively* loving self . . . is."

His hands found the rim of my face, framing it like a portrait of love. Cocky, but sincere smile. A world of understanding in those eyes. "You're right. We will never be that naïve again."

He kissed me. I let him.

Bold little sucker.

With a smile, a mere inch from my lips he said, "So let's be brave."

JANINE.

ME.

HIM.

US.

ൾ ൾ ൾ

"Mark Frasier isn't a man, he's a journey. He's on a path that few of us dare take or even acknowledge exists. His journey started him off as an idealistic teenager who dreamed of love in its purest, rarest form, experienced it briefly in college, and then endured the bitter agony of heartbreak just after graduation. In recent years, he has lost his way, only to find his way back again, stronger. His path has gone around yet forward at the same time. He's back where he started, but far more advanced. Mark Frasier may never get to where he's going . . . but he's on the right path." Pause. Smile. "And he has a terrific walking partner."

The Crossroad

S

By
E. A. Bagby

THE TONGUE's curved pressure at the teeth, a gentle dental whistle-hiss of wind, sustainable, a remembered softness. Ess. Yes.

> *Sinful Caesar sniffed his snifter, seized his knees, and sneezed.*
> *Silly Susie went ice-skating.*
> *The ice was thin, the weather brisk.*
> *Wasn't Susie slightly stupid,*
> *Her silly little *?*

Asterisk was treacherous, but so was *star*. He stopped after *little.*

"Go on," said Grace.

He shook his head.

"Mark."

He shook his head again.

"Do you not get it? I thought you'd like—"

"I get it."

"Well, say it then."

"I can't. You know I can't. It's"—he searched for the word—"it's vain."

"Vain?" she said, not understanding on purpose.

"Without a point," he said triumphantly.

"Did you want to say *pointless?"*

He nodded. "But I didn't."

"Well, you should have."

"But. I. Can't."

Grace started to say something, stopped, and took a long breath. Mark studied the tiny lines around her mouth and felt mean. He liked Grace. She tried. She talked to him; she listened to him. And she was beautiful in a strong, tough, experienced way, a way with which none of the girls at Valley View could compete, though a few of them tried. They smelled like smoke and went around with too much makeup on their babyish cheeks, and they said words they didn't quite understand, roughening their voices to approximate those of movie stars. Mark had stopped being interested in them almost as soon as he had noticed them. His lack of interest had become irrevocable two years ago, when he met Lisa. He was 15 then and had panicked: would his kisses give him away? But to his infinite surprise and gratitude Lisa never mentioned it, only kept kissing him with a mysterious fervor. In the morning she said he was a good kisser, but she was worried about the age difference. (He had told her he was 20; she was a senior in college.) After Lisa he pushed his age up gradually. He usually said 23. They usually believed it. But Lisa was—he thought of her as the firtht.

"Do you want to know what I did last night?"

Grace paused before she said anything; he could see her waver between actually answering and commending him for saying *last.* "What did you do?" she said finally, in a tone that indicated that, whatever he had done, it would not be news.

"Went out," he said. "Met a girl."

Grace sighed, and leaned back in her chair.

"Went home with her," said Mark.

"Do your parents know?"

"No. Why would I tell them?"

"What was her name?" said Grace, without real interest.

"Mel," said Mark.

Grace regarded him, unblinking. Damn her.

"Melissa," he said.

"Ah."

"Ergo, I knew it wouldn't be anything long-term," said Mark in a hurry, "and I didn't feel too bad—"

Grace interrupted: "Wait. I'm curious. What did you call her all night, if not Melissa?"

"Honey," said Mark. "Or dear."

"She didn't mind that?"

He shrugged. "Women like that."

"Women," said Grace, with a faint smile, "like it when men remember their names."

"I did remember her name."

"Say it for me again, then."

"Don't you want to know what happened?"

"Say her name first."

He did, quietly, slowly, carefully, contorting an unwilling tongue. It still came out wrong, and he went crimson at a sudden, unbidden memory of Melissa standing in her lamplit bedroom with her shirt off, cocking her head to one side and saying, "what?"

He had had no choice but to repeat the careless, unfortunate sentence: "I like kissing you." He meant it; he loved kissing. You could communicate without saying a word. It was the only time he felt he was making himself known. He hushed the inevitable word as much as he could, slurring it softly.

She gave him a searching look, aimed not at his eyes but at the near side of his head. He knew. Looking for the hearing aid.

"Something the matter?" said Grace.

"No," said Mark, trying to banish all traces of shame from his face.

"You sure?"

"Do you want to know what happened or not?"

"Mark. I'm not a therapist. I'm—" Grace remembered herself and lowered her voice. "Why don't you say what I am?"

What kind of cruel joke were the words *speech pathologist?* No one who needed one could say so. Mark glowered.

"Go on."

"You're a—"

Grace's face was relentless. He saw again Melissa, edged finely with lamplight, wondering and sad. Her mouth had been strong, decisive. But later her curious hands had crept over his ears, exploring, uncomprehending.

"Shpeech—"

"A what?" Grace hated his habit of slurring, said it would set him back. Not as much as other things, he thought.

"You're a bitch," he said.

Grace sat back in her chair. "Well."

The warm curve of Melissa's recumbent body. The two of them made an S, with their waists and their knees bent together. Other people called it spooning. He didn't.

"Are you going to stay all night?" said Melissa, unconscious of the miracle of the word in her mouth.

"I can't. I need to get home."

"Oh."

"I'm—"

"No, no, don't be sorry. It's all right."

"I am, though."

"Me too."

He stood up and began to dress. She watched him from the bed. "You're beautiful, you know."

He let out a startled laugh. "You are too."

"Not like you are."

He sat next to her to put his shoes on. "You shouldn't say anything like that." Out before he could stop it, with a hard whoosh on *say.* Something about Melissa was disarming him. That was two careless slips in one night. Not, of course, that he could tell her that.

Her lips parted; she tested the next words before she said them. "Do you have a hearing problem?" she said.

"No," he said, feigning astonishment. "Why?"

"My dad did, growing up," she said, "and he slurs his esses like that."

"Huh." He laughed again. "Well, I had a bit to drink tonight."

So easy: the possibility of truth rarely even crossed his mind. But what would he say, now? *I had an accident when I was thirteen*—fraught with problems. *I fell down the*—steps? stairs? basement staircase? all bad—*and damaged a nerve at the back of my neck and lost*—bad—*destroyed*—worse—*killed my ability to control my tongue. I woke up and couldn't talk. I had to learn to talk all over again. I learned everything but*—

But you could not describe it without saying it. I learned everything but Eth.

"Are you going to tell me you're sorry?" said Grace.

"I am." He was, too. Grace wasn't a bitch, and she was the last person he needed to offend.

"I need to hear you say it."

"I'm sh—"

"Don't slur."

"I'm—" His tongue was a foreign presence in his mouth, a fighting beast, a serpent; his teeth were unforgiving. Sharp and hard and stern. Mark swallowed and tried again and stopped, his eyes stinging with effort. Grace gave him another moment but he shook his head. Her patience was going to bring him to tears.

"Listen, Mark," she said, in a new voice, the same voice she might use with a colleague, "your mother called me. Because the school called her."

He nodded. He didn't trust his voice, even with the sounds he could master.

"Because you're failing five of six classes. Because you won't speak. Except in Spanish, is that right?"

He nodded again, and cleared his throat.

"Why is that?"

It was because Señor Rosen thought he was doing a Castilian accent. He could have explained it to her in Spanish. He shook his head.

"Mark. I'm not going to talk to you if you're not going to respond. It's just a stupid letter. You cannot avoid it forever."

She was going to do it, she was going to make him cry. Damn Grace, damn her, damn her—

"Do you know they blame me? They think I'm not doing my job. They don't see why they should pay me if you're not getting better, and they don't have any reason not to see it that way." Grace smacked her palm onto her desk and the force of the blow seemed to carry her up. Her chair rolled backward; the seat spun gently. "But the truth is, I'm pretty good. We've made progress. You can talk, for God's sake. And I'll be damned, Mark, if I let them think that about me."

She sat on the front edge of the desk, unavoidably close. Mark stared at his hands in his lap.

"Look at me."

He tried and the tears came. He looked away, pushed his hand at his eyes.

"So you can either start speaking the whole language—"

"They call me a faggot."

It was the last word he expected to escape his mouth. He wondered if there were some way to retrieve it, to gulp it back.

"What?" said Grace softly.

"Faggot," he said. "They hear the way I talk and they call me a faggot. They call me queer."

"Other students?"

He nodded. No use trying to hide the tears now. "What if they're right?"

Grace passed him the Kleenex wordlessly. Then she drew a deep breath and folded her arms across her chest. For a long time there was no sound but his hiccups and sniffles.

"Mark," she said finally.

He lifted his eyes to hers. Her face was tired and solemn and kind. And strong. And beautiful.

Mark had a list, a long scroll in his head, of the words he would say when he was finally able. *Sleep. Skin. Sex. Narcissism. Kiss. Sinister. Certain.* All the best words in English were out of his reach. *Strife, struggle, source, exult. Speak. Yes.* He would root for the 76ers, order the steak, sip a sophisticated scotch. He would slip through whole paragraphs when he could, long sinuous passages, curving and whispering with strength, with will, with skill. It would feel like love. It would yield like a kiss. Sometimes he nearly let it happen, esses be damned. Sometimes he almost forgot what was denied him, sometimes, rarely, but always in this room, always talking to Grace.

Grathe. Grashe.

Grace. That word was at the top of the list.

"I'm thorry."

She reached for a tissue and blew her nose. "So am I," she said faintly. "I wish I'd known."

"You couldn't have," he said. "I didn't tell you."

"That's true."

He leaned forward, resting his head on her belly, and she put a familiar hand on his head. "Do you think they're right?" she said.

"The guys at school?" He no longer bothered avoiding the words. It was easier, not thinking about it, just letting his tongue press in its bumbling way at the gap between upper and lower teeth.

"Mm hm."

"I don't know. I don't think so."

"Well," she said, "I guess time will tell."

He guessed it would. He hoped—he knew what he hoped. He hoped they were wrong. He hoped one day he could open the door and say her name cleanly and fearlessly. He would put his mouth against hers and kiss her. He would hold her with all his strength. She would keep her strong face close, quiet, breathing off of his lips.

The Storm that Loved a Bike

By
Diane Glancy

MY GRANDMOTHER, Molly McGivern, had a small walnut bed and side-table with one drawer in a back-room off the kitchen. I slept there as a child. It seems now I remember her baking biscuits in the mornings; the smell waking me. I had a wash-and-wear mother who'd married a Pottawatomie man, or *part-Pottawatomie*, he said. *Pottawatomie and some French.* I was the street sweeper that came along behind her. Paul Samuel was the Christian name my father had received in boarding school. My cousins lived with their parents; their mother being my mother's sister. Their mother was the sister who stayed married, whose husband did not leave her because they were of European descent and lived decently in the center of town. Only the Indians left their wives and families on the edge of Arkansas City; my mother wanting him to leave most of the time, but when he finally left, it devastated her.

On the walnut side-table was a doily and a lamp. The bulb was so dim it cast a yellow light in the room pale as the paper in the bottom of the drawer. My grandmother let me keep in the drawer: marbles, a twig, whatever I found. Some paper and a pencil . . . The Bible was on the side table also. Sometimes I read Ezekiel for his visions of cherubim. My grandmother was a Christian who let me know it was her Christian duty to keep me. I was the dark side of the light. The shadow. The black sheep that Jesus sought. At school I was ignored. Except for one girl from our church, it being her duty also . . . If there was a party I was not invited, but I heard the girls discussing it before and after.

On the walnut bed was a green quilt with a pattern of yellow and brown flowers. It was a small floral pattern I used to look at it. I kept my clothes in a lump on the floor. At one time, the room must have been a storage room or pantry. My mother breezing into the house now and then between boyfriends until after loud arguments and slaps, my grandmother wouldn't let her return. I was the low-water scum they talked about behind my back. I would fidget at my desk. My mind jumped from one thing to another. I couldn't light anywhere.

My grandmother had a house full of what would now be antiques. Walnut and oak and one of the chests I remember my aunt saying was cherry. When my grandmother died, the dealers came for everything. My aunt stayed angry at my mother because of the way the furniture was dispersed. Somehow the dealers knew my mother was the one to approach about the sale of the pieces. I don't remember how my mother could sell them with my aunt standing over her, but it happened. My aunt is dead now and sometimes when I leave flowers at the graves, I think I hear her say, your mother sold the furniture for walnuts.

That was the final break between them. The upstanding family and the one in fragments with a child who was dark as her father in a light family, some with hair that was almost white when they were children, though it darkened to blonde.

Who knew how many places my grandmother's things were? It always haunted my mother's sister. Maybe it was a way to get back at her sister for marrying a man who stayed with her.

I guess it was the usual story: a young woman running away from home to marry a man also on the run from a normal life. It was something outside of his realm. He never knew what it was, and if he did, he would have run faster than my mother. It broke my grandparent's heart; my grandfather a doctor and all. He demanded dinner sometimes when he returned home late in the evening. I remember the smell of frying chicken after dark; their voices outside my back-room. He made house calls and hospital visits and my grandmother fed him afterwards, even if it meant cooking another full meal after she had fed us— her and me, and sometimes a neighbor in need or someone from church. They came through our house all the time. Finally, my grandmother got back at him by dying.

My mother had a firm foundation, though she departed from it. My father had nothing. I knew little about him. He paced the kitchen of our house and usually ended up throwing something at my mother. He was caged in a world where he didn't belong. How do you face what you don't want to do? I knew that too. But I had my grandparent's steady life that pulled me back from running. When my grandmother died, she left some money earmarked, *Polly Samuel's education*. That was all it could go for. If I didn't go to college, the money would be added to the college funds of my cousins. That was all I needed to know.

I remembered my father's lack of focus. If he met friends, he wouldn't be back until he remembered us. If someone called, he was gone, no matter what had been planned. He always was sidetracked. He did not have steady work. There was tension between him and my grandparents that sawed them all in half.

I have lived in fear of his driftfulness. I too ran from Kansas to Minnesota to Texas and back, starting out sometimes not knowing where. I had no one to lean on, no one to turn to. What do you do when you're in it by yourself? I decided to learn responsibility. I would do what my parents could not. I would stop running. I would be responsible for myself. It had its drawbacks. I belonged to no one. I was no one. I did the clean-up after grandma's death, all those things no one else would do. I waxed the floors after the rugs were taken up. I carried her jars from the cellar, and her old magazines from the attic. My grandmother had left me money. I owed it to her. I went to college in Wichita the fall after I finished high school. I hated it, and decided to run from it too, but there was a conference, *The Native American Experience*, and it kept me there. I heard a man talk about the early Fort Michili-mackinac and the Mackinac-Prairie du Chien trails for fur trade in the northern territory. I thought maybe my father had been Menominee or Menominee-Winnebago instead of Pottawatomie because the man reminded me of him. I heard another panel on the southern removal trails. I heard the distances that my father's people had covered. The names Crow Wing and Oshkosh washed over me, the names of the past I belonged to, in part, anyway.

The walnuts ran away from the tree and I made up stories. They fell on the ground where they landed, something like my mother who would write from one place or another that when she had enough money she'd send for me.

Things didn't turn out like she expected, she said to me once. What did she expect?—Leaving her parent's house with a wild man.

I never knew my father's people. He took me to see them once or twice. There was a house somewhere on open land. No one said anything. My mother had been lured by the mystique of buckskin and images of brown warriors, braves and chiefs, the whole Winnebago line. She must have known right away it wouldn't work, but kept at it until I was born. I was like the sale of that antique furniture; I was the separating of the separation line.

My Grandmother McGivern and I would pick up walnuts on a corner lot. I saw the walnuts, their ridged shells. How did they make a bed and side-table from that? I knew the furniture was made from the wood of the tree, but I wanted to believe it was from the shells. I thought of them sending their workers into the field, gathering walnuts, returning to the furniture factory. In the thunder, I thought I heard them pounding walnuts, pounding and pounding out the ridges for long nights after. I thought of the magic that changed the walnuts into furniture, that was important enough for my aunt to be angry with my mother the rest of her life. I thought of the knobbed head and foot rails of the bed, the knobbed legs of the side-table. The walnuts had run away from the tree. They were taken from the ground where they landed.

My aunt came to my mother's funeral. She stood in the back and didn't say anything. The minister told us that Marsha McGivern Samuel was in the hereafter covered by Jesus' blood. And he asked if anyone wanted to say something, and no one did, and I thought it was my place, being her daughter. I said she was my mother and I remembered the flowered dress she wore that touched my face when she leaned down to tell me something, that she would be back tomorrow or the tomorrow after that.

If I could have any job, I would be a fire-eater in a traveling sideshow. I would be from Colstrip, Montana, or Ten Sleeps, Wyoming. But I was not any of that. I was from Arkansas City in southern Kansas, just off I-35. I was in college, and had papers to write, and books to read I didn't want to read. In desperation, I hitchhiked to another town, hitchhiked back, crying into my bed because I had to stay in school. I felt my father's need to flee. I felt my grandmother's gumption. I learned to make lesson plans and charts of whatever the instructor of the course asked for. I would rather have heard my parents scream at one another.

After graduation, the only offer I received was from a college on the edge of a great lake teaching six courses of freshman composition every semester and summer. I moved from Kansas to Duluth in a row of clapboard houses on a hill, ugly and grim as the climate itself. Behind in the alley, were ice-fishing houses with peeling paint. The clapboard weather, gray, cold, windy, was as hard to take as the Kansas heat. I heard the call of gulls for someone to take them away.

We had learned about the Indians hunting buffalo in grade school. My father was Pottawatomie. I didn't know if the Pottawatomie hunted buffalo, though I imagined they did. My mother was of German and Irish descent, another mix of heritages with boll weevils in it. But I was on the margins of it all. I was born in the days there was no multicultural recognition. No talk of mixed-heritages or displacement on the borderlands. I did not speak the Indian language. I did not have the land. I did not know the old relationship to the Maker, though I knew there was relationship. I was the usual mix: German, Irish, French and Pottawatomie. I was even born in a town that had the name of another state. Arkansas City, Kansas. Not *Ark-an-saw*, like the nearby state, but *Ar-kansas*.

My father hadn't come to the McGivern house unless he was drunk or nearly so. My cousins laughed at him. I remember once we rode in my grandfather's Pontiac looking for my father, my grandfather thinking he could form him into a family man, the way walnuts were transformed into furniture.

I was outside the main culture. I was outside the minority culture. I wasn't an Indian, though I had Indian blood. I wasn't white. Where was my place? If *place* defined one. Where were the ruins of the past that over-shadowed my present? I knew the blurring of boundaries. I knew the borders. Where was the land I was from? Who were my people? Plurality was my nationality. I was more than two in one.

If only it was easy and not a matter of visions. Traveling between Minnesota and my family in Kansas, the few times I visited the cousins, up and down I-35 dangling like a string. A *zip-way* to the northern shores. The next world coming. Already here. The sky ripped up. Highways snaking. I stopped in Kansas for the only toll gate. $5.00. How can they do that? The renovation of a country. The fractured place swept out, dusted, spray-painted. Pushed together. Crosshaired. Crosshatched. Spliced. Grafted—until what was it?—The first wave of the new stress? Taking a potshot at intercultural inexactness. Everything rattling that was not nailed down. How could any of them understand others? What made sense about cultures?

In my composition classes in Duluth, I had boys who hated English. Who hated writing. Who would not, could not write a sentence without chopping it up. I knew how they felt. They were not minority or mixed-blood, but they were outside the group of learners who could pass through classes and graduate. There was a program on television, Orange County Choppers, where a family, the Teutul's, made custom-built motorcycles. I heard the boys talking about it, and watched the program myself. I told them they could write essays on that program. A motorcycle is an act of composition, I told the students.

The wheels of a motorcycle are Biblical. I read about the cherubim in the first chapter of Ezekiel—He saw a whirlwind come from the north. A fire enfolded the whirlwind, and the fire was a great headlight. Out of the fire and the wind came other riders. They had wings, and under their wings were handlebars. They rode motorcycles and their wheels were full of eyes. Wherever the spirit went, they went. They were like burning coals of fire, shining with headlights. They rode as if flashes of lightning.

The composition students listened to Ezekiel. They watched Orange County Choppers on television. They listened to my visions of cherubim that were motorcycles. The students saw the composition of their papers as design and fabrication. They did research, planned an outline, made a cardboard cutout, and so to speak, used duct tape. They were under pressure to get it done. They particularly thought writing was like welding. They jerked their head forward, and their face masks fell over their face. To be honest with you, their sparks flew in a vision of nouns and verbs. They welded thesis statement, development and conclusion.

I didn't know what happened to my father, though I could understand his dislocation, his desperate spirit, his isolation and desperation. I went to a Pottawatomie cemetery in the country, but never found his name. Maybe his family buried him by his Pottawatomie name, the one I didn't know. I've stopped in other cemeteries on trips, but he was never there.

Sometimes I drive on my own to see the pines, the walnuts, the birch.

The Christians made the Indians strangers to their own land. They made them strangers to their language. They made them strangers to their ceremonies. They made them strangers to others. They made them strangers to themselves. Bi-marginal Christianity is itself a vectoring of marginalities. How does anyone understand?

Where are the altitudes? Latitudes? The geographies we pass through? Where are our dreams and visions? Our minds are story-makers, story-tellers. There's a place in our mind like a closet where dreams and visions are kept. A dream sees into the spirit world.

When I had visions of motorcycles, I prayed before the class, give us a place among the *being*-ones.

Why do we need dreams, even the bad ones? They help us remember there is more than we see. They help us see into the other world. We need our dreams to remind us. The bad dreams help us protect ourselves, to know the possibilities of harm exists. To not take our safety for granted. To haunt us so we look for answers. They make us face our fears. They make us know ourselves. Dreaming is like going to the movies, but we are the filmmakers.

I eat fire in my dreams.

I was a fire eater in another way than I wanted. I faced five days a week in composition classes. I graded papers nights and weekends. My life was in the furnace of composition. My running now was to academic conferences. I could say a mixed-blood heritage is dislocation, but I couldn't find the form in which to display that dislocation until I wrote a paper, The *Bi-Marginality of Design in the Construct of Motorcycle Fabrication*. It was published in an academic journal.

I wrote it between composition classes in the cold dampness of my small, drafty office I shared with colleagues off Lake Superior. This is a look into the structure of another culture. Another world. I had a woven knit skirt, and when I turned it over, the pattern looked completely different. The underside was its counterplane. I wrote the underside of Indian language in English. It was all I could see.

I think of it when I eat fire.

You can't write about a boring life in a boring way, but can you shape dislocation with dislocation? I would say, yes.

And what of this love, this engine blast, this passion that carries a rider? Where did it come from? Discouraged in school since the beginning, the boys barely making it through, but going nonetheless because of the hope of what was on the other end.

Once, a storm saw a motorcycle, and fell in love. Its thunder was a voice trying to speak the language of the bike.

I heard motorcycles at night, though I knew they were snow removal trucks. The neighbor down the street had a motorcycle he rode even in the frigid weather. Sometimes I heard him going by on the road. He had a cycle-shop past the truck-stop. Thereafter, the road unfolded across Lake Superior. Even heaven had motorcycles. I heard them in the storms. That's why I knew I could trust God. His cherubim rode bikes. Maybe his cherubim were bikes.

A motorcycle was fury. It was passage. On summer nights, I heard the lake shore traffic like migrating herds. I had a vision of this cross-cultural world. Something of the other crossed in me.

I got out of bed and looked at the sky during a storm. I loved the passionate wind. The bright flash of light on the lake. The different voices of the thunder. I felt the storm of displacement. Each night I heard the choppers that rode the whirlwind. I saw the blankness of earth under the sky. I heard the hum of traffic, turning down for an exit at the truck stop, to fill with gas or sleep for the night.

A motorcycle was a gift from the spirit world. A motorcycle was a landscape passing. A motorcycle was a lighthouse. It was a shore for those great lakes on the map hanging like three beehives from a branch. A motorcycle was a horse. The wheels of a motorcycle were twirlers before a marching band.

A motorcycle was language.
A motorcycle was radiance.
A motorcycle waged war.
A motorcycle was a desert warrior.
A motorcycle was a smooth wave.
A motorcycle was a desperado.
A motorcycle was a choice.
In church, the men passed the collection plate like a hubcap.
A motorcycle was a choir.
When the motorcycles understood what they were, they wept.

I understood that a motorcycle was a visit from the sacred world— if I honored it, if I spoke to it as a blueprint, a map of design, an abbreviation of something holy.

A motorcycle would help the students find the way to where they would go. In writing, they were as they knew they could be.

In the beginning (1885 I told them), a German, Gottlieb Daimler, invented an internal combustion engine and placed it on a frame with two wheels. That self-propelled vehicle was the first motorcycle.

I had a vision of how much could be imagined.

As they rode, the long shiny waves of the lakes rippled like oilcloth.

I have longed for a husband from time to time. But it never worked. No one wanted to share my meal. When I was in school, the boys used to think they could take advantage of me because I slept in the back-room of my grandparent's house, even though my grandfather was Dr. McGivern and had removed the tonsils of most of them.

The Bible was dislocation. It was for those of mixed-heritage. It was a contradiction of bimarginality. It was discontinuity. Disruption. The differing voices telling the different stories. No one telling the same story.

My grandmother, Molly McGivern, knew the use of disruptives. If she saw me concentrating, she interrupted me, trying to subvert my interest in finding out. I learned in spurts, doing several things at once, covering up the concentration I wanted. It affected my academic writing, my pedagogy; a moment here, a moment there. That was why I understood a motorcycle.

I delivered my paper, *The Bi-Marginality of Design in the Construct of Motorcycle Fabrication*, at a multicultural conference at Montana State University at Billings and received a crowd around me. Afterwards, I went to the Yellowstone Art Museum. In the museum I saw an albumen print, *Standing Holy*, the daughter of Sitting Bull, taken by David Francis Berry, 1854–1934. But when did Standing Holy live? What were her dates? How did she stand holy as her people were slaughtered? As her world was turned inside out and she saw a program she didn't want to see. What would she do as her children and grandchildren intermarried with the comers in an unholy mix? What did she do with the non-fit she felt in this world that replaced the one she knew? Did she handle it like my father? Or did she stand firm in the old ways? He stood firm, my father, in his desperation. He never got a job the way my grandfather said he should. He stood firm to what he was. In that, he stood holy, though it made him a failure in my grandfather's eyes. Maybe it was more than I had done. I lived a traitor to what I knew or felt sometimes when I woke in the morning and heard the old world of my father and knew why he ran from this one.

My vision for you all, dear students, is that you hold firm. *Stand Holy.* It's why walnuts are pounded flat and shaped into wood that is cut into furniture with a knobbed head and foot rail, so the little walnuts can become lovely furniture that is sold for nothing at a grandmother's death.

Dead Canadian Girlfriend

By
Philip Stone

I SHOULD not be here. The door opens in front of me.

"Oh lord, give me a break," the fat man says. "Her water ain't broke yet, eh?"

My legs move underneath me. A cloud of smoke hits my face. My eyes blink rapidly—I am not crying yet. I look down in wonder as my legs continue towards the bar. Snow falls to the floor from my pant legs. This place smells like apple juice and horseshit.

"No . . . I don't think . . . no it ain't broke," the short guy says. "Ya, but still . . ."

The stool scrapes across the sticky wood floor as my hand pulls it away from the bar. I look to see if the noise has disturbed anyone. There are only four people in this bar—a fat man, a short man, a bartender, and me. And I'm a ghost.

"Let me tell you there . . . ," the fat man says. "My old lady called me when I was at work there . . ."

I shake my head as my body props itself onto the stool and my hand motions for the bartender. My mind has given up control of the day. Its normally tight grip on the moment to moment has loosened. The body now seeks out alcohol without permission from the man upstairs.

". . . And she was yapping at me about 'my water broke, my water broke,' and all that there . . ."

The bartender does not see me. I turn to the two men sitting on my left. They do not see me either. I look down at my arm and wave it slowly in front of my face. Maybe I'm not really here. Thank God. I would hate for any of this to be actually happening.

"So what ya do then?" the short man asks.

The fat man sips his beer. "Hmm?"

"So what'd ya do?"

The fat man sets his beer on the bar. "I'll tell you, there. Nothing."

"Nothing?"

"Nope. I tole her, 'don't you be bothering me when I still got five hours of work left.' I had already put in some overtime that week, there, and I wasn't about to lose it."

"Oh."

"Ya. So I says, 'your water broke?' and she was like, 'ya,' and I was like, 'well, you still got at least ten hours before the bugger comes out, so ya know, just relax,' right?"

"Mmm hmm."

"I hang up the phone there, and finish my work, ya know? And I'll tell you, I'm a little annoyed about the whole thing, but I still get my work done, right? What's a man that let's a woman get in the way of his job, eh?"

"True."

"I roll into the driveway a few hours later, I load her into the car, and we're at the hospital at 10:30." The fat man takes another sip of his beer. "She has the baby at 10:41." He sets the beer down and stares at his friend triumphantly.

"Ya?"

"That's what I'm talking about. An extra two hundred on my check that week—overtime. Bought myself a new barbecue. And I had a son. That's what I'm talking about."

"Oh," the short guy says. He looks at his watch and shifts in his seat nervously. "Hmm."

"So, just relax there."

"I was gonna leave soon anyway . . ."

"Have another pint. She'll be fine." The fat man waves the bartender over. "Two more of these here."

The bartender drifts past me holding two pints. I hold my finger up only to be ignored again. A laugh escapes my throat. The sound startles me and I flinch. I cautiously look to my side to see if the locals heard the noise. The fat man is looking at me.

"You all right over there, shortstack?" the fat man says.

I clear my throat. They can see me. My head begins to spin. The fat man can see me. If the fat man can really see me, that can only mean one thing. My ass is really on this stool. If I'm on this stool, then I'm actually in this bar. In Toronto. I'm in fucking Toronto. My socks are indeed soaking wet from genuine Canadian snow. All of this shit is going down in Toronto. I am most certainly talking to this fat man in this bar in fucking Canada. I watch as my mouth opens and mimics what my brain has shown it to do a million times before.

"I'm thirsty," I say.

"Then drink something, pee wee. This ain't Ethiopia."

"It's fucking Canada," I say.

They laugh. The fat man points at the bartender. "Hey, how's about a pint for the thirsty geologist here, eh? Er . . . what are we calling the map guys? Geologer?"

A glass of piss colored beer appears in front of me. My hand reaches out towards the drink. I make a fist, making sure the muscles still work. The pint glass sticks to the inside of my palm. It is cold and heavy. I lift it in salute to the fat man and nod my head. My mouth opens wide, welcoming the awful drink. It hits my tongue and flows directly to my head. My brain begins to float in the malty soup. My stomach responds in acidic gulps. I feel as if I may vomit.

"Got a name, there, guy?"

I nod. "Ben."

The fat man smiles. "Enjoy the beer, Ben. I'm Dave."

I nod once more.

"And this here is Little Dave," Dave says, pointing at his short friend.

"Good to meet you," Little Dave says.

"Little Dave's about to be a father," Dave says. "But not before he has a drink with us, right, Little Dave?"

Little Dave looks at his watch.

"Right, Little Dave?" Fat Dave says. He leans into the bar and breathes on Little Dave's head.

"Right," Little Dave says.

"Congratulations, Dave," I say. "That's great."

"Congratulations for what?" Dave asks.

"Not you," I say.

Dave—fat Dave—grabs a handful of pretzels and shoves them into his enormous mouth. He is looking at me the whole time.

I hear a tapping sound. I look down and see my foot bouncing up and down on the barstool. Dave is still staring at me. I swallow and say, "What I meant to say is—"

"Yes?"

". . . Congratulations, uh . . . fucking uh . . . *Little* Dave," I stutter.

Dave explodes into laughter. "You hear that Little Dave?" he slaps his friend's shoulder again. "Ben's all right, eh?"

Little Dave shifts on his bar stool and giggles. "Ya, he's all right, there. He talks funny. Swearing and such."

"So, Ben," Dave says. "What's wrong?"

"What do you mean?" I ask.

"If you don't mind me asking," Dave sips his beer. "Well I did buy you that drink after all, but still . . . you have every right not to say . . . but ya know I gotta ask. What's wrong?"

"Why would you think that something's—"

"Ben, people don't come to this bar alone because they just won the lottery, eh?"

I look around. The bar is still completely empty, excluding the bartender, the two Daves, and myself. A video game sits dark and silent in the corner and all of the windows are covered with black spray paint. "Hmmm," I say.

"So?"

I finish the beer. The beer that the fat Canadian man bought me. Fucking Canada. Why am I still in fucking Canada? "I'll tell you Dave," I say. "I'm having kind of a fucking bad day."

The Daves laugh.

"Seriously, why is that fucking funny?"

Fat Dave frowns. "We're just not used to all that profanity, Ben. But don't mind us. Please go on, there. Or, as they say where you come from, 'please go fucking on.'" The Daves explode in laughter.

Profanity? Canadians? "I don't live here," I continue. "I live in Chicago. In Ameri . . . in the United—"

"I've heard of Chicago, Ben."

"Shit. Right, my girlfriend is—was—from here. She grew up here, and she was visiting her parents when this fucking goose—"

"What neighborhood?" Dave asks.

"What neighborhood, what?" I ask.

"Where'd she grow up?"

"Jesus, Dave," I say. "I don't know. Let me finish?"

"Leave the Lord out of this."

I shake my head. "I need another beer," I say.

Little Dave looks at his watch. "Hey Dave, Ben . . . I should get moving."

Dave plants his hand on Little Dave's shoulder. "Little Dave, what did I tell you about that?"

"She's having contractions. If I leave now, I can catch the 7:00 bus," Little Dave says.

"Okay okay," Dave says. "Have one more beer with us, and we'll give you a ride. Take you both to the hospital. That works, right?"

Little Dave nods. "Ya, I guess so."

"You have a car, right Ben?" Dave asks.

"Well, I do, but—"

"Perfect," Dave says.

"I can't give you guys a ride. I have to go back to fucking Chicago."

"Ben," Dave says. "Ben. The man's wife's having a child. A child. That's cold, Ben. Don't be cold."

Cold. Cold like Canada. Cold like my feet. Cold, like not crying at a funeral. My brain tries to pull my ass off the stool and move it to the warm car. Move it back to a warmer country. "I'm not cold, I'm just . . . " I look at the fat man and his small friend. He's so fat. There's no room for sadness in a car holding that man. "A'ight," I say.

"A'ight?" Dave asks. "What's that? Chicago talk?"

"It means 'all right.' As in, all right, I'll drive you guys."

"Fucking a'ight. Ben's fucking ai'ght." The fat man orders three more beers. I drink fast. As my hands grow busier, the absence of grief becomes less noticeable. My stomach tenses as the lukewarm piss climbs down my throat and drowns the guilt. It tastes so bad, but it's better than the alternative.

The glass empties into my belly and I wonder which is the greater feat: that I have not vomited, or that I am not crying. There is something awful inside of me trying to come up. Is it the beer, or that other thing? I hold it all down and press the mess into a ball of charcoal. It sits hard and sharp in a pocket somewhere between my stomach and my heart. I hold it there, knowing very well that it'll come up soon. But for now it is safely hidden in the shadow of the Great White North, guarded by an army of Mountees, a fat man named Dave, and his little friend named Dave in fucking Canada.

ᔕ ᔕ ᔕ

"Turn left here," Dave says.

"No not here," Little Dave says from the back seat. "It's the next street."

"Since when?" Dave asks.

"What do you mean, since when?" Little Dave asks.

"What I mean there, is when did you stop living on this street and start living on that there street, you dip."

"I have never lived on this street," Little Dave says.

"Oh ya, sure," Dave says. "And now I'm wrong. Is that what you're trying to say, there?"

"No, I'm just saying that—"

"It's always about that with you, isn't it, Little Dave? You always have to be right, isn't that right?"

"No Dave, I wasn't—"

"Dear God!" I interrupt. "You fucks are driving me crazy."

"Easy, Ben," Dave says.

"Dave, uh . . . er . . . fucking *Little* Dave, where do you live?" I ask.

"One more block, Ben," he mutters politely. "Number twenty-two twenty-two."

"Thank you," I bark. The words hang like daggers over the Daves' heads, begging them to say another word.

I pull the car to the curb. A body in an enormous beige coat passes through my headlights.

"Is that Char?" Dave asks.

"Ya, I think so," Little Dave says. "Where is she going?"

"Honk the horn," Dave says.

I honk. The woman turns and gives us the finger.

Little Dave rolls his window down. "Charlene, get in the car."

"Screw you, Little Dave," She says. "I'm taking the bus."

I roll the car slowly through the snow along side the walking pregnant woman.

"Get in, Char, we got us a ride here," Little Dave says.

Charlene stops and stares at me through the closed window. I look away.

"Why am I not surprised that you're late?" She asks. "I called you two hours ago." Charlene jumps into the back seat and slams the door. "And who's this guy?"

"That's Ben," Little Dave says.

"Shut up, Little Dave," Charlene says. "You can't talk to me right now. Dave, who's this guy?"

"That's Ben, Charlene," Dave says.

"Ben, eh?" Charlene says.

"Where are we going now?" I ask.

"The hospital, Ben. The hospital," Charlene barks. "I'm having a baby."

"I know that," I say. "I just don't know where that is. I'm not from fucking Canada."

"Listen to the mouth on this guy," Charlene laughs.

"Ya, isn't that something?" Dave says.

"Why you all dressed up, Ben?" Charlene asks.

"Huh?" I look down and see that awful black suit that I borrowed from my brother hugging my legs. "Oh . . . I uh . . . oh."

"Ya, Ben," Dave says. "You never told us what you're doing here."

"Ya, who is this guy?" Charlene asks.

"I uh . . . " the jet pumps in my stomach kick in like a jacuzzi and I taste bile on my tongue. I press it all back down and shift into drive. "We gotta get you to the hospital, Charlene. I'll tell you about the, uh . . . I'll tell you that shit later."

"Your what shit?" Dave asks.

"My what?"

"You'll tell us about what later?"

"I'll tell you about my day later," I say.

"Your day?"

"Yes," I say. "My day."

I burp vomit and quickly swallow it back down.

"Step on it, Ben," Charlene says. "This thing's going to come out whether we're ready or not."

"You're right," I say. It's already halfway up my throat and rising.

ઌ ઌ ઌ

The cold clean light from the fluorescent bulbs illuminates Dave's fat body in an unflattering way. I now see the pock marks on his face, the sweat stains by his armpits, and the hair creeping up his neck from the back of his shirt. As he fiddles with the waiting room vending machine coin return, his enormous pants battle gravity, desperately clinging to his non-existent waist. He leans into the machine and I see more of Dave than I had ever hoped for. "I ever tell you why I hate hospitals?" Dave asks.

"I just met you dude," I say. "You ain't told me much of anything."

"Dude," Dave mimics, "chill out . . . as they say. Fucking chill-out. A'ight?"

"I ever tell you why I hate fucking Canada?" I ask.

"Watch yourself there, eh." A pack of Lifesavers falls from the coil into the base of the vending machine. Dave sticks his sausage sized fingers in and grabs the candy. "I live here, you know, shortstack."

"I know."

"Ya."

"So?" I ask.

"So watch yourself," Dave pulls his pants up and steps towards me.

"Dave, all I'm saying is there's gotta be something wrong with a country where a goose—an actual fucking goose—can—"

"I want to hear this," Dave interrupts. "But before you finish, lemme say something here."

"What?"

"Lifesaver?" he holds the roll out in front of me.

"No thanks," I say.

"Your loss."

"So . . . ?"

"So what?" Dave asks.

"So . . . what where you going to say?"

"When?"

"When? Fucking now Dave. Now."

"I don't follow," he says.

I collapse into a chair and cover my face with my hands. "Never . . . fucking . . . mind."

Dave drops into the chair next to me. His fat leg touches mine. "Ben," he says. "Ben, it seems like you've got a lot on your mind. Let's go get a beer."

"We just had a beer," I say.

"We'll go get another."

"Little Dave's having a baby," I say.

"They can take a cab home," Dave says. "I'm worried about *you,* there."

I shake my head. "You're nuts."

"Watch it, eh."

"You are. You're fucking cuckoo. I should be at home. I don't know how I ended up here . . . "

"Where?" Dave asks.

I laugh. "In a hospital, maybe? In Canada? With you, perhaps?"

"Why don't you go home, then?" Dave asks.

"Cuz it's like a nine hour drive, Dave. Nine hours. I'm tired . . . "

"Well then, why don't you go stay at your girlfriend's house, sleep awhile, and then go home?"

"Dave . . . Dave, you see this black suit I'm wearing?" I say. My voice cracks.

"Yup."

"You wonder why I'm wearing this black suit?"

"Not really," Dave says.

"Cuz I was at a fucking funeral."

"Who died?"

"My girlfriend, Dave. My girlfriend died," I say.

Dave blinks several times and shifts the Lifesaver from the left side of his mouth to the right. "That's a tough one."

I nod.

"Did you love her?"

"I don't know . . . that's not the—"

"How'd she die?" Dave asks.

"A goose killed her."

"A goose killed her?"

"A fucking goose killed her. A goose attacked her, tore her jugular vein, and killed her. A goose killed her. She was walking in a park and a fucking goose . . . a goose . . . she's dead."

"That was *your* girlfriend?"

The contents of my stomach start churning themselves into a hot, bubbly butter. I grip my belly and lean forward in my chair. "What do you know about it?"

"Hard to miss that kind of news," Dave says. "Matter of fact, Little Dave and me were talking about it earlier today. And this is kind of funny, actually, cuz we had this theory . . . well shoot, you're here, why don't I just ask you. What'd she do to it?"

"Dave, she didn't . . . it was a fucked up bird. It wasn't something that she . . . ugh," I burp. "Just a freak occurrence. A fucked up bird is all. Tragic shit."

"That, as they say, 'is fucked up,'" Dave says.

Dave and I stare at each other. I am still doubled over holding my stomach. The sound of the Lifesaver hitting the inside of Dave's teeth fills the quiet room.

"Ben my friend, I ever tell you about the Carousel of Life?"

"Dude, you've told me like three fucking things . . . ever. You have never told me about the Carousel of fucking Life."

"Do you want to hear about it?"

"Not really," I say.

"Life is like a carousel—"

"I said, 'No.'"

"Tough shit," Dave says. He slaps me on the shoulder. "A'ight Ben? Tough shit. Cuz I'm talking and I love talking and you need to do some listening. A'ight? A'ight. Life is like a carousel. You sit on a horse—that's like your life there. The horse, it goes up and it goes down, there. And, here's the thing . . . it also goes round and round. It always comes back around."

"Oh god."

"You see what I'm saying there? It goes down, but it always comes back up . . . and everything always comes back around. Like a carousel, eh?"

And just like a carousel, my dinner twirled round and round my stomach. Where it had once gone down, it now found its way back up.

"I'm going to puke," I say.

"You go ahead and do that, there, Ben, a'ight," Dave says.

One hand grabs at my stomach, the other covers my mouth. My legs scramble across the shiny tiles towards the men's room. I ram my shoulder into the clean wooden door and lunge into the nearest stall. There on my knees, I purge Canada from my system: a Canadian cheeseburger, two cheap Canadian beers, ten Canadian cigarettes, two Canadians named Dave, a Canadian goose, and one dead Canadian girlfriend into the toilet. I rest my vomity chin on the seat of the toilet and pant.

Did you love her, Dave had asked me. I stare at my reflection in the vomit and toilet water . . . of course I didn't love her. I barely knew her. I was planning on breaking up with her. Then she died. I was going to break up with a dead girl. I am an American shithead.

Guilt creeps up my throat again. Now I recognize it. All this time I thought it was grief. One's easily confused for the other. Especially when you're drunk and you've switched time zones.

I spit into the bowl. The splash sends ripples out in all directions through my puke. Did I *want* a goose to rip her throat out? Fuck no.

"Good news."

I look up and see Dave standing behind me.

"Good news," he says again. "Char had her baby."

"Right on," I say. I flush the toilet and stand up.

"Probably right about the same time you were giving birth into that toilet, there, eh?" Dave slaps my shoulder.

"Fantastic," I say.

"It's a girl."

I wipe my mouth and push my way past Dave towards the sink.

"You feeling better?"

I fill my hands with water and rinse out my mouth. "I don't know," I say.

"You're sad, Ben, eh?"

"I should be," I say.

"Do you miss her?"

I pause. "You must think I'm a real asshole," I say.

"You don't miss her?"

"I should be really fucking sad."

"You mean because your girlfriend was murdered by a bird?"

A short laugh escapes my mouth. It feels good. "Yes. Yes exactly. So why am I laughing?"

"Not really sure about that one, there, buddy," Dave says.

"Me neither. She was young. Just out of college."

"Bright future, eh?"

"All that shit," I say. "And then a goose bit her on the fucking neck." I start laughing again. "A goose," I laugh, "bit her on the neck."

"That's what I heard," Dave says, chuckling. "Pretty tragic, there, eh?"

"Yes," I laugh. "Can you imagine? It's awful." The skin around my mouth starts to stretch as I laugh harder. "I mean, oh Lord, this shit must happen all the time here in fucking Canada, right?"

Dave's laugh grows louder with mine and his belly begins to shake, "not really, Ben."

"Don't you feed your geese up here? When they turn on humans for meat, you must know . . . " my laughter chokes out the rest of the sentence. I double over and grab my belly as it rumbles with giggles. Tears begin to creep over my eyelids and my stomach tightens with every wonderful laugh. I fall onto my ass as laughter consumes my body. I haven't felt this good since I left the U.S.

"This really isn't funny," Dave howls, one hand against the sink to prop up his body.

"Fuck . . . you . . . Canadian," I manage between gasps for air. Dave collapses next to me, laughing like an evil clown.

Dave manages to work his arm around his convulsing body into his pant pocket. "Lifesaver?"

"Yes please," I laugh.

"Have the yellow, eh?" Dave says, laughter subsiding. He wipes a tear from the corner of his eye.

I sit up and snatch the Lifesaver from his hand and pop it into my mouth. "Fuck yeah," I say.

"Feel better now?" Dave asks.

I suck on the candy for a moment and rub my eyes with my palms. "Yeah," I say. "Yeah, I think I do."

"Kinda happy even, eh, shortstack?"

I shake my head. "No, I'm sad. Very sad." I slap Dave on the shoulder. "I wasn't before. Funniest thing."

"That's a good thing, there," he says. Dave remains seated on the bathroom floor, sucking on a lifesaver. "I like to talk," he says.

"No shit."

"Yep," he nods. "I do it a lot. Fuck yeah, Ben. A'ight?"

Dave reaches up to the sink and tries to pull his enormous body up from the floor. His fat fingers slip off the porcelain and he collapses back to the floor. I spring up and grab him by his meaty arm. "On the count of three," I say.

The horse goes down, but it always comes back up. Same goes for the fat Canadian.

ꕥ ꕥ ꕥ

Welcome to the United States of America.

I smile at the sign as it floats past my car at seventy miles per hour. I pull a Lifesaver from the fresh pack on my dashboard and drop it on my tongue.

The horse goes down, but it always comes back up, the fat Canadian told me. I shake my head and laugh in disbelief.

We're naming her Kathy, like your girlfriend, eh? the little Canadian and his wife told me as I held their new daughter. I picture Little Dave standing next to Char and little Kathy in the hospital bed and my throat goes dry.

. . . it also goes round and round. It always comes back around.

I take the car off the next exit and park in front of the Motel 6. The neon glow of the motel saturates the inside of the car. I twist the rearview mirror and look at my face. My cheeks are shiny and glowing red from the nearby stoplight. My eyes are heavy and dry. I pull fifty bucks from my wallet and walk towards the motel office. The road to Chicago is long and lonely. I will tackle that task tomorrow. Tonight, I will enjoy the familiarity of an American bed, the quiet hum of an American highway, and the peace of my own grief—belated as it may be. Tomorrow the carousel will still be fucking spinning.

Reds

By
Gregory Pace

MARLBOROS.

And not Lights, either. Marlboro Reds. "Pussy cigs," Eddie would call the light kind and damned if I was gonna give anyone a chance to call me a pussy. No sir-ee, Bob. Just because I like the taste of the stuff, doesn't mean I wanna be one, ya know?

"Smoke Reds and you're dead," my older sister always said, but when you're a teen, dyin' ain't much of an option, is it? Nah, during the golden age of teen-dom, the dictionary of life is a bit lacking in words on the negative side. The letter A's reserved for alcohol and ass, and hey, do you really need much more than that? I mean, besides the occasional B for blowjob or J for joint every now and then when the money fairy was smiling my way, as far as I saw it, the dictionary could go to hell and don't come back. Don't call us, we'll call you.

That older sister of mine died when I was thirteen, by the way. And there wasn't a Marlboro Red within ten blocks of the scene, believe you me. Just a whole lotta guys with fancy degrees standing around, trying to look useful. All of 'em wearing those ugly green coats, the ones that smell like someone just pulled 'em out of a box of Band-Aids.

Why do the harbingers of bad news always gotta be good-looking? Hey big fella, the little lady in room two twenty seven just bit the big one. Sorry for your loss, life's a bitch. I'd love to do the Daddy knows best comforting routine till the cows come home, but I gotta meet the guys for a round of eighteen holes. Why don't you buy another carton or two of them Reds and I'll see you in a few years, okay? I got a stethoscope with your name on it, keep it nice and cold for ya, too, just the way you like it.

Fuck, maybe it really is like the bumper sticker says, maybe all we really need to know we learn in kindergarten. But all we *really* need to know about how to fuck up what we learned in kindergarten comes right around the time we start sproutin' little curly hairs in warm dark places and hearin' that voice. You know the one. Like a radio with a broken dial—one station, daytime, night time, anytime. All attitude, all the time. Helluva playlist, that one. It whispers nice and sweet, too, don't it? While the blessed real world is tellin' ya to take it easy, 'cause slow and steady wins the race, that station in your mind is playing a dandy game of last one to the coffin is a rotten egg. And you're falling behind, young man. Far, far behind.

I saw the man who I would later learn was named Walter B. Sexton (I imagine friends and family had probably called him Wally) outside a 7-Eleven on a Tuesday afternoon, just a few hours before some little kid takin' a squirt found a corpse just off Highway Five. I had just turned twenty-eight, was making ten bucks an hour at a job so insignificant that it's hardly worth mentioning, and I had a chip on my shoulder the size of, well, something *big*. I suppose Texas would be the most widely accepted whatchamacallit. Funny thing about a chip on your shoulder when you're twenty eight, though, because you're a helluva lot closer to thirty than you are to twenty, every now and then you get an inkling suspicion the big ol' bastard perched next to your left ear might just be dragging you down. As a matter of fact, you start to wonder if maybe it never really had your best interest at heart in the first place. A bad attitude just doesn't have quite the showroom appeal it had at thirteen, or eighteen, or even twenty-one. No, at twenty-eight it starts to feel a whole lot more like *a problem*. There comes a strange and terrifying moment for most guys when being a rebel starts to feel less and less like James Dean and more like every sadsack jerkoff you find in local watering holes on a typical Saturday night, guys who are so lacking in every other facet of their lives that they gotta down a few shots of Jack then prove they still got some pop left in their fists by starting battles over anything as simple as brushing against a pool table during a fifty cent game or surrendering a sideways glance when a woman who's been spoken for struts by with just the right amount of wiggle.

Some of us, if we're lucky, ease gently into that moment when we finally see the light, like slipping into a warm tub and knowing that you've got one helluva nice bath ahead of you. Of course, others aren't quite so lucky, and a state of awareness only comes by way of something about as subtle as a spiked mallet to the head. I was never blessed in the luck department, so I had a knowing feeling my day of revelation was gonna be one helluva ballbuster.

I was right.

"Those things'll kill ya," Walter offered as I walked out of 7-Eleven with my new box of Marlboro Reds. I had probably made a good two or three hundred trips to this particular 7-Eleven over the years (it was within walking distance of my apartment), and more often than not Walter was there, hanging around the parking lot like a bird keeping his eyes peeled for a scrap of moldy bread.

I slapped the box of Reds against the heel of my hand a few times —RAP, RAP, RAP—feeling pretty damn good about my chances that these babies were gonna taste just fine. Eddie taught me how to slap 'em like that when we were thirteen years old, trying cigs for the first time behind the old tool shed in my parents' back yard.

"What does the slapping do?" I had asked back then, being the Curious George (it killed the cat, I know) I've been since as long as I can remember. Looking back now I realize Eddie had no clue what that slapping was for, no clue at all, but had simply seen his father perform the gesture, probably upwards of a thousand times would be my best guesstimate. Like father, like son, they say. Makes sense to me, 'cause Dad smoked like a chimney.

"The slapping makes 'em taste better," Eddie had offered with a grin, crouched in the murky shadows of the tool shed, and that was plenty enough reason for me. Eddie had a way of grinning that could make you do just about anything. It was a grin that said life could be good if you let it. Years later I realize Eddie's grinning mug molded who I became more than anything my own two parents had ever said or done. With that grin at his disposal, Eddie could have sold a space heater to the devil. What he sold me, though, was a dream, a fantasy that you could have it all—the Marlboro Reds, the women, the booze. But more importantly, the belief that decades later you could still come out of it smiling, because that's what it's really all about in the end, isn't it? No regrets? Any amateur wiseass can play the game and dutifully pay the piper when he comes a' calling, but only a select few can play free of charge, as though the game was theirs to own in the first place. That was what I had been striving for ever since the day Eddie moved into my neighborhood and offered me my first Marlboro Red.

Only now can I sit back and wonder if I had been a fool.

"Can I get one of them cigarettes?" Walter asked from his position by the 7-Eleven pay phone, and although I may not have exactly set any records in my school days for perfect attendance or test scores, I still had enough brain cells going full throttle to see the irony in this question.

"I thought you said they'll kill you?" I countered with my best attempt at a smile. Granted, my grinning puss probably doesn't have quite the bite that Eddie's had, but it's done the job on more than one occasion when trying to get a pretty lady or two hot and bothered in all the right places.

Walter just eyed me a moment then, his bloodshot eyes gazing out from a face in desperate need of a decent meal and a warm bath. It was little more than just a moment our gazes touched, probably a span of a second, tops, but we all know there are times in life when one measly second ticking by can feel like a decade. And this was one of 'em. I saw something in his eyes, or maybe it wasn't so much what I saw as what I felt, deep down in my gut, like a wad of gum trying to pry itself free from a tangle of thick hair.

"I know," he said. It was as simple as that. *He knew*. And in those two words, I knew, too. Reds'll kill ya, sure, but Walter could smoke away, free of regret, because he had nothing to lose. But I still did. That's the crazy thing. I never fully realized it until that moment. Hour by hour, day by precious day, we're always searching for something. Beneath the jobs, the cars, the pretty ladies in pretty outfits on pretty magazine covers, we're searching for the right to believe, *really* believe, that we have a purpose, that the whole of our lives is far greater than the sum of its parts. Somehow it only took this complete stranger two words to let me know I still had a chance to find what I needed. *I know*.

I nodded, my senses briefly dulled, and peeled the plastic wrap off my latest treasure. As though jumping ahead just a half second in time, I somehow already had the precious Red in my hand, offering it to him, knowing deep down in that side of me that hides from truth that I was handing him his guaranteed demise. I can't quite describe what I felt then, but one word that comes to mind is ashamed. Ashamed at what I was, ashamed at what I had been for quite some time. Walter spent the majority of his days roaming that parking lot, fishing for the occasional handful of spare change or wayward cigarette, while I had a roof to call home. It wasn't the most spectacular roof ever built, but it was mine. If this man who I later learned was named Walter B. Sexton had the desire to be somewhere, well, he walked. That was a given. I, however, had a car. Would those four wheels turn any heads at a traffic light? Not a chance. My battered Plymouth had red electrical tape plastered to one of the broken tail lights, it sported a dandy crack in the windshield, and the exhaust was thick enough to choke an elephant, but damned if it didn't do everything in its power to get me where I needed to be. The queen bee may get all the press, but there's a quiet dignity in being a worker bee sometimes, too. And my Plymouth wore that distinction proudly.

As Walter took the fresh cigarette, so many things came to me in a heated rush. Ever since my sister died, life often had a way of grabbing me by the hair and dunking me headfirst into a dreamy state of both heightened self-awareness and frustrating confusion. End over end, front over back, one moment dull, the next bright and vivid, like waking up in the middle of a nightmare and feeling pretty goddamned sure tonight was the night you've finally gone mad.

"That was one of those moments for you?" a voice suddenly asked. Of course it was one of those moments I told it. Of course.

As Walter eyed the Red in his hand, taking in its image for what might have been an eternity, I couldn't help but wonder how long James Dean had been dead by the time he was my age. And when was the last time I had even talked to Eddie, anyway? We had been inseparable as kids, and now it had been—what? Five years since we last talked? Ten? Or did I just talk to him this morning?

Good ol' Walter, guardian of the 7-Eleven parking lot, smiled vaguely as he finally put the cigarette to his lips, like a death row inmate finding peace just a split second before the switch is pulled on ol' Sparky. That's when I noticed there was blood on his hands, bright and red and shiny. I wasn't sure why he had blood on his hands, but the closer I looked, the more I realized there was *alot* of it, dripping down his wrists and into his sleeves, like fire ants searching for a place to hide. If you've never seen a lot of blood in one place, consider yourself lucky, 'cause when you do, it takes the breath right out of you, believe me.

"Hey, you gonna need some help?" I asked him, a part of me feeling increasingly frightened, that wad of gum in my gut twisting and turning in directions I didn't want it to go. Afterall, this was just another day, wasn't it? Please tell me I had only walked here to buy a pack of smokes like I'd done so many, many times before. Please promise me I'd be free to go home and promptly forget about the man who was now bleeding by the 7-Eleven pay phone.

Walter just smiled again, even more warmly than before, as though he could sense my confusion, and actually wanted to help. But it didn't make me feel any better. Not in the least. I had hit the highest peak of the rollercoaster, and this, friends and neighbors, was the long plunge down. Something was not right here, not right at all. The nightmare was just beginning, and all the smiles in the world weren't gonna wake me up. Not yet, anyway.

"You still have work to do," someone tells me, a voice I have become quite familiar with throughout this journey. I used to think it was God taking time out of his busy schedule to assist me, but I eventually came to grips with the fact that God's last name probably isn't Weinbaum.

I looked up at the store sign above me and realized for the first time that one of the neon letters was on the blink. 7-Eleven had become 7-E even. It reminded me of another childhood friend by the name of Steven Bishop, a small for his age redhead who moved into my neighborhood when I was fourteen. Steven and I would often trade baseball cards for hours on end, the highlight of these heated trade sessions coming afterward, when negotiations were sealed with a handshake and my trademark line. "We're even-Steven, right?"

Steven Bishop, you had to love him, would always laugh at my not so subtle attempt at humor. It just never got old. Sure, other kids in our lives could use the "even-Steven" phrase anywhere they wanted—on the ball field, in the school lunchroom—but as far as Steven and I were concerned, I *owned* that phrase. I made it ours. When you're a kid, the smallest things can forge a bond, and sometimes, if you're lucky, those bonds can last a lifetime. But sometimes evil destroys them.

"He's not evil," Weinbaum tells me. "Remember that. There is no good or evil here. Only what you feel."

Tell that to even-Steven. At the time, I gave Eddie the benefit of the doubt. Afterall, he and I had been friends first, so could you really blame him for being jealous? I certainly couldn't. Not then, anyway. Looking back now, sure, I can remember the cold hatred that often lurked in Eddie's eyes, that look of *deadness* when something rubbed him the wrong way. Back then I was blind to it. I think sometimes I still am.

When they found even-Steven Bishop floating across the top of the lake, he was bloated to three times his normal size. Accidental drowning the papers had said. And Eddie no longer had to be jealous of someone else trading baseball cards with his best friend.

As I stood here now, staring at the gap created by the missing letter in the 7-Eleven sign, I was hit by a startling realization. It hadn't been years since I last spoke to Eddie. In fact, he had called me earlier today, wanting to get together for old times sake. And he had been missing a tooth. Just like the store sign, there had been a gap in that magical grin of his, and I felt sick to my stomach remembering how vile it had seemed when I first laid eyes on it, like God had played a cruel and twisted joke on me, akin to vandalizing the beatific smile of the Mona Lisa.

I swallowed down the lump in my throat that felt like nothing short of a bowling ball and looked across the 7-Eleven parking lot. My car was there, that busted tail light with the red electrical tape reminding me that the worker bees will always make the world go 'round. There were weeds growing all around my car now, some of them at least two feet tall. The worlds of my nightmare were coming together, gradually blending and shaping into something that would hopefully turn into the truth.

I was no longer at 7-Eleven. Why would I be, anyway? Eddie and I had left the store over an hour ago, with Walter as our passenger, poor Walter who was only along for the ride because Eddie had promised to buy him lunch. The three of us were now in a field on the side of the highway, Eddie's blank expression reminding me that no matter how many years go by, more often than not the deadness in a man's eyes will never go away. It was that deadness that left even-Steven Bishop floating like a piece of garbage, and it was that same deadness that allowed me to invite Walter B. Sexton out to lunch with little regret.

"Can you hear me?" Walter suddenly asked, and somehow he was once again standing next to his pay phone in the middle of the field. The last few hours were a hurricane of memories in my chaotic mind, fragments from one moment being stripped away, only to be superimposed on another.

When I looked at him, I realized it wasn't Walter at all anymore. It was a much younger guy, probably around my age. He was wearing some type of uniform, all dark blue corners and rubber gloves, with more blood on them. I was still sickened by the sight of that bright redness, but now I felt compelled to touch it, to rub it between my fingers and gently caress it back into the pores of my skin. It was mine, afterall, wasn't it? Can you recognize your own blood? Do we have some special bond with anything that's a part of us, even on a purely physical level? I imagine so, but why in God's name did this man have my blood on his hands?

Two more men came out of 7-Eleven, startling me. They were also dressed in uniforms, both with snakes on their shoulders. The snakes coiled around a golden staff on each of their arms, forming a symbol I vaguely recognized. I had seen it in the hospital when my sister was sick. It had haunted me back then. Today I felt compelled to welcome it. Today it meant help.

One of the men was pushing a shopping cart out of the store, and I tried to remember if I had ever seen someone use a shopping cart inside a 7-Eleven. I didn't think I had. I looked back at the guy by the pay phone, a guy who was no longer Walter, the poor sap who Eddie had invited to lunch for the sole purpose of bringing him into a field and torturing him, and I finally answered the question he had asked moments ago.

"Of course I can hear you," I told him, "Am I gonna be alright?" He didn't acknowledge me whatsoever. Please believe me when I tell you I have never felt so small, so utterly insignificant.

"Where's Walter?" I asked, this time injecting an urgency in my voice meant to convey my unwillingness to let this game go on any longer. "I only wanted to give him a cigarette, nothing else, I swear. Is he gonna be okay?"

Again, nothing. This was often the point where Weinbaum would tell me to relax, to gently wrap my mind around the idea that Walter was gone, but Weinbaum was silent this time, and I just knew the bastard wanted me to work through this on my own.

Becoming increasingly agitated, I turned and realized the other two men behind me didn't have a shopping cart at all. It was silver and it was metal, yes, but that's where the similarity between it and a shopping cart ended. They proceeded to unfold it into something else I had seen many times during my sister's battle with death.

A stretcher.

Sounds and images came to me suddenly, rapid-fire and fleeting. Eddie's whisper, telling me that we should have some fun, for old time's sake. Eddie getting out of the car as I pulled into the field. Eddie showing me the gun he had in his waistband. And the deadness in his eyes. Oh, God. The deadness.

The men with the snakes on their arms were touching me now, and all I could think about was Eddie, and how, after such a lengthy absence in my life, I had spoken to him earlier today. He had looked me up, simple as that. I was listed in the phone book, after all. Worker bees don't have unlisted numbers. Worker bees can be found at a moment's notice. And Eddie was here with me, right now, just as he has always been.

I looked to my left and saw a little boy, probably about ten years old. He was standing behind a yellow streamer, squinting at me, the sun in his eyes. The streamer fluttered in the afternoon breeze, making me think of that song. *Tie a yellow ribbon 'round the old oak tree.* I could hear Tony Orlando and Dawn singing from a car stereo, and then Eddie's voice drowning out Tony Orlando's, telling me with a full-fledged sense of kid in a candy store glee, that defaced, somehow unholy grin that was missing a tooth, announcing, "let's tie him up."

And I'm sick to my stomach. I want no part of this anymore. I had bargained for catching up on old times and maybe smoking a few Reds like we did way back when, but that's all. I try to tell Eddie I'm not the same person I was back then, but he doesn't care, not in the least. He still gets a thrill from pulling the wings off flies, and before I can escape his newly vile grin, I hear sounds coming from the man who I would later learn was named Walter B. Sexton, sounds that no man should have to hear. Something deep and resonant and ugly, and I feel a warmth spread through me, like someone has pumped hot chocolate into every pore of my existence, and I realize it is I who's crying out now, it is I who's screaming for the right to keep on breathing. Walter B. Sexton gave up long ago because he knew he had nothing to lose. But I still do. The game, as they say, is still mine to lose. Bottom of the ninth and it's time for me to step up to the plate.

"You can do it," Weinbaum urges, "take it slow."

The little boy is looking at me again, shielding his eyes from the sun, and I notice that his zipper is down. I can't really blame him for not remembering to zip up, not when he found what he did. Days later I will hear on the television in the rec room that he was taking a piss out here. Before Weinbaum can turn off the TV in time, I will learn that the boy was on the way to a swimming lesson with his mother when that big bottle of Gatorade he had been nursing proved too much for the confines of his ten-year-old bladder. His mother had pulled off the highway so he could relieve himself, a simple enough task, sure; that is, until they found Walter and me. I suppose after that day their lives were never simple again.

As if he can read my mind, the boy reaches down and pulls up his zipper, finally realizing his fashion blunder. The yellow streamer in front of him is advertising donuts, and I realize I would give anything, anything at all, to be sitting somewhere else, *anywhere else*, enjoying a donut right now. Jelly, please. And make it fresh. The freshest you got, 'cause I might not have much time left, so I'm gonna want the best.

"But would you give your life for the best we got?" someone asks, and this time I am quite sure it's not Weinbaum. There's a sense of finality to the question, an understanding that it all comes down to this, right here and now. And I don't even need a second to consider. The answer is no. I wouldn't make that trade. We are most certainly *not* even-Steven on that one. I want my life, dammit. And that's what this is really all about, isn't it?

So I promise everything under the sun, I promise to be the best little boy I know I can be, and what fills me with warmth is that I truly believe it this time. I realize I didn't even need that voice to threaten me, that voice that promised me the best damn jelly donut the world has ever known in exchange for my life. And just what the hell kinda fucked up deal is that, anyway?

In a moment of blessed clarity I realize the yellow ribbon 'round the old oak tree isn't advertising donuts at all. It's telling people DO NOT . . .

CROSS. Because that's what yellow ribbons tell people when a field on the side of a highway has become a crime scene.

I gaze up through the tiny gap between the heads of the three snake-wearing men crouched over me, desperate for an eyeline to the blue sky above. And I promise to keep my promises, every last one of 'em. You can keep your damned donut I cry out, someone else might want it someday, someone like Walter B. Sexton, who had awakened today to find out he had nothing to lose, and later learned that death was on its way in the form of a long lost grinning bastard named Eddie.

"Go on," Weinbaum urges gently, "work through it. You're almost there."

I see myself grabbing the gun from Eddie. To hell with that chip on my shoulder, and to hell with the booze, and the women, and fuck those Marlboro reds, the damned things. But life is never as easy as you think it'll be, that's the trick, it never plays out the way you want it to, and Eddie is strong. How could I have ever deluded myself into thinking I could take this bastard on?

He's grinning at me, both of us holding the gun now, that gaping hole where his tooth used to be like a little black window, and I feel like I'm being watched by someone from behind that window, like I'm in some very tiny movie that no one cares about, no one but me, Eddie, and the dead man lying in the weeds next to me, the poor soul who I would later learn was named Walter B. Sexton when I catch a glimpse of a forbidden newscast in the rec room.

Somewhere during the power struggle between Eddie and I there is a sudden burst of fire, and thunder loud enough to take away my ability to hear out of my left ear, even to this day.

As I feel the horrible warmth spread through me like a cancer (now I know how it must have felt, Sis), I watch frightened birds scatter from the trees above. My journey to the soft weeds below feels like an eternity. As I finally settle into what I am sure will be my final resting place, I see that Eddie has already completed his journey. He's lying next to me, eyes stuck wide open, that gap in his grin reminding me that I got lucky.

That's always where I close my eyes, and it's over. The next thing I know I'm here, in Weinbaum's office. He puts down his folder and smiles warmly. "Good," he tells me. "You're doing just fine." But I don't know if I really believe him.

Sometimes, late at night, when all the other patients are sleeping, I stand in front of my mirror and stare into that gap in my grin. Doctor Weinbaum (the good-looking bastard he is) tells me it's okay to look at the gap, or to touch the tangle of scar tissue on the back of my neck where the bullet came out. A millimeter to the left and I'd be dead, I once heard him say. It really is the little things that matter, I suppose, but when I hear him call it attempted suicide, it confuses me beyond repair. I was only trying to stop Eddie from hurting more people. Eddie, who I first met when my sister died and I needed a friend to help me work through the pain. I just couldn't do it alone, and I often thank God for the day Eddie showed up behind my parents' tool shed, offering me a Marlboro Red.

One time I peeked at Doctor Weinbaum's folder when he wasn't looking and I saw words like "schizophrenia" and "delusional." Sometimes he suggests that there never was an Eddie, that I imagined him to make myself go cold to what I was feeling when my sister died. He says I've been hiding Eddie ever since, first behind the tool shed, then later in the dark and forbidden corners of my mind. Sometimes I believe Weinbaum's theories, other times I laugh in his face. I like to imagine those are the times when I make Eddie proud.

There are no secrets in this place, and when others ask me how I feel about drowning even-Steven Bishop when I was fourteen, or picking up Walter B. Sexton when I was twenty eight and driving him out to that field to torture and shoot him, I often just shrug. I honestly don't know what I think most of the time. Sometimes it's hard to know what's real and what isn't. There are nights when I wake up in a cold sweat, haunted by the image of Walter tied to that tree just off Highway Five and asking me if he can have one of my cigarettes before I pull the trigger. Those are the instances when I'm truly sorry, when I pray for the day they'll let me out of this place so I can go to his grave and apologize for what Eddie did to him.

My life is little more than a blurred marathon of good and bad days now, and on the good ones I'm given access to the voice from above that I know is not Weinbaum's, the one that gets me through the nightmarish day in the field by telling me I'm gonna be okay, and offers me donuts, soft and warm and inviting.

On bad days, and there seem to be more and more of those lately, I crave Eddie's company, the comfort of the darkness that can handle my sister's death and any other heartache life might throw my way. We all need a friend now and then, I suppose, to make the marathon a little less painful.

As I stand before my mirror in the dark hours of night, trying to ignore the steel bars on my window, feeling beaten by the memories Doctor Weinbaum forces me to re-live week after week, Eddie finds me again and grins mischievously from behind the blank eyes of my reflection, the same eyes that would never allow me to shed another tear. He shows me a knife he has hidden under my mattress, a knife he made out of a piece of scrap metal he found during his allotted twenty minute exercise session in the institution's courtyard. He whispers to me that Weinbaum's days are numbered, and promises that the bastard will get what's coming to him for making me remember the things he's done.

The bottom line is that Eddie looks out for me, and as he passes me a Marlboro Red and hides the makeshift knife in my sock, knowing that I'll be seeing Weinbaum first thing in the morning. I smile my gap-toothed grin, once again feeling strong and ready to take on the world.

Jack and Jill

By
Gregory M. T. Colleton

"SHE GOT booty."

"I don't care."

"You a damn lie. Everybody cares about the booty," says Calvin. "And ain't nothing worse then a girl whose legs come out her back." Calvin pauses to laugh at his own joke. "This girl's supposed to be all kinds of slammin'. Even hotter than Mia."

Jaquin looks away, then over at his tequila. In one fluid motion, he grabs the shot and tips it down south. Cringing at the burn.

"Eh, man, it ain't that serious," smiles Calvin. "We're just talking about a roommate situation here. Think about it. You live all the way out in Skokie. You got to take a bus and the El to get down here. You got no crew, no car — shit, you ain't even got cable. All you got is a crap job and a one bedroom box with furniture left over from college."

Jaquin shrugs.

"I ain't hating. I still prop my TV up with cinder blocks. Still got plastic cups, too. But, I'm just saying — you should move to the city. The good life ain't nothing but a Ryder truck away."

Jaquin, sipping his beer, motions to the bartender to hook up another. "Who said she's hotter than Mia?"

"Kai," says Calvin. Jaquin swirls his beer so the liquid in the bottle makes a whirlpool. He watches the cycle slow to a still. Calvin continues, "I even found a practice space around the corner from my house. Equipped with a piano."

From the other side of the bar, an attractive looking woman passes by on her way toward the back room. The two men take notice. "That's what I'm saying, big dog," grins Calvin, noticing his grumpy friend peeping, "a new dime could make everything shiny again."

"Man, she's probably in line for the bathroom."

"No she's not. Women don't do that," smiles Calvin, "they don't pee alone."

"That's so dumb."

"Naw, dog, it's true. It's a rule. They like cigarettes, they gotta roll in packs and shit. See, we lucky. We can stand and aim. But they gotta squat. Which is a mad vulnerable position if you think about it. So they step at least three deep. One to guard the stall door, one to bring the strawberry lip-gloss, and one to hold a heel just in case something jumps off," chuckles Calvin, pausing to glance at the five women who laugh and sip cocktails on the other side of the bar. "Look at them. They just look like they getting ready to group urinate."

" . . . What the hell is wrong with you?"

"I'm just saying, playboy," says Calvin with a cocky grin. "That woman does not have to use that bathroom. So—if she's walking past us, she's doing it for a reason. You gonna holla or wha—"

"Goddamit, Cal, don't start! Don't you even start."

". . . Look Jaquin," says Calvin quietly after a moment, "you my boy and I'm just worried about you. I've given you a lot of space. We're talking months now." Jaquin's eyes glue to the bartender filling his glass. "But . . . shit's not right with you. For a good reason, I know. But, it's like you're getting lost. Or trying to get lost. And I . . . I think you should consider moving to the city."

Jaquin just stares at his drink, committed to the answer floating up with the next bubble. Calvin stares at his silent friend, defeated, "whatever, man."

Both men drink.

ꕥ ꕥ ꕥ

"Ugh," she cringes.

"I know, right?" agrees Gillian. "She's taking the last of her stuff as we speak. Worst part is, she couldn't even come correct about it. She said I didn't always give her her messages and something about too many dirty dishes."

"That's some bullshit," busts Kai, waving her arm like she's auditioning to be a def poet. "That girl was the nastiest! She can talk about dirty dishes all day long, but I don't remember you leaving used tampons in the toilet."

A woman gasps a few tables away.

Gillian shrugs, and takes a sip of her coffee. From her purse, Kai pulls out a pack of smokes. She shakes one free, puts it to her lips, and lights it from the candle on the table. "I'm thinking it's for the best, though," says Gillian. "She's caught up now. I mean, I could be as homey as Martha

Stewart, but at this point, the image is stuck in her head. I can't change that. And I don't want her afraid to be around me."

A little boy hurries by, stealing glances below their table.

"So it'll just be you," says Kai, annoyed her smoke rings keep getting punked by the ceiling fan. "Free to walk around the house naked."

"I guess," says Gillian, biting her lip, "but you know how I am. I get enough alone time. I'd rather eat with a friend."

A waiter drops his cups on the other side of the room. "You will, Gilly. I put the word out and Calvin did the same," says Kai. "Someone new is just around the corner. But until then, shit girl, enjoy it. Think of yourself as Conan, once Andy left the show."

"You know what else she said? She said I danced too much."

"Did you smack her? I would have smacked her."

"No," she says with a heavy sigh. "She said it made her uncomfortable. I take up too much room."

"I would have left a hand print on her cheek."

"But if I can't dance in my own home, what's the point of paying rent?" shrugs Gillian, pausing to make eye contact with a man sitting in the corner of the room. Embarrassed, the patron looks away. "I actually thought she liked me."

"She did like you. She does like you, it's just . . . well, you know how it goes," says Kai, putting out her smoke. "This is going to be a good move for you, Gilly. You just don't know it yet. Let's get out of here."

Kai heads for the register while Gillian finishes her cup. Gathering her purse, Gillian glances over the room. Faces turn away before she can catch them. Forcing a polite smile, Gillian stands up and joins Kai to walk out the door.

ღ ღ ღ

11:16 A. M.

Jaquin lifts his head up from the pillow, creases all along his cheek like a railroad track. The back of his neck glows red, threatening to hurt, as the sunlight comes in from the side window. He looks over at the clock on his nightstand before collapsing his head back down, deep into the folds.

5:48 P. M.

Beep

"Jaquin . . . where are you? Not again. This is highly irregular. Call the store as soon as you get this."

Beep

Jaquin's eyes peel open and blink for clarity. He sighs heavily. The fading sun lays tucked away, nicely snuggled in the small of his back. He rolls over and slides his hand down under the waistline of his boxers to scratch. He closes his eyes.

1:31 A. M.

Jaquins sits up. The light from the street lamp comes in through the window and shines down on his foot. The light politely points out just how long his toenails have grown. It also highlights all the little particles that are moving around his room. For the first time in awhile, Jaquin can see he is not alone. He waves to his friends and then lowers his head to slumber some more.

ග ග ග

Gillian yawns. Eight feet away a young intern, barely noticing the files slipping from her fingers, stares at her, mesmerized. Like she's found Carmen San Diego. "If you want to take a picture, I can autograph it maybe."

"Oh," says the startled intern, the files falling to the floor. "Sorry. Sorry. I'm so sorry, I didn't mean to—"

"Think of it like this," says Gillian politely, "remember Will Purdue?"

"Who?"

"Will Purdue. Used to play center for the Bulls. When they won all those championships."

"Like . . . basketball?"

"Yeah."

"Oh," she giggles nervously, trying to gather the files, "I don't watch basketball."

"Well," shrugs Gillian, "Will Purdue wore a size 21AAAAA shoe. Holds the record in the NBA. I think maybe on the planet, too. He's my hero."

"Your hero?"

"Yeah. I wear a 16."

". . . In men's?"

"Yeah."

"Oh my God!"

"I know."

"Dear God, 16!"

"I know," says a smiling Gillian, holding up her feet, "I'm special."

". . . They're so . . . "

"Long."

". . . Ginormous."

"Well," laughs Gillian, lowering her feet, "long is more accurate. They're actually pretty narrow. They're like skis. My dad likes to call me Picabo Street."

"But . . . how?" Like a quarterback after throwing a touchdown, Gillian smiles and points toward the sky. The intern stands there in awe.

"Yeah," nods Gillian, "pretty exciting stuff."

The intern remains unmoved, her eyes locked on her feet.

"You like the shoes? Shopping in my size gets tough, so I'm always proud when I find a cool pair. I'm looking for some LeBrons. So, you know, keep your eye out."

The intern continues to stare.

"Okay, well . . . you're new. You'll get used to it. Nice meeting you," says Gillian turning back to her computer and swinging her feet back under the desk to end the show. With only her memory left to guide her, the intern comes out of her trance. Embarrassed, she looks around at the other cubicals and hurries down the hall.

ꕥ ꕥ ꕥ

"It's Beethoven, actually. She uses bars from his Moonlight Sonata in that song. See, she's a classically trained pianist. And one of the first major pieces you learn on piano is Beethoven's Moonlight. Some teachers like to start with Shuman, but most go with Beethoven. That's pretty standard. Anyway, either out of homage or just to show off, she uses the arpeggios from the sonata as the baseline. They're both in E minor so it's an easy arrangement. And as far as pop music goes, it's pretty much why the song's so damn Billy Dee cool," says a heavy-eyed Jaquin, smiling at the pretty girl three stools down from him. He waits in hopeful silence.

". . . I just like the song," the girl says softly, taking her drink to a table in the back. Jaquin watches her go, his ego lacing up the boots to march down his shoulder.

"How you know?" says the woman on the other side of him. He swivels around. She has long hair, a nice smell, and a dress that exposes her back. She's unquestionably a hottie.

"What's that now?"

"Well, how you know all that stuff about that song?" She asks again.

" . . . I used to play it for my girlfriend."

"Used to?"

"Yeah," says Jaquin, lifting his glass, "used to."

"Lucky for me then."

Jaquin stops in mid-swallow and lowers his glass. He blinks. She grins. "Uh, I have more records at home . . . maybe you'd like to come listen . . ."

"I'd like that." A smile builds on both corners of his mouth and suddenly the bar doesn't smell like mildew and vinegar and corn nuts. The room maybe isn't lit with 15-watt light bulbs. Putting her hair behind her ear, she leans in close to him and whispers, "200 an hour, baby."

Jaquin deflates. His ego resumes lacing up the boots.

ᘓᘓᘓ

Gillian peers in like a mother standing outside the hospital nursery.

"You want to come in, sweetheart?" says a salesman from the door, his hair slicked and his tie clipped to the inside of a starched orange, metro shirt. "We have all the name brands and a variety of styles. Clogs, heels, sandals, pumps. You're welcome to—" He notices her feet and falls speechless. End of pitch.

"No, thank you. I'm good out here. But I would love a catalog if you have one."

"Sure," says the man lingering. "I'll, I'll . . . I'll be right back." While she waits, Gillian casually walks over to scans the kiosk shaded under a big Maple tree. An ad for a math tutor. An ad for a violin teacher. An ad for a used IKEA bed frame. An ad for a doctor that . . . Her eyes widen, and then skip backwards to re-read.

"Here you go, sweetie," says the salesman, who's brought the catalog as well as three of his co-workers. The gentlemen grin with gleeful surprise.

"Very nice," says Gillian, rolling her eyes and taking the catalog. She smiles pretty for the eye cameras, tears the number from the kiosk, and walks down the block.

ᘓᘓᘓ

"My friend says I'm lost."

The woman, dressed in a suit, sits in a cushioned chair across from Jaquin. She scribbles and looks up from the notebook, "and what do you think?"

"I don't know," says Jaquin.

"How do you feel?"

"I feel shitty."

The woman resumes her scribbling and pulls out her prescription pad.

ଓ ଓ ଓ

"You should write that down."

Gillian blushes.

"No seriously, love," he says, "you should document this. I know what I'm talking about. You're beautiful." Gillian takes a sip of her wine, mostly to dilute the grin amongst the grapes. "You ever consider modeling?"

"Well," says Gillian, riding the buzz, "when I was little, my mother had that idea. This whole plan for me, but . . . well . . . I . . . my fee —"

"Oh."

"Yeah."

"But what about the waist up, or even just your face?"

"That was an option. But, I don't know, fractions are for math class," says Gillian with a clever smirk. "I figure they get all or nothing. Plus, I like to eat lots of red meat. I couldn't see that changing. Even for the coin." The man laughs.

"Excuse me," says a voice from the stage, "I hope you all are having a good time tonight. We are the Aquatic Groove Session and for the next few hours, we'll give you a nice taste of jazz, funk, and blues. If you feel good about what we do, don't be shy, come on out to the dance floor." He turns to his band, counts to four, and . . . *Ta-dow!*

"On the phone you said you liked to dance," says the man, smoothly nodding his head to the music. He stands, buttons the top button of his jacket, and holds out his hand, "shall we?" Flushed with excitement, Gillian looks down as they head for the stage, trying to hide her schoolgirl grin in the vault under the floor. "You good?" asks the man. Gillian looks up, ". . . oh yeah."

With one hand on her waist, and one tangled between fingers, they begin to bump to the boom boom of the baseline. They come correct. Old school dirty. When dancing wasn't so shiny and sometimes just sloppy and hype. The Fly Girls before commercial breaks or Napoleon during Pedro's talent section. The cover of Camp Lo's only LP—except Gillian and her man have on a bit more clothing. They kind of got it going on.

"Ow!"

"Oh God," he says, staring down at her feet. "I'm so sorry."

"That's okay," she says smiling, "they're . . . there." She pulls him close again and resumes dancing.

"Oh, shit."

"It's okay," she says, reaching down to rub her toe. "It's no big deal. We're good." He shyly steps toward her and nods to the beat. It gets fun again. And they flirt with getting back into the zone.

"Aw!"

"Jesus!" he says, throwing his hands in the air. "I'm trying to be careful."

"I know. It's not your fault. Don't worry about it." She offers her hand.

"Maybe we should sit down," he says.

"Why?"

"Well . . . I'm nice with this. I know where my feet should go. And I'm trying to, I'm not used to—"

"Yeah, okay. So, we . . . we make do."

"Why don't we have a seat?"

"Look," says Gillian, "I'm having a really good time. You're a really great date. I don't want to sit down. It doesn't really bother me."

"But it bothers me!"

In Gillian's head, the music stops. The man continues, "and it's a bit too much for a casual night. I'm going to go." He walks away, leaving Gillian alone on the floor.

ɕɞ ɕɞ ɕɞ

"How you like me now?"

As if he were playing dominoes, Jaquin slams a scrap of paper on the table. Startled, Calvin and Kai jerk back, "what the hell?"

"I stepped to her just now. On the El. I saw her get on at Belmont," beams a pumped Jaquin, using his hand to describe the story, "didn't even let her sit. Just threw it down, right in front of the handicap seating. I was all, 'my name's Jaquin' and she's was all, 'how can I be down?' And then I was all, 'why don't you hit me with your digits?' and she's all, 'why don't I just give you my house key?'" Jaquin smiles proudly. Calvin rolls his eyes.

"Fine," he continues, "she didn't say nothing about the house key. But she looked like she wanted to. She's a stunner, too. I know you don't believe me with those charity looks you giving, but she's real cute. She looks like she could be Jessica Alba's little sister." Jaquin takes a moment to breathe.

"You a fool," laughs Calvin, "I ain't seen this cat in a month and he comes out the woodwork with battle scars and sibling fantasies. Eh, man, I done told you about that pipe."

"Ignore him, Jaquin," says Kai, staring at the girl's phone number, "he's just happy to see you. And I'm glad to see you're getting back out there. You gonna sit?"

"Let me get a drink first, my mouth is crazy dry," says Jaquin, as he lays his coat on a vacant stool. Jaquin orders at the bar. Looking over his shoulder, he discreetly pulls a prescription bottle from his pocket, shakes out a pill, and pops it in his mouth. He washes it down with a Corona wave and returns to his friends. "So what's good?"

"Man, Kai wants me to build a deck. Do I look like I can build a deck?"

Jaquin shakes his head, "I don't even think you can find Home Depo—" Jaquin's thought accompanies his eyes as they drift toward a group of women entering the bar. They find a seat in the corner. "Will you guys excuse me for a minute?" says Jaquin, getting up to walks across the room and sits down with the ladies. He friends watch in puzzled awe.

ᘓᘐ ᘓᘐ ᘓᘐ

"Are you confused?"

"No, I'm fine," says Gillian nervously.

"Good," says the man in the white coat, "then let's keep going." On the wall, he begins to circle areas of the X-ray with his finger. "This section here is called the metatarsal bone. It functions as a bridge, mostly used to hold structure. It also protects the nerve endings that control a portion of your lateral movement. We plan to cut here," he says, dragging his finger across the transparency, "to here. And then, with a laser, bond the two remaining piece."

Gillian leans back and exhales. "That's incredible. I mean, I read the ad and I looked stuff up on the internet, but—God . . . I can't believe this is possible."

"I know. It's a lot to absorb," agrees the man. "Most clients are skeptical at first. It's scary stuff. And I want to be unconditionally honest with you—while I expect success, there are drawbacks. Unavoidable ones." He reaches into his coat pocket and pulls out a pamphlet. He hands it to Gillian. "You will have permanent, while varying, tenderness when you walk—you'll likely take routine painkillers. Because the process will kill nerve cells, you will have permanent paralysis from the point of incision to your toes, which may cause difficulty with your balance and permanent loss of much of your vertical and lateral movement. And you will have to have regular injections of antibiotics, so the tissue does not become gangrenous."

Gillian sits speechless.

"But," says the man, holding both ends of his stethoscope, "they will be smaller."

"Shorter. They're already pretty narrow. Like skis."

"Shorter then," nods the man. He flips off the X-ray light and sits in his chair. "So, it's really a question of what's most important to you."

ᔕ ᔕ ᔕ

Scratching the inside of his naked thigh, Jaquin lowers the volume on the answering machine.

Beep

"J . . . Dawn. My head was throbbing like a Janet Jackson song this morning. I barely made it to work. It was fun as hell, though. Call me soon, Papi. Peace."

Beep

"Jaquin? Hi, this is Kelsa. We met last week at the Buddha. You tried to bite me. I know you were kidding, but I guess I'm curious now. I can't tell if that makes me a freak. Anyway, call me, okay? 312-520-1003."

Beep

"No more messages at this time."

The bedroom door opens, and a woman wearing only a t-shirt walks out. She squints at the light. "You coming back to bed?"

"Yeah, girl," says Jaquin with a triumphant chuckle, "I'll be right there."

ᔕ ᔕ ᔕ

Gillian stares at her entire shoe collection and holds a permanent marker in her hand. She picks up a loafer and measures about two thirds of the way down the shoe. She draws a thick black line all the way across the width. She continues the line up to the toe and back around to where she started. Like first grade homework, she colors in the outline. She does the same routine to the other loafer.

She slides both feet in, stands up, and examines the pair from above. And then in the mirror. She smiles sincerely, "I'd love to." Gillian holds out her arms, grips tightly to the air, and begins to sway.

ᔕ ᔕ ᔕ

"This is a delicate matter, Jaquin," says a man in the black suit, staring at a computer screen from behind a long oak desk. "I'm a bit torn. Within the last few weeks alone, you've gone from almost being fired to landing 167 new accounts. Those are employee of the month numbers!"

Jaquin, from a cushioned chair on the other side of the table, clears his throat, "people are simple, sir. You just got to talk to them the right way."

"That's correct, Jaquin. The right way. Now let's talk about that for a minute." Shrugging, Jaquin adjust his tie. The man with the suit lifts a memo from his desk, clears his throat, and begins to read, "you like a baby with all this crying. You went over your minutes? Too bad, you little punk. Your limit's printed on the statement every month. Learn to read. Quit being such a douche bag!"

Jaquin covers his mouth to hide his Joker impression.

ᔓᔕ ᔓᔕ ᔓᔕ

"It's only playing here or in Evanston."

"Here's fine. I'm going to Evanston next month for my niece's birthday party," says Gillian. "I still have to get her a gift. They have Toys R' Us in Evanston?"

"They got everything in Evanston," says Kai, unzipping her coat and stomping off the snow. "You never told me, what happened with Jamie?"

"Not too much," says Gillian, "I showed her around the place, but I don't know that she was paying attention."

"Caught up?"

"Yeah."

"That sucks."

"Yeah."

"You got the Junior Mints in your purse, right?" asks an anxious Calvin coming through the doors and handing his ticket to the doorman.

"Yes, Calvin. For the 100th time, I've got the Junior Mints, the Sour Patch Kids, the Dots, the Reeses, the Milk Duds, and the grape pops. And don't say nothing to me about popcorn or Twinkies unless you're willing to bring a purse next time too. Now I want you to meet my friend. Calvin," says Kai proudly, "this is Gillian. Gilly, this is my Calvin." They shake hands. Calvin examines Gillian, looking her up and down. Or, at least to her ankles. Startled, his eyes race upward, locking on her breasts, as if a safer spot to glare.

"Like my shoes?"

"Huh?" stumbles Calvin, "I don't . . . I didn't . . . "

"She's just playing, baby," says Kai, hugging Calvin.

"Oh. That's a fun game. Maybe we can play again later. Eh, I told my homeboy about your place."

"Really?" Gillian says, pausing to visualize it, ". . . I could live with a guy."

"Let's go," interrupts Kai. "I don't want to miss the previews."

Calvin pulls open the door, and the three walk into the darkness.

ᔓᔕ ᔓᔕ ᔓᔕ

3:13 A. M.

"I know . . . it was kind of hot," says Jaquin softly, moving the receiver closer to his mouth. "Naw, naw . . . sleep's overrated. It's early. Come on now . . . work ain't no thing—" Jaquin jerks up from the couch, eyes ovaled. "Hold on for a second . . ."

He drops the phone, jets for the toilet, and drops to his knees, "Uuuhggg."

ᔓᔕ ᔓᔕ ᔓᔕ

Gillian wipes her mouth and lays the napkin on the counter. She digs into her wallet to pay the tab. "Let me get that for you," says a man no taller than a doorknob, who climbs onto the stool next to her and puts money on the counter.

"No, thank you," says Gillian, her face still digging in her purse. "I'll manage."

He looks her up and down and beams, "you're beautiful."

"Excuse me?" she says, finally looking up. She gasps.

"What are you, 5'7? That's amazing," says the man in a voice to match his size. "We're never this beautiful."

"I'm sorry, do I know you?"

"Oh, no. This is a chance encounter. Fate, really," says the man, pointing to a table. "See, I was here, eating my breakfast, when I noticed you. Just sitting there. Alone. Waiting." Wary, Gillian slowly leans back. "Oh, now," smiles the man, "please don't be scared. I am harmless. I just look different."

She forces a smile, "I gotta go, I'm late for work."

"Hm. What is it you do?"

"I work down at . . . wait, this is silly," she stands up.

"Hear me out," he says, holding up his palms, "you don't have to do this. You don't have to eat alone. You have a family."

"Aw, man . . ."

"It's okay," says the man, digging in his breast pocket, "you might not be ready. Take your time." He lays a card on the counter, slides off the stool, and waddles away. Gillian picks up the card to read.

Timmy's Traveling Circus

ထ ထ ထ

Jaquin puts a pill on his tongue to make friends with a tequila shot.

"Anything else?" shouts the bartender over the music.

"What else is there?" he shouts back. "I'm in a room full of kittens and I'm a big old bowl of milk. Black shirt, far corner. Church."

Jaquin pushes off the bar and walks out onto the crowded floor. With flashing lights and a pulsing snare, he is a bit annoyed by the scene, taking a minute to adjust to the bodies. Steam rises to the ceiling as hundreds of people rub and grind up against each like videos on BET. Pushing past packed people, Jaquin finds his way over to the black shirt. He taps her on the shoulder. She turns.

"Oh damn . . . "

"Ain't this some shit?" says Kelsa.

He forces a smile, "you got my messages, right?"

"Don't. Don't even do that. Makes it worse."

"Aw, girl, it ain't ev—"

"Go away," she says calmly.

"Come on, now," he says. "Let me buy you a drink."

"I don't want a drink," she says, shaking her head. "I just want you to go away." She turns back to her friends. Embarrassed, Jaquin forces a full-on belly laugh. Kelsa turns back around, "fucking jerk! You laughing at me?"

"It's just you all mad and shit," he says over a grin.

"It's funny? I liked you."

"I like you too, you know," he says, continuing to laugh.

"Whatever," she says, folding her arms, "it's on me for being dumb. But do me a favor, okay? When you tell your friends about all the girls you hit and never called back, don't forget to tell them you had trouble keeping it up." Jaquin's smile drops. Her friends break into laughter.

"That ain't true!" Jaquin shouts out with high school conviction. Gloating, the girls walk away. "It ain't true! She messing with ya'll! Don't believe her! She's an internationally known liar! If you were smart, you wouldn't even be associating with her! . . . I can prove it . . ."

ଓ ଓ ଓ

"You're going to throw it out there like that?"

"Yup."

"Babe, we just met."

"I don't care," says Gillian, "just answer the question."

"'Will I dance with you no matter what?'" He considers, "I don't get it. What's the catch?"

Gillian pushes aside her plate, and leans forward on the table, "you've seen my feet, right?"

"Yeah, you just put them on the table, remember?"

"Right," she says, moving the bread aside. "So, when we get on the dance floor, you will step on my feet."

"I will?"

"By accident. But it'll happen."

"No, it won't."

"Yes, it will."

"Babe, I'm gold on the hardwood."

"Doesn't matter. You're going to step on my feet."

The man envisions it, "you want me to step on your feet?"

"No."

"Then I'm confused."

"Listen to me," says Gillian, almost on top of the table now, "when we dance, you will step on my feet. When you step on my feet, I don't want you to freak out. Can you do that for me?"

"I already told you, I won't step on your feet."

Gillian thumps her fists on the table, "dammit!"

"Don't get upset," says the man. "You want me to step on your feet, babe, I'll do it. It's cool."

"Genius, it isn't a fetish."

"I don't mind."

"It's not like that."

"I've heard worse. It's all good."

Gillian gets up and pulls her chair right next to him. She leans in real close, "it's a little different, I realize. But I'm looking for some guarantees here. I'm wanting to know that before we even go through the hassle of small talk, before you even tell me what's on your Tivo "to do list," I can be confident that you'll do me this favor at the end of the night. Can you understand that?"

"You mean like when I meet a chick, and I wish she'd hurry up promise me some loving instead of having to listen to her babble all night? That kind of thing?"

"Exactly."

He smiles slyly. "Babe, I'd like to . . . have some loving tonight."

"Fine. Great. That's sound like fun. But first we have to dance."

". . . And you want me to step on your toes while we do it?"

Gillian drops her head. She gets her purse and walks out.

ళ ళ ళ

"She is kind of hotter than Mia."

"Are you really sweating me about that apartment shit right now?" says Jaquin from his stool. "It's about to be on in this piece. Let me have this, Cal. I'm already got enough static blowing up my BlackBerry."

Calvin shrugs, "maybe you should chill on the females for a minute."

"You bullshitting, right?" laughs Jaquin, shaking his head. "You make me jump through hoops to get some face time. And then you come at me sounding like Kai? Dog, don't you have a deck you should be building?"

"I told you about the practice rooms right around the corner from my crib, right? That conservatory mess was a while ago. A new semester starts in a month, I looked it up."

"What are you, my mother? You gonna dress me too? What the hell has Kai done to you?"

Calvin blinks, "that's your second Kai joke, J. See what happens if you say one more."

"You gotta be kidding me?" says Jaquin, his mouth wide open, "you claiming noble? Of all people, you ain't clean."

"No," says Calvin calmly, "I guess I'm not."

From the other side of the bar, a nice looking woman comes by on her way toward the back room. Both men take notice. "Oh my God," says Jaquin with a grin.

Calvin shakes his head, "she's probably just using the bathroom."

"Not when she's alone, remember?" Jaquin downs his shot and slides off the stool. Calvin places his hand on Jaquin's chest, "please don't."

"You best take your hand off me."

"You ain't right, Jaquin. I think you need to calm down."

"I swear to God, Cal—"

The woman comes out from the back room. Jaquin steps in front of her, "what's your name, girl?"

"What?"

"I said what's your name?"

"Don't mind him," interjects Calvin, "we're sorry to bother you."

The woman begins to walk away. Jaquin again steps in front of her, "I still didn't get that name, love."

"Get out of my way, asshole," she says.

"Jaquin, don't—"

"Don't be like that," Jaquin pushes, "let me buy you a drink."

"What are you, stupid?" The woman smacks Jaquin across the face. His smile fades. Calvin gets up and stands in front of Jaquin, "we're really sorry about that. Have a nice evening, okay?"

She glares at a seething Jaquin, his eyes red and angry, unfocused. His neck vein pulsing. She tries to push passed the men, but Jaquin grabs her by the wrist, yanking her around.

"Jaquin . . ."

"You another one, huh . . ."

"Jaquin, come on . . ."

"You walk by like you don't remember . . ."

"Let go, asshole . . ."

"Jaquin, let her go . . ."

"You fucking bitch . . ."

"Let go . . ."

"Jaquin, don't do this . . ."

". . . Like what we had wasn't special!" he shouts, spit flying from his lips. ". . . Goddamit Mia . . ." Enraged, Jaquin takes his glass and shatters it against the wall.

The room falls silent. Jaquin stands motionless, his heart pounding out of his chest. He takes in the room. There's the bartender who slowly reaches for the bat behind the counter. There's the elderly man who grabs his fedora in disgust and shuffles towards the door. There's Calvin who can't even look up from the floor. And then there's the girl who cowers behind the stool, hiding from him.

Jaquin steps back and slowly lowers himself into a chair. "Oh my god . . ."

❧ ❧ ❧

Gillian looks down at her feet, at the nice white pumps that match her dress. Her eyes shift to the taxi cab between her feet. From this distance, it looks like a Kracker Jack prize. Except topped with snow left over from last night's fall.

"Can I come too?" asks an anxious little girl standing by the door, goose bumps forming on her bare arms.

Smiling, Gillian brings her legs back over the ledge and joins the girl, "no, that's nowhere to be. Why aren't you inside?"

She folds her arms, "because I look stupid. No one else is wearing a dress."

"I'm wearing a dress."

"You don't count, you're a grown up."

Gillian quickly peers in the window and scans the room. With the exception of the other five or six who don't count, sure enough, most wear baggy denim, baggy warm-ups, and a few scattered pair of baggy Khakis. It's possible the entire room shops at Old Navy. "That just means you're special," reasons Gillian. "Your father rented out this whole ballroom to make sure you know that."

"I asked for a pizza party."

Gillian laughs, "well, sometimes we don't get what we want."

"I hate boys."

"Yeah," smiles Gillian, "sometimes that happens, too."

"Fine. But I still don't want to dance with him."

"Who?"

"Chucky."

"Why not?"

"Because Chucky's stupid. He's got a watermelon head. And I've seen him eat his boogers."

"Gross."

"Anyways," she says, "I'm seven now. I'm too old for dancing."

Gillian laughs, "you might like it."

"With stupid Chucky?"

"Well," says Gillian, "let's start with me." Embarrassed, the little girl breaks into uncontrollable giggles. "What? You too old for your Aunt Gilly?" The child continues to laugh.

Gillian subtly glances over her shoulders, looks suspiciously at the band playing on stage, and leans forward as if others should not hear, "I'll make you a deal. Give me ten minutes on the dance floor. Ten minutes and I can guarantee that not only will this night go down as one of the greatest displays of 847 antics, but it'll have the brain of little Chucky spinning and bouncing like his name was Tigger."

Worked up, Gillian grabs a truly chilled glass of Champagne that was left on an outside table. She downs it. "Trust me, boys like girls that dance. Even stupid boys."

Gillian holds out her hands to the little girl. Shyly, the little girl shrugs, "but, I . . . I trip over myself."

"That's the best kind." With the whole party watching, Gillian leads her niece back into the ballroom onto the middle of the dance floor. "But I don't . . ."

Gillian offers a comforting nod, "just follow my lead." Slowly, as if not to rush something so good, the little girl places one foot on top of Gillian's. She does the same with the other. There is plenty of room. Gillian and her niece, both beaming, begin to sway.

*** * ***

Jaquin sits on his couch, the phone lies in his lap. After a few moments, he dials. "Yeah . . . Calvin, listen . . . I know I haven't seen you for a minute . . . things got, messy. I hope to change that . . . I was wondering if you still have the number for that apartment we talked about. If it's still available . . . Hit me. Peace."

He puts the phone back on the cradle on his desk next to the garbage can. Inside the can is a half-empty bottle of pills.

*** * ***

"Hello, my name is Gillian Wade," she says into the phone, "I have an appointment scheduled with you guys on Thursday . . . yeah, that's right. 4:30 . . . I'm going to have to cancel . . . no, no need to reschedule. Thank you."

Smiling, she hangs up and slides a catalog onto her lap. She briefly glances at the open page and dials. "Hi, I'd like to place an order. I'd . . . sorry . . . I'd like #82176 . . . those are the LeBron's, right? Sweet . . . I know, right—"

She pauses. "I'm sorry, could you hold on for a second, I got . . . just hold on, okay?" Gillian pushes down on the flash button, to switch over to the other line.

www.ingramcontent.com/pod-product-compliance
Lightning Source LLC
Chambersburg PA
CBHW070629310726
48982CB00001B/219

* 9 7 8 1 4 9 8 2 4 9 9 5 9 *